HALLOWDENE

GEORGE MANN

TITAN BOOKS

Hallowdene
Print edition ISBN: 9781783294114
E-book edition ISBN: 9781783294121

Published by Titan Books
A division of Titan Publishing Group Ltd
144 Southwark Street, London SE1 0UP

First edition: September 2018
10 9 8 7 6 5 4 3 2 1

Names, places and incidents are either products of the author's imagination
or used fictitiously. Any resemblance to actual persons, living or dead
(except for satirical purposes), is entirely coincidental.

No part of this publication may be reproduced, stored in a retrieval system,
or transmitted, in any form or by any means without the prior written
permission of the publisher, nor be otherwise circulated in any form of
binding or cover other than that in which it is published and without a
similar condition being imposed on the subsequent purchaser.

A CIP catalogue record for this title is available from the British Library.

Printed and bound by CPI Group (UK) Ltd, Croydon, CR0 4YY

What did you think of this book? We love to hear from our readers.
Please email us at: readerfeedback@titanemail.com,
or write to us at the above address.

To receive advance information, news, competitions, and exclusive
offers online, please sign up for the Titan newsletter on our website:
www.titanbooks.com

FOR MUM

CHAPTER ONE

Overhead, the crows were circling.

Jenny Wren watched them turn in concentric wheels, stark against the pale sky. Their crowing had grown impatient, expectant – as if they knew what was about to happen. As if they were calling out a warning. If she'd been disposed to such things, Jenny might have considered it an ill omen, but she knew it for what it was: the natural instinct of the birds, accustomed to the turning of the earth in the nearby graveyard and expecting a feast of newly exposed earthworms.

Well, today they were going to be disappointed. It wasn't worms they were about to unearth. She glanced at the jagged hunk of granite beside her. It was huge and misshapen, slick with moss – a pagan marker that hadn't been moved in centuries. It must have taken scores of villagers to drag it all the way up here – it weighed at least a ton, and standing beside it, it was almost as tall as her hip. Even the crane operator had sucked his teeth dubiously when he'd seen it.

"So, could you provide our viewers with a little

insight into what you're expecting to find beneath the stone, Jennifer?"

Jenny sighed. It was only half past twelve in the afternoon, but she was already beginning to feel weary. Why she'd ever agreed to this foolish invasion of her dig, she didn't know. A few seconds of madness, perhaps... or more likely the thought of seeing her face up there on the TV screen, running about enthusiastically like some latter-day Tony Robinson, pointing at stratified layers of mud and pretending to be positive about the lack of finds. Now, she was regretting ever entertaining the idea.

Too late now, she supposed.

Painting on her best winning smile, she turned to face the lens, almost recoiling at the proximity of the camera. Behind the cameraman, Steve Marley, she could see the young presenter who'd asked her the question, looking preened despite the waxed jacket and wellington boots.

Jenny wondered if she should have made more of an effort for the camera. She'd grown accustomed to thinking about comfort, rather than appearance, while she was out on a dig. Her hair was coming loose, and while she'd made an attempt at doing her make-up before leaving the house that morning, it was nothing compared to the pristine elegance of Robyn Baxter. And then there was the fact that the woman was almost twenty years her junior. Jenny was dowdy and parochial by comparison.

Still, what were people expecting? She was an

archaeologist, not a TV presenter. Archaeologists were never glamorous, were they? Everyone had seen the endless re-runs of *Time Team* on the telly. She was just living up to the stereotype – even if she did look more like Phil than Carenza.

She told herself off. She was being too harsh on herself again. Her cheeks were burning. The truth was, being around these people made her feel old. She supposed that was only to be expected. She'd been at this for years, and needed to remember that her experience counted for something: she was the expert here, this was her dig, and they were her guests. She took a deep breath, and let it out slowly. *It's all going to be fine. It'll be over in a couple of hours, and you'll be sat in the Rowan Tree, sinking a pint and congratulating yourself on a job well done.*

She glanced at Robyn, who offered her an encouraging smile, and then looked straight to camera, just as she'd been taught in her briefing that morning.

"Well, Robyn, it's long been believed that this stone–" she patted the huge, moss-covered rock beside her "–is a 'witch stone', relating to a form of superstitious burial that, on rare occasions, was given to women who'd been denounced as witches. The practice is thought to originate from the seventeenth century, but has its roots in much earlier mythology." She cleared her throat. "The stone was placed upon the witch's grave as a means of containing her spirit, to prevent her from returning in the afterlife to seek revenge upon those who had judged her." She smiled, and looked to Robyn. The camera was still pointing squarely in her face.

"And legend has it that this particular stone," said Robyn, "marks the grave of the notorious witch Agnes Levett, who's a figure of some fame, locally, isn't she?"

"Absolutely," said Jenny, nodding. "Surviving records suggest that Agnes Levett was discovered by local villagers performing a ritual with the body of Lady Grace Abbott, wife of the then Lord Cuthbert Abbott, upon whose grounds we're now standing. She was hanged for her crimes, and buried here, beneath this stone. Or so we believe."

"And… cut."

Jenny looked to Robyn, who was wearing an easy, practised smile. "Perfect. We'll get out of your hair so you can carry on with your dig."

"Okay, thanks." Jenny heaved a sigh of relief to be out of the frame once again. She watched as the cameraman set up in a new position, taking the opportunity to grab a brief insert from Robyn.

Jenny listened for a moment as the presenter reeled off a practised speech about how Agnes Levett had become something of a tourist attraction in the local area, and was now the centrepiece of the Hallowdene Summer Fayre, during which the villagers all dressed up in bizarre costumes and paraded an effigy of the witch through the streets, much to the delight of the local children.

That was why the TV crew were really here – to film a piece on the festival for their rural affairs programme, an example of how the British, in the wake of Brexit, were returning to their old traditions and pagan roots. It was nonsense, of course, but Jenny had jumped at the chance to have them along at the dig, to capture her moment of triumph when they lifted the stone to reveal the remains of Agnes the so-called 'Hallowdene witch'.

She only hoped that she was right, and the local legends hadn't led her astray. If they lifted the stone and there was no grave to be found… well, she'd look like a prize fool, and no matter what positive spin she managed to put on it, people would see her failure writ large on screens all across the nation.

She glanced around, catching sight of the crane driver, leaning against his machine and sucking surreptitiously on an e-cigarette. She couldn't help grinning at the sight – progress was all well and good, but people rarely changed. Nevertheless, she felt a brief pang of envy. She'd given up smoking years ago, and even though they now made her feel nauseated – she'd learned this to her regret – she still craved the occasional cigarette.

Around her, the bustle of the television crew continued. She hoped they'd be done soon so she could press on.

In the distance, Hallowdene Manor was a jagged silhouette, jutting brazenly from the hillside; a bleak, man-made interloper that didn't belong in such an otherwise unspoiled landscape. Beyond that, the trees of Raisonby Wood – once a part of the former Wychwood, which had formed a leafy mantle over this area for centuries – stood sentry-like on the horizon. To her right, the crumbling old church of St Mary erupted from the loam like a crooked finger, its lopsided spire pointing warily to the heavens. To Jenny, it looked somehow unsure of itself, as if the building itself were questioning its faith. The graveyard around the church was crowded with listing headstones – a silent audience, presiding in judgement over the events unfolding in the next field.

She'd explored that graveyard, more out of curiosity than professional interest, wandering around late one evening with a torch and checking off the names of the dead. Centuries' worth of villagers had been laid to rest here, including Lord and Lady Cuthbert Abbott, interred in a rather ostentatious tomb inside the church itself. Agnes, on the other hand, had been buried out here, in the mud, away from hallowed ground – moved from her first grave after superstition got the better of people, and they believed her to be enacting a curse from beyond the grave. She'd been carried out here, into a field, and re-interred beneath the heavy stone. It seemed a particularly cruel fate to Jenny, a final insult for a terribly misunderstood woman.

Jenny had no time for talk of witchcraft and curses – no one did, in this day and age. She'd spoken to a number of the villagers down at the pub, and they'd all said the same thing: that the village obsession with their historical 'witch' was just a bit of fun, and that the truth of the matter was really rather sad – that a woman had been lynched by her fellow villagers for crimes that everyone knew to be impossible now. There seemed to be some disagreement as to whether the woman had committed murder – she'd been accused of killing Lady Grace Abbott during a 'ritual' – but there was no surviving evidence, and no way of settling the matter either way. That the woman had been persecuted on grounds of witchcraft, though, like so many other poor souls of her age, was, as far as most people were concerned, something of an embarrassment. Jenny found the whole thing fascinating.

She heard a polite cough and turned to see Avi Dhiri, the show's producer, standing by her shoulder. He was a smartly dressed, tidy man, but practical, lacking Robyn's sophisticated glamour. A bit more down to earth. He'd dressed for the occasion, opting for a stiff pair of brown leather boots, jeans, a jumper – the cuffs of which she could just see, poking inquisitively out of the ends of his sleeves – and a navy waxed jacket.

"You did great," he said. He'd known she'd been nervous, and he'd been a great encouragement throughout the process. "Just what we needed."

She fought the urge to correct his grammar. He was being nice, after all. "Thanks. It's all a bit unfamiliar, that's all."

He smiled. "Don't worry, I know exactly what you mean. I've been doing this for years, but the few times I've had to face the camera myself I've gone to pieces. Something about having that big lens looming in your face."

She laughed at his awkward expression. Maybe this wasn't going so badly, after all.

"Are you ready for the big event?" he said.

"We're ready," said Jenny. "We've already recorded everything we need, at least until the stone is lifted. That's when the real work starts." She lowered her voice. "Although I fear it's not as climactic as you might expect. We've no dramatic music or anything." She grinned. "The crane will come in and lift the stone, and we'll get our first view of what's lurking beneath."

Dhiri laughed. "Don't worry, we can add the dramatic music in post-production." He offered her a wicked grin. "Particularly if the curse is true, and the witch comes crawling out to get us all."

Jenny shook her head, finding herself charmed by the young man, despite herself. "You've been watching too many late-night movies," she said.

"Still, it's all a bit creepy, isn't it? I mean, she must have done *something* to warrant all of this. I know they were a superstitious lot, but to bury the woman beneath a rock like this..."

Jenny shrugged. "I don't suppose we'll ever really know the truth. Most women accused of witchcraft were victims of jealousy, panic and misunderstanding. Like you say, people were terribly superstitious. People paid for it with their lives. I suspect her death simply coincided with some other phenomena that couldn't be readily explained by the people of the time – a bout of a particularly virulent disease, or what have you – and as a result, the poor woman was blamed for that, too, despite already being dead. That's why they shifted her body and placed this rock on top of her grave – to keep her unquiet spirit from enacting its revenge."

"Thank God people have changed," said Dhiri.

Jenny had to force herself not to laugh out loud at the irony. "All right, let's see about getting this thing moved," she said.

Her assistant, John, was chatting to the two young students they'd brought along to help with the digging and recording of the finds. Dhiri had already turned his attention back to Robyn and Steve, the cameraman, so she made a beeline for John, putting a hand on his shoulder. He looked somewhat disappointed at having to break off from trying to impress the two young women, who in turn seemed somewhat relieved.

"We about ready?" said John. His accent was broad West Country, and always made her smile.

"Yes. I think our friends are getting anxious for some excitement," she said. "You'd better move everyone back to a safe distance. I'm not taking any risks with that rock."

"Worried about the curse?" said John.

"Yeah," said Jenny, "the curse of the Health and Safety Executive."

John grunted, amused, and then set about shepherding people back to a safe distance. Jenny noted that a reasonable crowd had begun to gather around the edge of the field: a mix of folk from the village, she presumed, and people from the manor house, come to watch the excitement unfolding in the grounds. Or else hoping to catch sight of themselves later on TV. There'd be a lot of that in the coming days, she suspected, as the preparations for the Summer Fayre began to unfold and the film crew went about cataloguing everyone's lives. There seemed to be something of a party atmosphere amongst those who'd gathered to spectate; they formed a loose perimeter, chatting and laughing with one another. A woman in a blue raincoat was pouring people cups of tea from a large, silver flask. Jenny could have killed for a cuppa. Right after she'd finished that non-existent cigarette.

Sam, the crane operator, blew a nonchalant stream of vapour from the corner of his mouth when he noticed her approaching, unaware of the torture he was putting her through. Then she caught a whiff of what he'd been smoking, sweet and sickly and tinged with a hint of berries. She wrinkled her nose in disgust. Is this what the world had come to?

Sam prised himself away from the filthy yellow machine he'd been leaning against. He scratched absently at his nose with one gloved hand. "All right, boss?"

"I will be when this dog and pony show is over and done with and I can get on with the real work," she said. Sam had worked with her before, on numerous digs throughout Oxfordshire, and was well adjusted to her temperament and humour. He always laughed at her jokes. It was one of the reasons she liked to keep him around.

He grinned, one foot already up on the footplate of the crane. "This won't take a minute. Just give me a thumbs-up when you're all clear."

Steel chains had been carefully looped around the edges of the stone for ease of lifting by the crane. Jenny had supervised the process earlier that morning, monitoring how Sam had carefully dug out around the base of the rock, allowing him to work the chains in and around it, to secure a tight grip.

Theoretically, lifting the stone should be a simple matter – but Jenny knew from bitter experience how theory and reality were rarely comfortable bedfellows. Too many times, she'd been proved wrong by the data, or something had gone awry when they'd brought in the machines and the finds had been churned or damaged, or they'd dug a hole in completely the wrong spot.

She backed away, ensuring that everyone was clear. "Okay, Sam. Let's get on with it." She motioned to him to raise the arm of the crane.

With a mechanical chug, the crane arm began to rise, clanking and hissing like some ancient beast angry at being disturbed from its slumber. Jenny watched as the chains slowly lifted, pulling taut, catching on the underside of the jagged stone.

For a moment the arm stopped and the crane seemed to rock forward slightly as it took the weight of the enormous stone. Then the gears made a deep grinding sound, and the stone pulled free of the clinging earth with a wet sucking sound; a laborious sigh, as if whatever lay beneath had been holding its breath all of these years and could now, finally, exhale.

Sam pivoted the crane to the left, swinging the rock aside, revealing the damp soil beneath. Jenny fought the urge to rush forward. Aside from the fact that she was intent on remaining composed on camera, she had to follow procedure and wait until the stone had been secured.

Sam slowly lowered his payload, accompanied by a cacophony of more clanking and beeping. And then it was done, and the witch stone was sitting, rude and proud, about five feet to the left of the grave.

Slowly, Jenny walked forward. John, the students and the TV crew fell in, too, remaining one step behind, allowing her to be the first at the graveside. Whether this was out of respect for her position, or fear of what they might find, she didn't know.

Her stomach churned. She felt a rising sense of unease. She peered down at the grave. She realised she was holding her breath and let it out. Her heart was thudding.

John was standing beside her, arm extended, proffering a trowel. For a moment she hesitated, but then she took it, glanced back at the camera, and then lowered herself to her knees and began to dig.

The grave was shallow, and within minutes the edge of her trowel had struck something solid. She scraped carefully at the soil, drawing it back in layers, as if peeling back time itself. Slowly, the ground divested itself of its macabre bounty.

There, as she'd predicted, were the remains of a human being. She'd found the edge of the collarbone. She followed the line of the bone with the tip of her trowel, scraping at the damp earth, until she exposed the vertebrae, and then finally the jawbone and the lower part of the skull. She worked carefully around it, clearing away the clinging mud, ignoring the sudden gasps of the others behind her.

When she had finished, she straightened her back, peering down at the eerie visage before her. There was something unnerving about the skull – the way it was turned to face her in the soil, as if the dead woman were peering up at her and grinning, right across the centuries.

Jenny felt a shiver pass along her spine. "Right, everyone, keep back. Let's get the boring stuff over with. John, get on and notify the coroner, and let's get the paperwork signed off so we can take a proper look at her."

Around her, the crew began to disperse, none of them having said a word. No triumphant cries, no high-fives. Nothing. There was a strange, melancholy atmosphere about the place, as if no one wanted to acknowledge what they'd just found, to give voice to their fears.

Jenny looked back at the dead woman's grinning skull, and then turned away. It was time for that cigarette.

CHAPTER TWO

The café – Elspeth supposed it *was* a café, despite the odd appearance – was buzzing with the clatter of mugs, the hiss of steam and the chatter of at least a dozen other patrons. It was at once comforting, and maddeningly distracting. At least they weren't playing any thumping music. Small mercies, and all that. Still, there was no way Elspeth could concentrate on her book. She tucked a serviette inside to mark her place, and sat back in her chair, sipping at her coffee, annoyed at herself for allowing it to go cold.

The café – known as Richmond's Tearooms – was an odd sort of place that seemed to have one foot in the past and another in the present. This was evident in the overall décor – the tables were laid with red gingham and lace doilies, and the waiting staff were dressed in old-fashioned black and white uniforms – as well as the menu, which featured an eclectic mix of traditional teas, cakes and scones, alongside an array of paninis, fancy lattes and chorizo stew.

Even the place itself seemed unable to decide what

it really was; while most of the old building had been given over to the café, the area behind Elspeth had been lined with racks of cheap trinkets and books; a gift shop, of sorts, in which most of the stock related to the local legend of the Hallowdene Witch. The figure leered at her off the shelves: a caricature of a crooked old woman with a hook nose, claw-like fingers and black robes, with a mane of ragged white hair. Her image was emblazoned on the front of the menu cards, too, and the tables were adorned with black candleholders in the shapes of cats and broomsticks – she'd clearly become something of a mascot for the village. Broomsticks hung from the roof on fishing wire, and the soup – Elspeth could see someone cautiously sipping the hot liquid from a spoon at a nearby table – was served in little cast-iron cauldrons.

Presently, the witch was a hot topic of conversation amongst the tearoom's patrons. Elspeth took another sip of her coffee, surreptitiously turning her ear to the table across from her. An elderly lady, fingers stained yellow from years of nicotine abuse, was chattering loudly about the archaeological dig going on up at the manor, and how they'd better all watch out because of old Agnes's curse.

"In my experience," she said, "things that are buried should remain that way. No good ever comes from stirring up the past. These young ones would do well to remember that."

Her companion, whose fading glamour reminded

Elspeth of a television or movie star whose time on the silver screen had long passed, nodded enthusiastically. "Aye. Leave well be, that's what I say."

Others, clearly, had different ideas – as she'd arrived, Elspeth had overheard a man and a woman talking excitedly about how the dig might drive up attendance for the coming fayre. Most people, she'd gathered, seemed to see it all as a bit of fun, wilfully playing up the stories, tongues firmly planted in cheeks.

Elspeth had vague memories of the Hallowdene Summer Fayre, of people parading through the streets dressed as Jack-in-the-Green, or wearing elaborate masks in the guise of birds or foxes. Her mum had taken her as a child, but she'd been scared, hiding behind Dorothy's skirts, peeking out between her fingers as the villagers had marched the crooked effigy of the witch to the village cross. She'd been horrified by its twisted visage. The image had haunted her for weeks.

She must have only been six or seven, and hadn't understood the history and ritual behind the parade. The following year, when Dorothy had insisted they return, refusing to acknowledge her daughter's complaints, Elspeth had hidden under her bed, amongst the boxes and the dust bunnies, and refused to come out until her mum had relented and agreed to take her shopping in Oxford instead.

She hadn't really thought about it since, and had never had cause to return to Hallowdene, at least until the previous week, when Meredith – her editor at the

Heighton Observer – had asked if she'd be interested in covering the fayre for a local-interest article. This year, interest was particularly high because of the dig excavating the supposed resting place of the 'witch'.

Elspeth had jumped at the chance – her freelance instincts kicking in – and had come over this morning to be on hand when news from the excavation broke. She'd tried to get really close to the dig, to be there when the grave marker was moved, but the site manager had refused any close access to allow a national television crew to gain uninterrupted footage. The best she'd been able to do was arrange an appointment with the lead archaeologist, Jennifer Wren, once the stone had been moved. In the meantime, she'd camped out at Richmond's, having purchased one of their local books on the origins of the myth. It was an interesting read – if in need of a good edit – detailing the known facts surrounding Agnes's death, alongside the more lurid and fanciful tales of occult wrongdoing. Elspeth had been busily making notes in preparation for her story.

Agnes, although clearly a beloved cult figure – if only for the local tourist industry – was portrayed as near demonic, a stooped and crooked spinster with a hideous visage, spindly fingers and wiry grey hair. It was claimed that, in 1643, she'd been caught performing a ritual with the body of Lady Grace Abbott in a copse in the Wychwood, close to her home. Her hands had been steeped in the dead woman's blood, and Lord Cuthbert Abbott – desperately searching for his missing

23

George Mann

wife – had overheard her chanting some kind of wild incantation. Consequently, she'd been hanged by her neighbours in the village square, and then buried under the witch stone on un-consecrated grounds on the outskirts of the village.

Elspeth couldn't help but wonder what had really gone on. If the rumours were true, Agnes had apparently committed a terrible murder. But to what end? There had to be a human story behind the caricature that she'd become. Now, no one really believed that Agnes had been a witch – the so-called witch trials of the seventeenth century had long ago been debunked – but the question that Elspeth was interested in exploring was whether she'd really been a killer. That was the story here. Was a woman who was wrongly accused of witchcraft still rightly accused of murder?

There were few surviving accounts from the time – according to the book, and a bit of digging around on the internet – so real evidence was scant. Nevertheless, she had to admit, the story had her intrigued, and she found herself wondering what Jennifer Wren would find beneath that crooked old stone, pictured there in the book in a faded black and white photograph.

She checked her watch. There was an hour before she was due up at the dig site, and the skies outside were brooding, threatening rain. She downed the rest of her tepid coffee and caught the eye of the young waitress, who was buzzing about between nearby tables, balancing a near-impossible array of crockery on her arm.

24

Elspeth pointed at her mug. "Can I get another coffee, please?"

The waitress nodded, offering her a lopsided grin. She was young – in her early twenties – and despite the rather formal uniform had a rebellious twinkle in her eye, a flash of blue in her otherwise blonde hair, and a matching blue plaster on her eyebrow where she'd clearly covered a piercing. The hint of a tattoo poked out from beneath the sleeve of her uniform. Her black eyeliner and slash of pink lipstick all added to the overall impression. She blew a loose strand of hair out of her eye, and tottered past, carefully stepping around the blue-haired lady's chair leg.

"With you in a minute," she said.

It was more like five, but Elspeth wasn't in a hurry, and she smiled when the woman made a beeline for her table, coffee pot in hand. "Right, here you go." She sloshed coffee into Elspeth's empty mug with a practised flourish. "New round these parts, are you?" She placed Elspeth's bill on the table, tucking it under the sugar pot.

"Yes, I suppose I am," said Elspeth. "Recently moved back to the area from London."

The woman cocked her head, her expression wrinkling in confusion. "You moved back *here*, from London?" She sounded utterly incredulous, as if the very idea of it was simply outlandish.

"Well, Heighton," said Elspeth, sounding a little more defensive than she'd intended. "It's not so bad…"

The woman looked doubtful. "Well, I suppose not.

Still, I'd prefer something a little more cosmopolitan. I'm Daisy, by the way."

"Elspeth." She reached for her coffee. This time, it was too hot to drink. She blew on it. "You looking forward to the fayre?"

Daisy laughed. "Not really. I mean, it's a funny old thing, isn't it, all these people getting dressed up and parading through the streets. Besides, I imagine I'll be tied to this place by my apron strings. We always get busy around the fayre, and this time it's only going to be worse because of the dig."

The café door opened with a tinkling bell, and Daisy glanced up. She issued a low groan. "Here we go," she said, under her breath.

Elspeth looked over to see a man bustle in, making a show of unbuttoning his coat and stamping his feet, as if he'd just wandered in from an Arctic wasteland. He was wearing wellington boots spattered with mud, and leaving a trail of it right over the floorboards.

Daisy placed the coffee pot on Elspeth's table and went to intercept him. "Lee, you know you're not supposed to be in here with those muddy boots. If Sally gets hold of you..."

"Sally?" said the man. He fixed Daisy with an intense glower. "Is she here?" He stretched up onto his tiptoes, trying to see over Daisy's shoulder. The man looked to be in his fifties, with dark hair going to grey, a stubble-encrusted chin, and a greasy complexion. His eyebrows bobbed as he looked from table to table, as if searching for someone. "Sally?"

"She's busy, Lee," said Daisy. She sounded exasperated. "Look, I'll tell her you called."

"Sally!" called the man, this time loud enough to elicit a response from most of the café's patrons, who noticeably paused their conversations and turned in their seats to see what was going on.

The man was growing increasingly agitated. Elspeth wondered if she should try to intervene.

"Sally!"

"I'm here, Lee." Elspeth turned to see a woman standing by the door to the kitchen. She looked flustered, red-cheeked, and had a tea towel tossed over one shoulder. She was of a similar age to Lee, with a frizz of blonde hair and pale blue eyes. She was wearing a thin-lipped smile. Behind her a younger man – who, aside from the badly healed broken nose, resembled her so closely he had to be related – was glaring over her shoulder, his face like thunder.

"Right, good," said the man, visibly calming. "I need to talk to you. About all of *this*." He waved his hands at the witch-related produce on the shelves behind Elspeth.

"We've *had* this conversation," said Sally. "And it's no use going over it all again. Let's not bring it up in front of all the customers?" She edged forward, ushering him back. Daisy retreated, coming to stand by Elspeth's table, hugging herself with obvious concern.

"Look, it's not right. Selling all of this. Turning it all into a tourist attraction. It's *dangerous*," said Lee.

"Dangerous?" Sally sighed. "Don't you think you're taking this a little far? It's just a bit of fun. No harm can come of it. We all know she's not real. It's just a few postcards and trinkets."

"She doesn't like it, Sally. I'm telling you. And now they're out there digging her up. You're all messing with things you don't understand."

"Right, that's enough, you stupid old fool. Out, now." This from the young man, who Elspeth assumed to be Sally's son. He pushed past his mother and took the older man by the arm, causing Lee to wince and try to squirm free.

"Get off me, you little thug. You can't do this."

"You'd better be off, Lee. You're disturbing the customers." Sally sounded somewhat apologetic, but didn't move to intercept her son as the young man forcibly dragged Lee towards the door.

"All right! All right! I'm going." He yanked his arm free, and turned in the doorway, glancing back at Sally. "But don't say I didn't warn you."

The door shut behind him. Within seconds, a wave of quiet muttering passed amongst people sitting at the tables.

"Thank God for small mercies. But you didn't have to be so hard on him, Christian. He doesn't mean any harm. Not really," said Sally, her voice low.

"He's a mad old fool, and I'm tired of his bullshit," retorted the young man. "Maybe this time he'll get the message." He stalked off into the kitchen, leaving his mother looking weary and embarrassed. She forced a smile, apologised politely to the guests for the disturbance, and slipped away after Christian. Moments later, there were muffled voices in the kitchen. The general hubbub amongst the patrons returned, soon drowning out all sounds of the disagreement.

Daisy retrieved her coffee pot from Elspeth's table. "Well, that's enough excitement for one day," she said, rolling her eyes.

"Waitress!"

Elspeth turned to see a man in his late sixties beckoning rudely for attention. He was shabbily dressed, his shirt poorly ironed, his jacket – which had clearly once been expensively tailored – worn and frayed at the cuffs. He was grey and balding, clean-shaven, and might have been handsome, too, if it hadn't been for the sour expression on his face.

Daisy rolled her eyes. "Nicholas Abbott," she said, beneath her breath. "Still thinks he's the lord of the manor." She turned and approached his table, forcing a smile.

"Yes, sir?"

"You've ignored me for long enough, prattling on with your stupid chitchat. I want more coffee, now." Clearly, this was a man who didn't believe in niceties.

"Of course," said Daisy. She leaned over the table to slosh coffee into his mug, and to Elspeth's horror, she watched as the man reached out and cupped his hand around Daisy's behind. "And I'd like a piece of that, too," he said.

Daisy slammed her coffee pot down onto the table, stepped back, and glowered at him. "Do that again and you'll pay for it," she growled.

"I'd gladly pay for it," said Abbott, slyly. "Just let me know how much."

"Get out!" barked Daisy. "Before I do something I regret. Go on. Get out, now!"

The other customers had all turned around in their seats again to watch this new unfolding drama. Elspeth couldn't help but wonder if it was always like this, in here.

"Oh, don't be like that. It's only a bit of fun. I'll finish my coffee first, I think," said Abbott. He reached calmly for his mug.

"I've asked you to *leave*," said Daisy.

Abbott calmly took a sip from his mug. In the kitchen, the argument continued to rage between Sally and Christian. They were clearly too preoccupied to have noticed what was happening out here.

Elspeth couldn't stand it any longer. She pushed back her chair, got to her feet and marched over to stand beside Daisy. "You heard her," she said. "I don't care who you are, you're lucky she didn't ring the police." She took out her phone. "But they're only a quick call away."

Abbott looked up at her, seemingly weighing her up. She didn't like the way his eyes seemed to linger. "Well, look at you, Miss High-and-Mighty. I bet it's only because you're jealous. After all, the younger model is getting all the attention."

Elspeth opened her phone and began dialling.

Abbott seemed to consider this for a moment, and then sighed, and got to his feet. "I'm going. For now."

Elspeth lowered the phone.

Abbott grabbed his jacket from the back of his chair, slammed a five-pound note on the table, and headed for the door.

Beside Elspeth, Daisy breathed a sigh of relief.

Elspeth slipped her phone into her pocket. Around them, the room was silent, save for the bickering still taking place in the kitchen. Everyone was watching Elspeth and Daisy. Elspeth crossed to the door and stepped outside. Nicholas Abbott was marching away down the lane, his back to her.

"Good riddance." Elspeth turned to see Daisy had followed her out, and was standing on the threshold, watching Abbott recede into the distance. She was shaking.

"Are you okay?" said Elspeth.

"Just angry," said Daisy, and Elspeth realised it was that, more than fear, that was making her shake. "Men like that – they think they can do whatever they want. Well they bloody well can't."

"Do you want to report it to the police? I know someone you could talk to."

Daisy shook her head. "No, thanks. You were great, though."

"Are you sure? I'd give a witness statement. You could have him barred too," said Elspeth.

Daisy shrugged. Elspeth followed her back into the café. "He'll get the message, one way or another. It's not the first time." She touched Elspeth's upper arm briefly. "I really do appreciate your help. I'd best be getting on, though. Doesn't sound as if I'm going to be getting much help this morning." She nodded towards the kitchen, where the argument was still playing out.

"You sound as if you're used to it?"

"The sexual harassment, or the arguing?"

"Both."

Daisy laughed, but it was humourless. "Yeah. I suppose you're right." She collected her coffee pot and went to fetch the bill for a woman who was making a fuss of gathering up her bags. Elspeth looked at her watch. It was probably time she got moving.

CHAPTER THREE

Detective Sergeant Peter Shaw slammed the car door shut and started the slow trudge up to the dig site in the grounds of Hallowdene Manor, feeling more than a little weary.

He couldn't help but think he'd been handed the short end of the stick, being called out here at two in the afternoon. It really was a perfunctory matter, amounting to nothing but a waste of police time. Of *course* they'd found a body on site. That's exactly what they'd been expecting to find. And now here he was, forced to traipse through the mud, just to take a quick look and exchange a few words with the coroner to ensure it wasn't a police matter.

Still, at least he'd be able to get it over with quickly.

It was cold out, and the wind was beginning to stir, ruffling his mop of unruly auburn hair. He'd had to force himself out of bed that morning, scraping shaving foam and stubble from his chin in the bathroom mirror and ponderously brushing his teeth while still half asleep. The morning had passed slowly, drowned in coffee and paperwork at the station. He couldn't help feeling as if all his days were like this at the moment – going through the motions. Since all that business with the Carrion King murders, things had returned to a somewhat more measured pace, dealing with the gangs of teenagers who'd taken to loitering around the back of the High Street in Heighton, or investigating the occasional burglary or missing person who always turned up hours later.

It wasn't that he *wanted* to see anyone murdered, of course. Quite the opposite, in fact. It was more that, after successfully bringing the Carrion King case to a conclusion, he knew that he had something more to offer. He supposed it was a little arrogant of him, but he couldn't help feeling he was treading water at Heighton; that he'd be able to do more to help people at one of the bigger stations elsewhere, where there were more serious criminals to be brought to account.

It seemed the Commissioner agreed – there'd been recent talk of a promotion, but Heighton was a small station, and he knew that meant moving on. Possibly to a city like Manchester or Birmingham: places in need of police officers who had the stomach for some of the more harrowing work that the job sometimes entailed. The thought was appealing... but then, there were other things keeping him here.

Still, he wouldn't miss all the pomp and circumstance that seemed to accompany village life. Take for example the Hallowdene Summer Fayre. It was still days away, but as he'd driven through the centre of the village, he'd seen people up ladders, draping bunting from street lamps, someone hanging Halloween decorations in their window, another person erecting a 'temporary car park' sign in a vacant lot behind the village hall. It all seemed a bit parochial and mad to Peter, even as someone who'd grown up surrounded by it all. They all seemed to take it so *seriously*. Still, he supposed it made people happy.

Short of breath after marching quickly up the incline towards the manor house, he veered left, heading towards the silhouette of the old church.

There was something eerie about the crooked building, dark and sombre against the pale skyline. He felt a sudden sense of foreboding, but quashed it quickly. He'd had a few moments like that since the Carrion King case, flashbacks to the terrible things he'd seen, but worse, to the things those sights had *suggested*, the things he hadn't properly understood. For all his thoughts about rolling his sleeves up, making more of a difference, he was in no hurry to find himself involved in another case like that one. It had raised too many questions that he wasn't yet ready to answer.

He hopped over a stile and splashed down into a muddy field, spattering his boots and the hems of both trouser legs. Muttering a curse beneath his breath, he found a path by the hedgerow, and marched across the field towards the dig.

Up ahead, he could see a small crane sitting in the adjoining field, and beside it, a large slab of grey rock, which was still attached to the crane by a series of chains. People had gathered around a large hole and were peering in.

Another group of people were standing off to one side, behind a loose perimeter of metal posts and fluttering yellow tape. He recognised Elspeth as one of them, her arms folded across her chest to stave off the chill. He made a beeline.

"Morning, you," she said, beaming as she saw him approaching. He felt a sudden twinge of guilt for even thinking about a transfer.

"Morning," he said, trying to remain on a vaguely professional footing, when what he really wanted to do was sweep her up into a big hug. They'd only parted a few hours ago, after he'd crawled out of the pit of his comfortable bed in Wilsby, and made his way up the hill to work.

"This is Hugh and Petra Walsey," said Elspeth, indicating the people standing to one side of her. "They're the owners of the manor house and the sponsors of the dig."

Peter shook hands with the enthusiastic-looking man. He looked every inch the modern country squire, with an expensive navy shirt tucked into faded blue jeans, a brown, waxed jacket and a flat cap. He was thin, and relatively short – about the same height as Elspeth – and was wearing the day's grey-flecked stubble as if he'd been up since the crack of dawn, watching over the dig. He was holding a steel flask in his other hand.

Peter guessed him to be in his mid-forties.

"Hello. DS Shaw," said Peter.

Beside Walsey, his wife seemed somewhat less enthused to be out in the cold. She offered her hand, but her expression showed clear disinterest – in Peter, in the dig, perhaps even in her husband. Unlike Walsey, she had clearly made an effort to look good for the cameras – a long, form-fitting flower-print dress, a small bolero jacket, perfectly applied make-up. Even her long, dark hair seemed unruffled by the breeze. It was a studied appearance, and impressive, too, but nevertheless, Peter couldn't help but wonder about how cold she must be, and how long she'd been forced to stand out here in the mud.

"Quite the event," said Peter. He glanced across at the dig, where another woman was talking hurriedly into a television camera. Others were standing in the shallow recess revealed by the removal of the stone, scraping away with trowels and brushes. He recognised the coroner, Dr McCowley, dressed in a grey over-suit and talking quietly to a woman in her fifties, whom he presumed to be in charge of proceedings.

"Yes, all rather exciting, isn't it?" said Walsey. "We're just waiting on the coroner to make his pronouncement so we can get a better look."

"I'm sure it won't be long now," said Peter. "You know what these experts are like. One glance at an old bone and they can tell what the person had for breakfast."

Walsey laughed. His wife sighed and rolled her eyes impatiently.

"Now, this could be interesting," said Elspeth, peering over Peter's shoulder. He turned to see what she'd spotted.

An older man in a raincoat was ambling across the field, heading in their direction. "Why? Who's that?"

"He's called Lee. He caused a bit of a fuss at Richmond's café earlier on. He was claiming that the witch was unhappy with the café for selling souvenirs, that it was dangerous. He got quite agitated and they had to throw him out."

Beside her, Walsey groaned. "Yes, we're all quite familiar with Lee Stroud. We've had a stream of handwritten letters through the door, protesting about the dig, and he came up here yesterday and started sounding off, too. The cameraman, Steve, saw him off with a few harsh words." He shrugged. "I suppose every town or village has one."

"One what?" said Peter.

"Oh, you know what I mean," said Walsey. "One of *them*. A weirdo. A strange old man with funny ideas."

"He's probably just lonely," said Elspeth.

"Be that as it may, we can't have him disrupting the dig," said Walsey.

"Leave it to me," said Peter. "I'll head him off."

"No, don't worry," said Elspeth. "If it's all the same, I wouldn't mind a quick word with him. Maybe I can dissuade him from making a fuss."

"Be my guest," said Peter. "I'll be over with the coroner if you need me."

* * *

Lee Stroud looked akin to a deer caught in headlights as Elspeth hurried over the muddy field to intercept him, her boots squelching in the thick mud.

She hadn't yet worked out what she was going to say to the man, but she saw in him an opportunity to present a different perspective in her article, an alternative local voice. Surely he couldn't be the only one in Hallowdene with reservations about the dig? For a start, there were the two elderly women she'd overheard in the café, insistent that no good was going to come from disturbing the burial site. As a journalist, surely her job was to present things from a variety of different perspectives?

At least, that's the way she justified it to herself. The truth was, she couldn't quite shake her own nagging doubts. Recent experience had proved to her that sometimes you had to retain an open mind. And Lee Stroud had seemed particularly anxious. She wasn't yet prepared to write him off as a 'local weirdo' as Hugh Walsey had.

"Mr Stroud?" she said, marching forward, her hand extended.

He narrowed his eyes suspiciously. "You were in Richmond's earlier. I saw you there, watching."

"That's right," said Elspeth. "I'm Elspeth Reeves, a journalist. I heard what you said back at the café, and wondered if you might have a moment to talk? I'm writing an article on the Hallowdene Fayre, and the dig."

Stroud looked suspicious. Clearly he wasn't used to people taking him seriously. "What do you want to talk about?" he said.

"What you said, about it being dangerous. Could you tell me a bit more about what you meant?"

Stroud sighed. "The thing is, I'm just trying to help. That's what they don't seem to understand. You've seen the frivolous way they treat our village's history: the dolls and lollipops and postcards and guidebooks. But that woman, Agnes Levett, she was a force to be reckoned with. She did terrible things. And people like that – they don't go quietly, Ms Reeves. And now here they all are, stirring it all up again."

"You believe there's some truth in the old curse?" said Elspeth, careful to avoid any sense of judgement in her tone.

"I believe that atrocities have echoes, is all, and those echoes can be felt through the years, like the aftershocks that follow an earthquake. It's happened before, and it'll happen again, as surely as the world will keep turning."

"I'm not sure I follow," said Elspeth.

"Aye," said Stroud. "But then you don't seem like the type to sit still for long enough to see it. My family have lived in these parts for hundreds of years. We've seen it all, Ms Reeves, and if there's one thing that's clear to me, it's this: everything comes around again. There ain't nothing new in this world."

"So what do you think is going to happen?"

"Stirring up things that have lain long buried," said Stroud, "you're likely to find things that people don't like. And as I said, people like Agnes – wild people, who lived by a different law – they don't rest so easy. When they first buried her, in an unmarked grave on the edge of that there churchyard–" he indicated it with a wave of his arm "–she let her presence be felt. People ended up dead – the very same people who had put her in the ground."

"There were further deaths?" She hadn't got this far in the book, yet.

"Yes. Three people. Peter Loverage, Gwyneth Coombe and Simon Kirkby. Three of the people who dragged her to the gallows. They were all struck down in mysterious circumstances, and there were reports of strange sightings and unearthly voices. That's why they moved her here and buried her under that stone, to keep her presence at bay."

"Like a prison, you mean?" said Elspeth.

"Aye. Like a prison. And now they've gone and opened up the cell."

Despite herself, Elspeth felt the hairs on the nape of her neck prickle. Whatever the truth of it, the man really believed this stuff. To her mind, it was a jumble of superstition and fear, but she'd seen too much to dismiss the idea entirely out of hand.

"All right, Mr Stroud. Thank you for your time. I might want to talk to you again, if that's okay with you?"

Stroud looked surprised at the very notion. "Well,

yes, I suppose so. Look, here's my number." He took a scrap of paper from his coat pocket and scrawled down his phone number on the back with a cheap biro. She took it and placed it in the pocket of her jeans.

"Now, the police are up here at the moment, so if I were you, I wouldn't worry about trying to warn anyone off. It's a little late for that already, I think. But I promise you, Mr Stroud, your concerns have been heard, and I'll call in the next couple of days to talk to you again."

Stroud seemed to consider this for a moment, before giving a satisfied nod. "Very well. Thank you, Ms Reeves. You give me hope for the future."

Elspeth smiled, then watched as he turned and ambled off across the field. When he reached the stile and disappeared from sight, she turned back towards the dig.

Peter was standing to one side, deep in conversation with Hugh Walsey. The coroner was already packing up his equipment, and the film crew were busy getting shots of the grave.

"Ah, well done," said Walsey, as she approached. "What did you say to him?"

"Very little," said Elspeth. "I just listened to him, showed a bit of interest. That's all he wanted, really. To be heard."

"Well, I admire your patience," said Walsey. "I'm not sure I could listen to that claptrap for very long. Did he go on about unquiet spirits and the echoes of the past?"

"Something like that," said Elspeth, feeling slightly defensive. She supposed a certain amount of arrogance was to be expected from a man who owned a manor house. She looked to Peter to rescue her.

"All done," he said, with a relieved grin. "McCowley has confirmed the body is of no interest to the police. Thinks it dates back a few hundred years at least."

"So it could well be Agnes Levett?" said Elspeth.

Peter shrugged. "Quite possibly. I'll leave that to the experts to decide." He bid Walsey goodbye, and she walked with him as far as the border of the adjoining field.

"See you at home tonight?"

"Yes. Of course. You haven't forgotten Abigail's coming to stay tomorrow though, have you?"

"Abigail?"

"Yes. My friend from London. I told you, she's coming to visit. I'll have to stay at my place to keep her company."

He looked a little crestfallen. "Yes, yes. Of course. I forgot. It'll be good to meet her."

Elspeth laughed. "You'll get on, honestly."

"I'm sure we will. See you later, then." He leaned in and kissed her lightly on the lips.

And then he was off, following the same track that had taken Lee Stroud back down to the road a few minutes earlier.

Elspeth turned back to the dig. The TV crew were packing away their equipment, and she had an appointment with Jennifer Wren.

* * *

"Whoa! Steady now!"

Daisy smiled gratefully at the dark-haired young man who leapt up from his seat to catch hold of the tottering stack of teacups she was in the process of dropping, after she'd been forced to hastily sidestep an octogenarian who'd pushed his chair back into her path without any hint of a warning.

He steadied the tower on the tray, and then met her eye, grinning broadly. "That could have been a disaster."

Daisy laughed. "Yes. Thanks. You were quick off the mark."

The man shrugged. "Always happy to help a lady in need." He returned to his seat amidst a ripple of applause from the people at the nearby tables, and Daisy carried on her path towards the kitchen. Christian, who'd seen the whole thing from his position over by the till, made a beeline to intercept her.

"Here, let me help you." He scooped up an armful of teacups and pushed the kitchen door open with his foot, so she could pass.

"Thanks, Christian."

"No problem." He followed her into the kitchen and set the dirty crockery down beside the sink. There was no one else around. "You need to watch out for people like that," he said, lowering his voice.

"Like what? The old man who nearly sent me flying?"

"Like that fella out there, the one who was so keen to try to rescue you."

Daisy sighed. "He was only trying to help, Christian."

"I saw the look in his eye. He had other things on his mind. I'm just trying to say – you're a pretty girl, you need to be careful. I don't think you realise what men are really like." He wouldn't meet her eye, picking at his fingernail as he spoke. He looked a little lost, like a boy at school trying to hold an awkward conversation with a girl. He'd been like this as long as she'd known him. It was as if he'd never quite managed to shed the gawkiness of his teen years. The two of them had never really grown close, despite living under the same roof for a while, and both spending time in Sally's orbit. Daisy had tried, but he'd maintained a cultivated reserve, and she supposed that was just how he was, and that perhaps he'd seen her as a bit of an interloper, impinging on his relationship with his mum. For years it had just been the two of them, him and Sally, and then Daisy had been thrown into the mix and perhaps he'd seen her as a bit of a third wheel. She knew he was fond of her in his own way, though – and fiercely protective, just like he was with his mum.

"Not everyone's like Nicholas Abbott, you know. You don't have to worry so much. I can look after myself."

She saw him wince at the sound of the other man's name. "No, no. I suppose not. We're not all like *that*." He looked up, then, meeting her eye. The moment stretched.

"Look, I'd better be getting back. We've left Sally to cope on her own."

Christian gave a dismissive shrug. "She'll be okay for a moment. Take a breather. You nearly had an accident just then. Let me fetch you a glass of water." He fetched a glass tumbler and ran the water for a moment, then filled it and passed it to her. "Here."

"Thanks." She drank it down.

"You and I should stick together, you know. I've been thinking – we're similar, in many ways. We've both lost people..." He looked away again, returning his attention to the hangnail on his left thumb.

"Is there something on your mind? Something you want to talk about?" said Daisy. There'd been a few moments like this in recent weeks, strange little asides, comments that suggested he wanted to say more.

"No, no. I'm fine," said Christian. "It's you I was worried about. I know how upset you'd have been if you'd dropped all of those teacups."

"Well, thankfully that nice man was there to make sure I didn't," said Daisy. She set her empty glass down on the work surface. "Now I really should be getting back to work."

CHAPTER FOUR

"So, what are we looking at?" said Elspeth. "Besides a skeleton, I mean."

Jennifer Wren grinned, and it was an expression of pure and unabashed glee. She was bristling with excitement, and it was utterly infectious. Elspeth could feel herself getting drawn in. "We'll have to excavate properly. We'll be erecting a tent in a short while to protect the site from the elements. But it's likely this is the grave of Agnes Levett."

"How can you be sure?" To Elspeth, it looked very much like a muddy depression with a few jagged bones poking out. The weight of the stone had pressed everything into the soft earth, reminding her of when she'd played with modelling clay as a child, how it had oozed when she'd hidden copper coins inside the pots to dig out later.

"The skeleton is remarkably well preserved, considering," said Jenny. She stepped down into the depression. "See here. The body was still relatively intact when it was moved and re-interred. And here, these are the remains of witch bottles – jugs or pots stuffed with hair and believed to counter the witch's curse."

Elspeth studied the bones, trying to see whatever Jenny was seeing. The skull was looking straight up at them, its jaw hinged open in a silent scream. The mud and the passing years had caused the bones to discolour, too, mottling them with yellows and browns, which made it appear to Elspeth as if there were still remnants of flesh and blood and other organic matter clinging resolutely to the remains. It didn't help that the wind was blowing in the stink from a nearby farmer's field, leaving Elspeth with the distinct impression that the grave still smelled of rot and decay. Something about the sight of the bones, still here, in situ, left her with a sharp feeling of disquiet.

It wasn't like seeing bones in a museum, where they'd been cleaned and presented as part of an exhibition, a story, with little information cards, or like finding a recently deceased body – which she knew from bitter experience. It was more like looking in on someone sleeping, like somehow invading their privacy, and she felt both privileged and uneasy to be a part of it.

"So the villagers placed these witch bottles in here with her corpse?" She took out her phone and grabbed a few pictures. Most of them had been reduced to jagged fragments, their contents now little more than discoloured patches, exposed to the light for the first time in centuries.

"I'd assume so, yes. Charms, of a sort, to keep her evil

spirit at bay." Jenny straightened up, rubbing her lower back with a groan. "Archaeology. It's a real back killer."

"I empathise. Being chained to a desk isn't much good for my neck," said Elspeth, unconsciously rubbing the sore spot between her shoulder blades. It was one of the reasons she was enjoying getting out and about so much, digging up stories to sell to a growing portfolio of newspapers and online news sites. She supposed, in some ways, her job and Jenny's weren't that different – both of them were looking to uncover the truth, digging down through layers of obfuscation and assumption to get to the real story. And both of them seemed to include bodies. She'd certainly never expected that.

"Have you excavated anything like this before?" said Elspeth.

"Never quite like this, lifting a witch stone and all. I know of others, but it's a pretty rare opportunity," said Jenny.

"But you've examined the graves of other so-called witches?"

Jenny shrugged. "A couple. Sadly, most of those poor women were buried in unmarked graves and are lost to us now. It's all pretty shameful."

"And you've never worried about a curse?" said Elspeth. "I mean, the villagers obviously believed it. Their witch bottles are surely evidence of that. Have the locals had much to say about the dig?"

Jenny smiled. "One or two of them cling on to their superstitions, I suppose. Most of them recognise the truth – that Agnes was most likely the victim in all this. They like to play along, though. You've seen this village – the trinkets they sell in the café, the fuss they make about the fayre. Agnes – or rather, the caricature that's been painted of her – is the story of this place."

"So you think they're clinging on to her out of a desire to hold on to a tourist attraction?"

"No, nothing so cynical as that," said Jenny. "I think they're worried that the dig is going to show everyone the truth – that Agnes was just another victim, a woman who was tried and executed as a witch, along with hundreds of others. Let's face it, we all know that's what I'm going to uncover here, and it's a lot more mundane than the stories that have sprung up around her, isn't it? I think it's high time this woman's dignity was restored to her. She needs to be seen for the victim she is. Even if she was responsible for the death of another woman, we don't know the circumstances. History has already found her guilty, but the truth is likely to be far less salacious. I think that's what people are afraid of, whether they realise it or not. People don't like change, and they cling to their traditions. If there's no witch, what does that mean for Hallowdene?"

"You don't believe that Agnes committed the crimes she's accused of, then?"

"I didn't say that. She might well have committed murder. But to what end… I don't know. That's the real story, here, the one you should be writing about. What did Agnes really do, and why? Because one thing's for certain – she was no witch, and she died a horrific death because people were scared." Jenny held out her arm. "Give us a hand up, would you?"

Elspeth obliged, clasping the other woman by the arm and helping to heave her up over the lip of the depression. They walked together, back towards a small tent on the other side of the field. Here, a couple of trestle tables had been laid out, ready to receive the finds as they were removed from the grave.

"There's nothing in any of the material I've read – and it's admittedly scant – to suggest that Agnes Levett actually committed that murder. She was found with the body, yes, and there's reference to 'pagan symbols', but how are we to know what she was trying to do, three hundred-odd years later?"

"If I'm understanding you right, you're saying your aim here is to set the record straight? To prove that Agnes wasn't really a witch *or* a killer?" said Elspeth.

"Oh, nothing so grand as all that," replied Jenny, laughing. "I don't think anyone *really* believes she was a witch, do you? My job is to lay out the facts, just as I find them in the grave. It's a fascinating insight into village life in the seventeenth century, and the witch trials that took place all across the country. Those little witch bottles, for example – they may be unique to this case, this situation. Isn't that exciting enough?"

"I suppose it is, yes," said Elspeth. "Okay, last question. Why now? People have told stories about the Hallowdene Witch buried under the stone for hundreds of years. Why choose now to excavate and try to find her?"

"That's easy," said Jenny. "It's all down to Hugh."

"Walsey?"

"Yes. The previous owners, the Abbotts, would never allow anyone to dig. It's as simple as that. People have been trying for years, but every time they asked, the Abbotts would shut them down. Now that Hugh's bought the house, things are a little different. He's got plans, wants to develop the land, so he had to bring us in. Besides, it's all good publicity for his venture, too. And for the village."

"And what *is* his venture?" asked Elspeth. She had visions of one of those enormous outlet malls, or a garden centre or housing estate suddenly springing up to mar the landscape and continue the slow march of homogenisation across the country.

"You'll have to ask him. Something to do with books, I think," said Jenny.

"Books…" Elspeth perked up at the thought. Maybe she'd misjudged the man after all. "Well, thanks for your time," she said. "A photographer from the paper will be along later to get some proper pictures, if that's okay?"

"I'll be sure to show them my best side," said Jenny, grinning. Elspeth felt herself warming to the woman. She appreciated the no-nonsense approach, the fact that Jenny was there to do a job, and didn't want to wrap it all in airs and graces.

"Oh, and I've got to ask – I presume your parents were Dickens fans?"

Jenny groaned. "You can't imagine what I went through as a child!"

Elspeth laughed. "I'll give you a call if I have any more questions."

CHAPTER FIVE

The sun was low in the sky as Elspeth traipsed up the long driveway towards Hallowdene Manor.

The house was a glorious gothic mansion, partially fortified, with crenellations running around the lip of the roof and a small tower – complete with arrow slits – which had clearly been added sometime after the main building's initial erection. Elspeth supposed these additions were an affectation of previous generations of the Abbott family, but regardless, they added something spectacular to what was already a rather grand and impressive house. She'd read that parts of the building dated back to the early seventeenth century, but that it had been extensively remodelled during the Gothic Revival of the nineteenth century.

Now, it was encrusted with all the trappings of modernity – CCTV cameras, burglar alarms, reinforced windows, and floodlights. Through one of the large bay windows she could see the flicker of a massive TV, and where once horse-drawn carriages might have stood on the gravel forecourt, now there was a top-of-the-range

BMW, and a Range Rover. She suspected there were other cars tucked away in the garages, too.

Still, whoever was in the process of modernising the building was doing so sensitively. The grotesques still loomed over the main entrance, and years of accumulated ivy still crawled over the brickwork, lending the place an authentic, rural charm. It was picturesque, and very appealing.

Elspeth approached the main entrance, conscious of the state of her boots, which were thickly encrusted with mud. She'd walked up here from the dig site, rather than heading back down to the road to collect her car. Now, she couldn't help thinking that was a bad idea.

The front door – an ancient, iron-banded construction of heavy wood, mottled with age – stood open, revealing the passageway within. The walls here seemed to lean outward, the wood panelling warped and uneven, giving the place a strange, organic feel. The floor was flagstone, and an ancient side table stood against one wall, bearing a telephone and a heap of papers. A cable modem sat beside the phone, lights blinking incongruously. Beyond that, she could see the sweeping balustrade of a grand staircase leading up from the larger hall.

Elspeth hovered on the threshold for a moment, unsure whether to go in. She'd agreed with Hugh Walsey to come up to the house after she'd finished at the dig, but she didn't want to intrude. She considered using the large cast-iron knocker in the shape of a lion's head on the door, but it looked as though it was there for decorative purposes, rather than practical use.

After a moment of searching, she located a small plastic box on the outer wall, and pushed the button. She heard an electronic bell trilling inside, and then a burst of static issued from the box, followed by Hugh Walsey's echoing voice. "Yes, who is it?"

"Elspeth Reeves," she said. "About the dig."

"Ah, yes, come on in," said Walsey. "I'll meet you in the hall."

"Shall I take my boots off? I've been down at the dig," she called.

"If you don't mind," replied Walsey.

Feeling less like a snoop, Elspeth entered the house, kicking off her boots just inside the door, where she found a heap of other, similarly encrusted footwear.

Inside, the building was gloomily lit, the only light filtering down through a large stained-glass window at the top of the landing. Red, gold and blue formed a shimmering pattern on the polished floorboards. The window itself was beautifully crafted, and must have dated back to the creation of the house. It appeared to depict a scene of an archangel descending from the heavens, surrounded by a flock of cherubs heralding its arrival with thin-necked horns.

"Stunning, isn't it?"

She turned at the voice to see Walsey watching her, a look of wry amusement on his face.

"Sometimes I stand just where you are, at the

foot of the stairs, and look up at that window, and think to myself 'how did I end up here?'" He sounded genuinely moved.

"It's a beautiful house," said Elspeth. She could see why he was so in love with the place.

"Ever since I was a child, I've dreamed of living here," he said. "I used to sneak into the grounds with my friends to play hide and seek. The Abbotts had a groundsman who would chase us away if he caught us, but we knew just where to hide to avoid him. We'd run through the fields, hide in the sheds, climb the trees to pinch apples, and sometimes even come right up to the house to peer in through the windows." He laughed. "Once I even plucked up the courage to sneak in." He looked scandalised. "Can you imagine? At the time it seemed as if I had no choice, even though I knew it was wrong. I just had to see inside, like it was calling to me. I know that seems strange. But that's what it felt like.

"The door was standing open, like it is now, and I went right up to it, standing on the threshold, peering in. And then, before I knew what I was doing, I was creeping down the hallway. I could hear voices down there, in the sitting room, but I carried on regardless. I didn't even think about getting caught. I just kept on going, until I found myself right here, standing just where you are now, looking up at that magnificent window. And that's the moment I knew I had to live here someday."

Elspeth realised that she'd been completely caught up in his story. "Is that true?"

"Every word of it," said Walsey, with a wistful smile.

"And did they catch you?"

"No, no. I legged it when I heard someone coming out into the hall. They saw me, came chasing after me, but they can't have recognised me, because nothing was ever said. For days afterwards I kept on expecting a knock at the door, a scolding from my parents, even the police, but nothing. I didn't set foot inside again, though, until I came to make arrangements for the purchase from Nicholas Abbott earlier this year."

Nicholas Abbott was the man she'd seen in Richmond's earlier that day, grabbing Daisy's behind and making lewd comments. She found herself feeling pleased that he no longer had this magical old place to himself. "What made him sell? I mean – if I had a place like this, with such a long family history attached to it, I'd be pretty reluctant to give it up."

Walsey shrugged. "I guess it was just the right time. I'd made a few approaches over the years, but he'd never given any sign that he'd consider selling. Then one day late last year, I decided to try again, and lo and behold, I get a call from his solicitor two days later, saying that he was willing to entertain my offer. I jumped at the chance. It's cost me a fair bit more than I'd anticipated to renovate the place, but it's worth it."

"What about the family? Aren't there any children?"

"No children, but there is a younger cousin, Thomas. He was furious with Nicholas for selling up. Said he'd destroyed the family legacy. He's on something of a crusade, trying to get me to sell the place back to him. But it's not going to happen. Not now I finally have it." He shrugged. "To be honest, I can't help thinking that Nicholas sold the place simply to spite him. There's no love lost between them, and they're a difficult family at the best of times."

Elspeth turned at the sound of raised voices from the top of the stairs. Petra, Walsey's wife, was shouting something in a hoarse, Polish accent, and a younger woman was yelling back at her in total defiance.

Walsey sighed. "But then all families are difficult, aren't they?" A young woman in her late teens wearing cut-off jeans, black tights, black boots and a T-shirt emblazoned with the image of a cassette tape came hurtling down the stairs. She didn't even acknowledge Elspeth or Walsey as she ran across the hallway and straight out of the front door. A moment later they heard the sound of a car engine revving.

"My daughter, Lucy," said Walsey. He beckoned towards the drawing room. "Come on, this way. I'll fetch you a drink. I know I could use one."

"Just a soft drink for me," said Elspeth. "I'm driving."

The drawing room was more like a library, lined with antique bookcases, serried ranks of garish paperbacks stacked haphazardly upon them. So often, traipsing around the musty old houses of the National Trust, Elspeth had seen shelves such as these housing crumbling old volumes bound in vellum or cracked leather, their titles embossed in Latin or French. It made her smile to see them put to proper use, housing a collection of books that were actually read – crime, mystery and travel writing, rather than ancient treatises on philosophy, or Christian tracts, or weighty tomes about law. She couldn't help but scan the shelves as Walsey poured her a glass of lemonade, grinning as she recognised many of the names on the cracked spines.

"These yours?" she asked, as he handed her the drink. He tapped the rim of his own drink against hers, before taking a long draught.

"Yes, mostly. I'm something of a bookaholic. It's my biggest indulgence. After the house, of course. I grew up in a house where every book was treasured, because we never had the money to buy more. We used to cling on to them until they fell apart. Even now, I still can't let them go."

"I know exactly what you mean," said Elspeth, thinking of the wall of Ikea bookcases that Peter had recently helped her to assemble for her new flat. She'd already filled them twice over after unpacking the boxes she'd fetched from London, cramming more and more books into every conceivable space. It was nothing compared to the magnitude of Walsey's collection, but she recognised the impulse, and she knew she'd be the same if she had the space and the money to indulge herself. She'd already started leaving piles of books at Peter's house. He hadn't mentioned it to her yet, which she'd taken as a sign that he was growing comfortable with her constant presence. She wondered how he'd feel if and when the time came to move the rest of them over, too.

Walsey drained his glass, and returned to the cabinet for a refill. "What is it they say? You're never alone with a good book."

"Jennifer mentioned something down at the dig site, about your plans to develop the land. She said it was something to do with books?"

"Yes! I'm planning to build a few cottages down there, along with a small office. The idea is to use the cottages for readers' and writers' retreats, and the office will be the base for a small publishing business." He had the same gleam in his eye that Elspeth had seen in Jenny's earlier.

"What sort of things will you publish?"

"Mostly crime and fantasy fiction," he said, gesturing at his shelves as if to underline his point, "but anything I fancy, really. It's an extraordinary privilege to have money in the bank; I feel I should use some of it to give voice to people who don't."

She couldn't tell whether this was grandstanding, arrogant, or wonderfully philanthropic. She supposed it was a nice story, amongst all the talk of witches and murders and curses – the tale of a local boy made good, who'd worked hard to achieve his goals. "Well, I look forward to seeing how it all develops. Maybe I could do a piece for the paper when you're ready to set out your plans."

Walsey inclined his head in thanks.

She hadn't yet established how he'd come into so

much money, and was fishing for a way to broach the subject when Petra Walsey stormed into the room, heading straight for the drinks cabinet. She flung open the cabinet door, grabbed a glass and poured herself a very large measure of brandy, which she downed in a couple of gulps. Elspeth was amazed the glass didn't shatter in her hand.

"You're going to have to do something about your daughter," said Petra, accusingly, fixing Walsey with a contemptuous stare.

"Look, Petra, I've already said she's as much right to be here as you or I—"

"It's not about that. It's about respect. Or rather her distinct lack of it." She crossed to one of the tall windows between the bookcases and peered out, brushing the curtain aside with the back of her hand. "If she wants to live under this roof, she needs to show me the respect I deserve."

Walsey bristled, and Elspeth started to wonder how she could politely extricate herself before things got any more heated. She was already feeling like she'd accidentally wandered into an episode of *Downton Abbey*. "Respect has to be earned, darling," said Walsey, his voice dripping with sarcasm. "Perhaps if you made a little more effort trying to understand her…"

"Don't you think I know what it's like to be a nineteen-year-old girl? I know better than you."

And you're behaving just like one now, thought Elspeth. For the life of her, she couldn't understand what

Walsey could see in the woman, besides the obvious. She *was* startlingly pretty.

"I'll be off now, then," Elspeth said, during what she imagined would be nothing but a momentary lapse in the argument. "Thanks for your time. I'll see myself out." She ducked towards the door, only to find Walsey following after her.

He caught her arm in the hallway, lowering his voice. "I'm so sorry about that," he said. "It's the dig, and the move… it's all got a bit much for her. You understand?"

His expression looked so hopeful that she didn't want to disappoint him. "Of course," she said. "You've got a great deal going on." She smiled, and he let go of her arm. "I'll call with any further questions," she said.

"Please do. And perhaps when my imprint is up and running, we could talk about a writing project."

"Oh, no. Thank you. I learned long ago that my strength lies in reporting stories, not making them up. But I appreciate the gesture."

Walsey gave her a forlorn smile, as if reluctant to see her go. She supposed he'd much rather continue talking about books than return to the argument that awaited him in the drawing room. But she had somewhere to be, and she didn't want to put herself in Petra's line of fire.

CHAPTER SIX

"You're not reading another of those dreadful books about the supernatural, are you?"

Elspeth looked up from where she was lying on the bed, her book propped open on the pillow before her. Peter was standing in the bedroom doorway, grinning, in a T-shirt and boxer shorts.

"No. Not tonight," she said. "And yes, I know most of it's hokum, but after everything we've seen, I just want to see if I can get to the truth."

He crossed the room and flopped onto the bed beside her. "You know, I still can't believe it."

"The supernatural?" she said, taking his hand.

"No. That I get to come home on a night, and come to bed and find you here, waiting for me." He leaned in and kissed her, then rested his head back on his pillow.

"I'd have thought you'd be getting used to it by now."

He shrugged. "I'm not sure I'll ever get used to your snoring."

"What?" She slapped him playfully on the arm. "I do *not* snore!"

"How would you know?"

She gave him a withering look, and he laughed. "What are you reading, anyway?"

She turned the book so he could see the cover. "It's that book I picked up at Richmond's. The one about the Hallowdene Witch, Agnes Levett. It's such a sad story."

"I thought she was a murderer?" said Peter.

"So the story goes. But I wonder what led her to do it. According to this, she was well known to most of the villagers at the time. She lived alone, in a cottage on the edge of the woods, and her sister and surviving family had moved away because of the Civil War. She was a wise woman who the villagers went to for help with their ailments."

"That's most likely where the witchcraft connection comes in," said Peter. "She was probably using herbs to heal people and ended up getting accused of all sorts. That's what usually happened, wasn't it?"

"Well, the story goes that one night, some of the villagers heard screaming coming from the woods near her house and went to investigate. They found her crouched over the body of Lady Grace Abbott. The woman had been stripped and covered in strange markings, and she'd been beaten and stabbed. The villagers claimed that Agnes had been carrying out some dark ritual, and they lynched her, dragging her through the streets to the village green, where they hanged her for witchcraft and murder."

"That's pretty dark," said Peter.

"Isn't it?" said Elspeth. "But why would she do it?

There's no real record of what happened – just folklore and stories – so there's no clear motive."

"But surely it's all largely superstition. I mean, witches? No one really believes they were real." He stretched, rolling his neck back and forth to work the muscles.

"Well, it's what happened afterwards that's interesting. I've been reading up on what Lee Stroud said at the dig this afternoon."

"The guy who was getting all worked up about the 'terrible curse'?" The scepticism was clear in Peter's tone.

"Yes," said Elspeth. "And I know it's probably all nothing but superstition, too, but it's *interesting*."

"Oh, very," said Peter, smirking.

"Look, if I'm boring you, I can just as soon turn the light off and go to sleep…"

Peter laughed. "And miss the end of my bedtime story? No, you carry on."

She narrowed her eyes. "I'm watching you."

He leaned in and kissed her again, running his finger along the line of her back. "No, seriously, I'm listening."

"It's the story of how Agnes's remains were moved that's got me intrigued. Apparently, as she was dragged away, she told the villagers that she'd have her revenge. No one thought too much about it, but a few days after they buried her, people started to die in mysterious circumstances. There were reported sightings of the dead woman in the village at night. Three people, Peter Loverage, Gwyneth Coombe and Simon Kirkby, all members of the gang that had lynched her, were found dead."

"But this was the seventeenth century. They were probably riddled with some horrible disease."

"Quite probably," conceded Elspeth, "but the rest of the villagers didn't think so. They persuaded the Reverend from the local church to assist in her reburial. They moved her body, digging a fresh grave, and had the Reverend bless a 'witch stone', which they placed upon the grave to keep her spirit at bay. Afterwards, the mysterious deaths stopped completely."

"And that's the stone that Jenny Wren was digging up today."

"Yup."

"Spooky…" said Peter. He reached over and closed Elspeth's book. "Then we'd better watch out, and think about making the most of the time we have left, before the witch comes for us all." He wrapped his arm around Elspeth and pulled her in, kissing her neck.

She laughed, wrapping her leg around his, running her hands down the fold of his back. "Well, when you put it like that," she said, "there's only one thing for it." She reached over and turned out the light.

CHAPTER SEVEN

Nicholas Abbott popped the CD from its case and slid it into the machine. Moments later, the delicate strains of Chopin's Nocturne No. 2 were swirling through the room. The edginess he'd felt all day finally started to slip away. He crossed to the cupboard in the alcove and searched out his bottle of Scotch, sloshing himself a large measure. In the corner, the TV was playing with the sound down, showing images of men and tanks and people on the other side of the world blowing each other up. He couldn't care less what they did. Why did *he* have to see it? He fumbled for the remote, flicking the channel over. Michael Portillo was lurking in some dustbowl in the arse-end of America, standing beside a ridiculous-looking steam train. He tossed the remote away in disgust.

The answering machine was flashing again, and he knew it would be bloody Thomas, moaning again about the house. Well, bugger the house, and bugger Thomas. He'd never deserved to inherit it. He barely deserved the Abbott name. He'd been a wheedling little child, always moaning, and he was just the same now. He supposed it was too late for the man to change. They were all too old. And to think – it was Thomas's sickly little brats who'd continue the family legacy. Well, at least he hadn't given them the satisfaction of the family seat, too.

He didn't even miss the place, with its creaking beams and rickety old floorboards. The cottage was much more manageable. Here, he could while away the last few years of his life in peace, away from all that ruddy nonsense about who was going to inherit what. He'd never have to speak to any of them again, not if he didn't want to. And they could stop their bloody moaning, too. The manor had been his to sell, and sell it he had. Let that idiot Hugh Walsey spend all his money doing the place up, installing cameras and fixing the roof; he had reached the point in his life where he didn't want anything to do with all that.

He walked through to the kitchen. The microwave had almost finished. He fetched a plate from the dishwasher and collected a knife and fork.

A few minutes later he was safely installed in his armchair by the fire, fish pie on a tray on his lap. He'd put the fire on to warm the room, and was starting to feel a little dozy. He'd probably drunk his Scotch too quickly. Still, after he'd finished his meal, there'd be time for a little nap before he took himself off to bed. He'd become accustomed to drifting off in his chair, dreaming of that young lass from the café and her shapely behind.

He scooped up another forkful of fish pie, and glanced again at the telly. Portillo was still going on about ruddy trains. What was it about trains? Thomas had developed a thing for them as a boy, always messing about with the little electric set he'd been given one Christmas, faffing about laying out tracks on the dining-room table. Nicholas had never seen the attraction. To him they were just machines, and bloody useless ones at best. Why take a train when a car would get you straight to wherever you were going? He'd never understood that. Why did people persist with these things? Were they all idiots?

Shaking his head, he finished shovelling the last of his pie into his mouth, and then sat back in his chair, closed his eyes for a moment and allowed the music to roll over him.

He snapped awake, sitting bolt upright in his chair. He must have dozed off. The music had stopped, and the television was showing some athletics programme. The gas fire had warmed the room, and he loosened the collar of his shirt, feeling a little uncomfortable. He reached down and turned the fire off.

He must have been asleep for hours. A quick glance at the clock on the mantelpiece told him it had gone midnight. Silly old fool. He'd only meant to close his eyes for a few minutes.

He cocked his head at the sound of something tap-tapping against the window.

"What is it now?" he grumbled, levering himself out

of his chair. The muscles in his lower back creaked in protest. He'd spent too long sitting in the wrong position.

There it was again: a sound like someone tapping lightly with a fingernail against the glass pane. Who could it be at this hour? Who would have reason to tap on his window, rather than knock at the door? Probably drunks, staggering back from the pub, he decided, as he walked over to investigate. He pulled back the curtain with a groan of frustration, expecting to see the leering faces of a gang of youths, pale and eerie in the moonlight. But there was no one there.

"Must have been a bird," he muttered to himself, tugging the curtain back into place. He turned back to the television. He couldn't be doing with the athletics, and he supposed it was a bit late for another whisky. He'd do his rounds, lock up and head to bed.

When he stooped to collect his tray from the floor, Nicholas stiffened at the sound of the front door creaking open. So there *had* been someone at the window. And now they had the temerity to let themselves in.

"Who's there?" He heard a footstep in the hallway, beyond the sitting-room door. "Who do you think you are, letting yourself in at this hour?"

No response.

A sudden spike of fear curdled his guts. What if it was a burglar? Everyone around here knew who he was, that he'd moved most of his family's accumulated treasures from the old manor to this little cottage. What if someone had decided to chance their arm, figuring the old man wouldn't be able to put up much in the way of resistance?

Well, he'd show them.

He turned, scrabbling for one of the pokers he kept in a bucket by the fireplace. It was a gas fire, but like all the other furnishings here, he'd brought these with him from the old house, too attached to them to let them go.

Behind him, the door creaked open.

"*Without grace or remorse.*" The voice was an eerie whisper, right in his ear.

Panicked, he started to turn, brandishing the poker, but his attacker was too quick, and they were on him within seconds, gloved hands reaching around his throat from behind, squeezing so hard that stars burst before his eyes.

He kicked and punched, tried to swing the poker, but his assailant was simply too strong, and he was too old. The last thing he saw was a woman on the television screen, pole-vaulting over some impossibly high bar.

CHAPTER EIGHT

Usually, she didn't mind the cold, but tonight it was bone deep, the sort of chill that set in and wouldn't let go, no matter how much she stamped her feet, or blew into her cupped hands. She wished she'd brought her scarf along, or worn more than a jacket over her T-shirt, but it was early summer, and it was supposed to be *warm*.

Daisy exhaled, watching her breath plume before her face, as if the air itself was trying to leach the warmth from her body. Around her, the shadows were deep and long, liquid-like, pooling amongst the brambles and the trees. She thought how easy it would be to lose herself in that inky blackness, to disappear into the night. She'd been tempted to do it before, to just up sticks and run, to get away from this little town, with its small-minded people and oppressive air. But she supposed there were things keeping her here, for now. She'd just have to stick it out. She wasn't about to let it crush her spirit. She wasn't the type to give in.

Still, tonight she was dog-tired. The shift at

Richmond's had been a trial in and of itself. Not only had she had to deal with Nicholas Abbott and his disgusting advances, and Geraldine Finch getting all pernickety about the size of her scone, she'd had Sally and Christian at each other's throats for most of the afternoon. She could have cut the tension in that place with a knife, and the customers had noticed it too.

What Daisy couldn't understand was why Sally seemed so insistent on defending Lee Stroud. His outbursts had become a regular occurrence, and Daisy had started to wonder if it was turning into some sort of dangerous obsession. Was he the sort that was just going to flip one day, and stagger in with a shotgun or a kitchen knife? She certainly got the sense that he wasn't all there, that he'd been damaged in some way.

Daisy supposed it demonstrated a streak of naivety in Sally, but Daisy could never see that as a fault. Sally had been there for Daisy when she'd needed someone, and she'd always be grateful for that. She'd taken her in when Daisy had lost the house, letting her sleep on the sofa bed for a couple of months, giving her a job at the café, offering her moral support. She'd even paid the deposit on Daisy's little rental cottage, and bought her art supplies to keep her going. She owed the woman a lot.

Christian didn't see it that way, of course. He couldn't understand how his mother could lavish all of this attention on others, while paying such little heed to him, her only child. Daisy didn't think it was like that, of course, but she knew that was how Christian saw it; she'd overheard enough arguments in her time to piece it all together.

She turned the corner, passing down Hulston Lane. Here, the solitary glow of a single street lamp cast a weak pall over the rooftops. Everything seemed still. In the distance, she could see the light was still on in Nicholas Abbott's new cottage. The dirty old bastard was probably still up watching porn.

She walked a little way along the road, her fingers drumming a nervous beat on her left thigh. The hairs on the nape of her neck prickled. Was there someone there, watching her?

She sensed movement behind her and turned, but the street was silent, empty. Around her, window blinds and curtains were pulled shut. The village was asleep, its people dreaming.

She shrugged and carried on her way.

"*Without grace or remorse.*"

Daisy turned on the spot, her heart hammering. The whispering voice had been right in her ear, so close that she was certain she'd felt the person's breath on her cheek. There was no one there.

"Hello?" she said. Her voice was tremulous, loud and rude in the absolute silence. "Who's there?"

She scanned the road in all directions. Had someone ducked behind a garden hedge, keeping out of view? It had been a woman's voice, clear and insistent. She bunched her hands into fists. "I know you're there. If this is some sort of joke, it's not funny. Come out where I can see you."

Silence.

Her mouth was dry. She swallowed, feeling the adrenaline coursing through her system, the metallic aftertaste, the heightened senses. Whoever it was must have gone. She wondered whether she'd simply caught the tail end of something spoken on a television or radio show in one of the darkened houses. But even she was far from convinced.

She hesitated to turn her back on the road again. She was nearly home now, though. Just a few more streets.

She turned and hurried off, quickening her pace into a near run.

"*Grace. Remorse.*"

This time the words felt as though they were *inside* her head. She stopped, panting for breath, leaning against the lamp-post with one hand. Her head was spinning. She retched, choking back a stream of bile. The world was spinning. She clutched at the lamp-post, trying to anchor herself, to hold on as the world seemed to shift all around her. The darkness swam in, as if the shadows themselves were alive, swirling like liquid, embracing her.

Her vision shifted.

She was standing in the woods. Around her, the trees loomed; ominous silhouettes, branches like scrabbling limbs. She gulped for air, heady with the aroma of damp earth and mouldering leaves. She realised a light sheen of sweat had formed on her forehead and cheeks.

Her legs felt tired, lactic acid causing a dull, deep ache in her thigh muscles. Had she run here? What the hell was going on?

She felt the dizziness returning, and fought to hold it at bay, leaning forward, hands on her knees, drawing ragged breath.

She was in the woods.

One moment she'd been standing in Hulston Lane, by the lamp-post. The next she was here, somewhere deep in the Wychwood, alone in the gloom.

For a moment she wondered if she was dreaming, if she'd passed out on Hulston Lane, and this was her mind attempting to make sense of what had happened to her. Some kind of seizure, perhaps? Something about it felt too real, though.

Daisy looked up, trying to catch sight of the moon through the canopy of leaves, but the light was diffuse, the shadows all-pervading. She thought about her phone, and scrabbled to find it in her jeans. It was still there. She flipped open the case. The light of the screen seemed so bright that she had to squint, and tears formed in the corners of her eyes. The time flashed up in big, white letters: 2.46 am.

She'd lost nearly two hours. Had she been walking all that time, stumbling out here alone, delirious?

She checked the battery – 76 per cent left. She could use it as a torch. That would have to be enough. She could find her way with that. How far could she really have come? She was probably on the outskirts of the village, where the farmland gave way to the woods and everyone walked their dogs in the nice weather.

She glanced again at the screen, thumbing through her contacts. It was no use calling anyone. How could she explain what had happened? Besides, she didn't even know where she was. It wasn't as if Sally could drive over to pick her up. She'd only worry everyone unnecessarily. She'd also have to explain what she'd been doing out so late, wandering the streets. That certainly wasn't a good idea. No – she'd have to make her own way home. Maybe in the morning she'd be able to make more sense of it all.

She heard a rustle of leaves and looked up. At first she thought it must have been a bird or a badger, ferreting in the undergrowth, but there, standing beneath the twisted bough of an oak tree, was the silhouette of a person, picked out in a silvery spear of moonlight.

Daisy couldn't quite make out their face, but she guessed from their size and build it was a woman, wearing what appeared to be a thick overcoat. Had someone heard her and come out to see if she was okay?

"Hello?" she said, her voice cracking. "Can you help me? I think I must be lost. I need to get back to the road..." She trailed off. The figure hadn't moved, hadn't even acknowledged she'd spoken. "Hello, can you hear me?"

"*Grace in death.*"

The whispered words were like a short, sharp punch to the gut, and Daisy wheeled, thrashing at whatever had spoken them in her ear. She lurched into the darkness, and the world seemed to unbalance again. She went down, throwing her hand out to catch a tree stump, scraping her palm on the jagged end of a broken branch. She hit the ground, sliding forward on one elbow down a short incline, scoring a slippery path through the thick moss.

She came to rest with a loud sob, tears running down her cheeks. She dabbed at them with muddy fingers, wincing at the bloody gash on her palm. What was happening to her? Her mind reeled in confusion. Were the voices in her head? Somehow, the thought of that seemed even more terrifying.

She remained there for a moment, lying on the ground, catching her breath, and steadying her nerves.

After a moment, she felt strong enough to sit up. Her hands were shaking. She could see her phone, lying in the moss a few feet away, back up the incline.

"Thank God for small mercies," she mumbled, echoing one of Sally's oft-used phrases.

Slowly, she picked her way up the mossy bank to retrieve it. She looked around for any sign of the woman, but she was gone.

Perhaps she'd simply been a figment of her imagination, Daisy considered, or a malformed tree trunk, caught at just the right angle to appear like something it was not. She repeated this to herself as she used the light from her phone to pick her way through the woods and back to the road.

She was still repeating it as she staggered to her
bed a short while later, hand wrapped in a makeshift
bandage, and slipped into a deep, dreamless sleep.

CHAPTER NINE

"Well, as much as I hate to speculate, the contusions around his throat suggest the poor bastard was choked to death from behind," said Dr Nijjer. "Of course, I'll know more later, once I get him back to the lab."

"Thanks, Raf. Are we looking for a ligature, a rope, a garrotte?"

"It doesn't look like it. From the pattern of the bruising and the marks on the throat, I'd say the killer was wearing gloves, and throttled him with their hands."

Peter nodded. They were standing in the living room of Nicholas Abbott's small cottage at the end of Hulston Lane. It was the last in a row of similar cottages on the east side of Hallowdene village, close to the communal green with its large children's play area and its imposing village cross, supposedly erected in the fourteenth century by monks from a nearby priory. All that was left of the priory now was a lumpy field full of foundation stones, and a single gothic arch which stood on the hill, looking down upon the village and marking the border of Raisonby Wood. He guessed the main building was probably destroyed during Henry VIII's dissolution of the monasteries.

The cottage itself was pleasant enough, but not exactly the sort of thing he'd have expected for someone of Nicholas Abbott's standing, a man who'd spent his entire life walking through the ancient surroundings of Hallowdene Manor, surrounded by opulence and his own extensive lands.

Men like Abbott, Peter knew, tended to have a skewed perspective on life. Abbott had probably never had to worry about money, never feared how he was going to pay the next electricity bill, or been forced to save for months on end to treat himself to some minor luxury. People envied that lifestyle, that freedom, but what did it really amount to? Isolation, recalcitrance and a lack of empathy for others, in Peter's brief experience. He'd dealt with Abbott's type before, had to put up with their arrogance, their assumption that they were somehow above the law that governed others.

But then Nicholas Abbott had sold up and moved here, to a small cottage close to the heart of the village. What did that say about him? Was he somehow trying to make amends for his past behaviour? Was he trying to prove something? Or had someone been leaning on him, slowly edging him out of the house? He'd have to look into Abbott's affairs more closely to find out.

With a sigh, he turned his attention back to the room, unconsciously rubbing his throat. The room itself was cluttered with furnishings that looked as if they belonged in a house three times the size of the cottage. Which, Peter conceded, they probably did. By all accounts, Abbott had left as little as possible up at the manor house, squeezing much of the furniture in here, including an ungainly jardinière – along with accompanying dead houseplant – and an antique oak sideboard that dominated the entire rear wall of the room. God only knew how the removal men had managed to manhandle the thing into place.

He'd evidently been a man with a taste for the finer things in life – three portraits on the wall looked like seventeenth-century originals, and an impressive skeleton clock sat under a glass dome on a nearby side table, quietly counting away the seconds. Everything about the room spoke of such refinement, a man who'd enjoyed his luxuries, and had the money to indulge such tastes. Which made it all the more pitiable that he had died face down on the rug before the fireplace, surrounded by the detritus of his microwaved meal.

Dr Nijjer had returned to examining the body, down on one knee, leaning so close that his forehead was nearly touching the dead man's chin. Abbott looked as if he'd known someone was coming for him. An iron poker, its surface gnarled and tarnished through age, lay on the rug just a couple of feet from Abbott's lifeless hand. He'd evidently grabbed it from the bucket on the hearth to try to defend himself. It seemed unlikely he'd been quick enough to retaliate, however – if his attacker had grabbed him from behind, there would have been little he could do to fight back. Analysis of any skin or hair beneath the fingernails would help, but Peter didn't hold out much hope.

Nor was there any evidence of forced entry. The SOCOs would dust the place for fingerprints, of course, but from what he'd already heard from Nijjer, it looked as though the killer had worn gloves.

He made a mental checklist. His first job was to identify anyone who might have had a grudge against Abbott, a motive for wanting him dead. He suspected it would be a relatively healthy list.

He'd start by looking into the family while the PCs did a door-to-door; see if anyone witnessed someone entering the house yesterday evening. He'd already questioned the housekeeper, who'd discovered the body that morning – Chambers could deal with her formal statement. She'd had a key, but claimed to have found the door unlocked when she'd arrived. She'd also given a reasonable alibi for the previous evening, which Chambers could check out with a quick phone call. Peter didn't think it likely she was involved, but he couldn't rule anyone out just yet – it wouldn't have taken much to overpower the older man. The killer could have been a man or a woman.

"Any chance you've got a time of death for me, Raf?" he said.

Nijjer shrugged. "It was warm in here, so the body's taken longer to cool. If you twisted my arm, I'd say sometime between 10 pm and 4 am, but don't go quoting me on that."

A six-hour window, right in the dead of night. Someone on this quiet street must have heard something?

His phone trilled in his pocket, and he took it out, glancing at the screen. He thumbed to accept the call, and made a beeline for the door.

Outside, a couple of PCs had set up a cordon, but so far, the only onlookers were the people in the neighbouring houses, concerned faces peeking out from behind twitching curtains.

"Ellie," he said.

"I've just heard." Her voice was tinny on the other end of the line.

"Heard what?"

"Nicholas Abbott's been murdered," she said.

"Jesus, that got around quickly."

"The housekeeper called her sister. You know how it is," said Elspeth. "I'd expect the usual circus within an hour or two, as news spreads."

A pause.

"Look, I can't get you onto the scene, Ellie. It's more than my job's worth. You know what happened last time…" DCI Griffiths had come seriously close to demoting him, following his somewhat flexible approach to his partnership with Elspeth during the Carrion King investigation. If it hadn't been for the result he'd achieved, and the killer's subsequent conviction, then he suspected all current talk of promotion would have been a distant dream.

"Don't worry, that's not why I'm calling," she said, and he breathed a silent sigh of relief.

"Then what's up?"

"It's just... I saw him yesterday, at Richmond's, the tearoom in the village. It's probably nothing, but there's something I thought I should mention."

"What is it?"

"I saw him grab hold of one of the waitresses. A young woman called Daisy. He put his hand on her behind. She told him if he did it again, he'd pay for it. He made some filthy comment and I intervened, threatening to call the police. In the end, she threw him out, saying he'd better leave before she did something she'd regret."

"So you think she might have something to do with his death?" said Peter.

"I don't know. It seems unlikely... I just thought it was worth looking into. If nothing else, it tells you a bit more about what he was like, why someone might have held a grudge against him. She didn't seem like the type who would seek him out and murder him in his home."

"They rarely do," said Peter. "But thanks. I'll look into it. Daisy, you said?"

"That's right," said Elspeth. "She seemed nice, but she did threaten him openly in public. If nothing else, you might get a few calls about it when people around Hallowdene hear about what's happened."

Peter glanced at the house across the street; saw the curtain fall back into place. "I should think the whole village will know in the next half hour," he said. He turned at the sound of a car engine starting up. They were getting ready to move the body into the ambulance. "Look, I'd better get on. It's chaos here."

"Well, you did say you were looking for more excitement."

Peter laughed. "Yeah, I did, didn't I?" He paused. "See you for lunch?"

She hesitated, as if weighing up her options. "I've promised Abi... but how about coffee beforehand?"

"If I can get away," said Peter, somewhat gruffly. "I'll call you."

CHAPTER TEN

Peter found Daisy easily enough, working the morning shift at the tearooms Elspeth had told him about, no more than ten minutes' walk into the village from Nicholas Abbott's cottage.

The place was bustling, even at this hour. People were hunched quietly over their bacon and eggs, coffee mugs steaming, fortifying themselves for the day ahead. His stomach growled at the rich aroma, and he considered for a moment taking a table and filling up for the day, before dismissing the idea. He'd call at Lenny's later when he returned to the station, somewhere where he wasn't expecting one of the potential suspects to serve him his food.

He'd spoken briefly to the owner of the place, Sally Jameson – who he'd found attending to the customers – and she'd pointed him in Daisy's direction, the only other waiting staff working that morning.

Daisy Heddle was a young, pretty woman in her early twenties, with a clear independent streak and a love of pop culture. The latter he deduced from the tattoo of a wide-eyed porg from *Star Wars* on her upper left arm.

This morning she looked tired: her eyes were sunken pits, her pupils like pinheads. Her hair, too, was loosely tied back and hadn't been washed, and she was wearing a bandage around her left hand. A hangover, perhaps? If so, this was going to be a relatively easy interview, followed up with a quick call to the pub she'd been drinking in.

"Daisy Heddle?" he said, approaching as she refilled a coffee pot by the counter.

"Yes, that's me," she said. Her voice cracked slightly as she spoke, and she cleared her throat.

"DS Peter Shaw," he said. He showed her his warrant card, but was careful not to make a show of it. He didn't want people in the tearoom gossiping. "Can I have a quick word? In private?"

She frowned, but nodded. "Yes, of course." She finished refilling the pot and placed it on a hotplate. "We can talk in the office, out the back. We'll have to keep it quick, though – I'm on shift."

She led him through a door into the kitchen area, where a young man in an apron, about Daisy's age, was standing over a griddle, frying another batch of breakfast. He glanced up inquisitively, catching Daisy's eye, but she shook her head and he returned to his work without a word. Peter tried to ignore the smell of the sizzling bacon.

The office was a small side room just off the kitchen

and opposite a flight of stairs that he presumed led up to the flat above. The room was barely larger than a store cupboard, with a desk piled high with paperwork and teapots missing their lids. He hoped the place wasn't about to be audited by HMRC – if this was the state of the accounts, they'd have a hell of a job on their hands.

Daisy propped herself on the edge of the desk and beckoned for him to take a chair.

"I'll stand, thanks. This shouldn't take long," he said.

"What's it about?"

"Your name has come up as part of an investigation, that's all. I'd like to know where you were last night."

"Why?" The question was breathless, nervous.

"As I said, your name has been brought to my attention." He found himself feeling sorry for the girl. She looked like a deer caught in headlights. She brought her hand up to her face, and he noticed she was shaking. "Are you okay?" he said. "Maybe you should sit down for a moment. I can fetch you a glass of water?"

She shook her head, forced a smile. "No, thank you. I'm fine. It's just... I'm a bit tired, that's all."

"Heavy night?"

"Something like that."

"So... your whereabouts between the hours of ten and four last night?" he pressed.

She hesitated, as if casting her mind back. "I was at home. In my cottage, painting."

"Decorating?"

"No. Watercolours, acrylics... I dabble," she said,

with a shrug. "They have a few of my paintings out there, in the shop. Sally's always been very kind and supportive."

"Was anyone with you?" said Peter.

"No, I'm afraid not. I was alone all night. I got into the groove, and before I knew it, it was three o'clock in the morning. I had to get up for the breakfast shift this morning. That's why I'm so knackered."

He could tell she wasn't giving him the full story. The way she kept fidgeting, looking over his shoulder at the door. There was something on her mind, and she couldn't wait for this to be over and for him to be gone. Perhaps there was more to it than he'd imagined. "So there's no one who can corroborate your whereabouts?"

"I'm afraid not," she said, as if that was an end to the matter. "I'm sorry. I don't even know what this is about."

"How did you hurt your hand?" said Peter. "Looks nasty."

She frowned. "Oh, it's not that bad, really. Can you believe it – I cut myself opening a tin of beans?" She looked down at her bandaged hand, and then curled her fingers up into a fist.

No, I don't believe it, thought Peter. *Not for a minute.*

"Tell me about Nicholas Abbott," he said.

She met his gaze, before her eyes darted off again. "That old git? He's always in here, making lewd remarks, trying to put his hands where they're not wanted. An over-privileged fool, is what he is. Thinks he's entitled to whatever he wants, just because of who his parents were."

Present tense. Does she know he's dead? "He was in here yesterday?"

Daisy nodded. "Until I threw him out, yeah. Look, are you going to tell me what's going on?"

"In a minute. I want to hear more about Nicholas Abbott. You were overheard making threatening remarks."

"Threatening…?" She seemed to consider this. "I told him to get his hands off me, if that's what you mean."

"Before you did something you might regret?" finished Peter.

"Yeah. Maybe. Something like that." She waved her hand dismissively. "You know how it is in the heat of the moment. You say things you don't really mean. I was trying to get him to leave. Look, has something happened?"

Peter considered for a moment, and then decided to see what sort of reaction he'd get. "Nicholas Abbott was murdered last night."

"*Murdered*," echoed Daisy, her hands going involuntarily to her mouth. "Oh, God. That's awful!" He let the silence stretch, waiting to see if she'd fill it. She wouldn't meet his eye. After a moment, she looked up. "What happened?"

Peter sighed. "I can't disclose that sort of information," he said. "You're sure you didn't follow up on your threat, go to confront him about what happened in the tearoom? Now would be the time to tell me if something happened."

"I… I…" she stammered. She looked as if she were

about to reveal something. Then her shoulders dropped and she shook her head. "No. I told you, I was at home, painting until late."

"But you did hold a grudge," said Peter.

"What? No!" She looked pained. "Well, I suppose a little bit. Wouldn't you, if someone kept on grabbing you, making horrible comments about what he wanted to do to you? He followed me home, once, a few months back, and tried to grope me in the street. I fought him off and ran home. You should have heard the things he said to me."

Peter had to admit that, in the same position, he would probably hold a grudge, too. "Why didn't you call the police? Make a complaint against him. We could have helped."

She sighed. "It's par for the course in a waitressing job. Besides, calling the police would hardly be good for business, would it? And I owe Sally so much. I didn't want that sort of story going round about the place, and Nicholas Abbott wasn't the type to keep it to himself. If the police issued a restraining order, he'd have blatantly broken it, just to get a rise."

"So Sally asked you not to make a fuss?"

"God, no. She'd never do that. She just… she has a tendency to give people the benefit of the doubt, that's all. She thought it would all blow over, that he'd realise he was making me uncomfortable and give it up. And besides, she only knows about the stuff that happened in Richmond's. I've never told her about that night he followed me home. I don't want to make things difficult for her." She scratched her knee absently. "Of course, that was part of the fun for him, making me squirm. But I tried not to give him the satisfaction. Yesterday... the truth is, I'd just had enough. Lee had been in, shouting the place down, and then all that with Abbott..."

"Lee Stroud?"

"Yes, that's him. Another of Sally's projects. He's always in here, going on about how we shouldn't be disrespecting the legend of the Hallowdene Witch by selling those silly knick-knacks. Yesterday he caused a big argument between Sally and her son, Christian – that was him in the kitchen – and then that dirty old man started touching me, and I just... well, you heard about what happened."

"You gave him a piece of your mind."

"Exactly," she nodded. "And then one of the customers helped me to see him off."

Elspeth, thought Peter. She'd mentioned that.

"All right. That'll be it for now. I may need to talk to you again," he said.

Daisy smiled and nodded, but he could tell she was spooked, and it wasn't just the result of his questioning. Something was definitely going on with her. Something she wasn't prepared to talk about. He'd come here looking to rule her out of his investigation, and ended up with a potential suspect. What had she *really* been doing last night? And how had she really hurt her hand?

"I'll show you back through to the tearoom," said

Daisy, hopping down from the desk. She smoothed her skirt, took a deep breath, and seemed to paint on a professional cheerful face.

"Thanks," he said, "but I can find my way." He started out of the door, and then turned back, reaching into his jacket pocket. "Here's my card. If you think of anything that might be useful, or there's anything you want to tell me, just call me on that number."

She took the card and tucked it into the front pocket of her apron. "I will."

Peter watched her for a moment, and then turned and left, steeling himself against the lure of a greasy fry-up.

CHAPTER ELEVEN

Judging by the look of the place, Elspeth was surprised that Thomas Abbott felt he had anything to complain about.

The house was almost the size of the manor, nestling in a natural alcove in the woodland and flanked on two sides by extensive farmland. A private lake glistened in the morning sunlight, blue and clear, speckled with an array of white and brown water birds. The house largely comprised tall glass panels fitted over a steel frame, providing what she guessed must be a glorious vista of the local landscape for those within.

She'd parked down by the lake, in a small car park set aside for local fishermen. The signs warned of penalties for those without a permit. She didn't have a permit, of course, but nor did she expect anyone ever bothered to check.

The walk up the long driveway to Thomas Abbott's house had left her feeling as if she was participating in some bizarre, modern-day version of a Jane Austen drama, trudging up from the village to the big house to take tea with the lord and lady. Only this wasn't the lord and lady, and this was no light-hearted drama. Thomas Abbott's cousin had been brutally murdered, and – she had to presume – Thomas Abbott himself was likely to be one of the prime suspects, particularly after making such a fuss about the sale of the manor house.

She'd thought twice about keeping her appointment this morning, which had been made in haste yesterday afternoon, after her interview with Hugh Walsey. She'd arranged to speak with Thomas about the witch stone, to get a little background on why the Abbott family had always refused to allow any excavation. It might add some interesting flavour to her article – particularly if the Abbotts admitted to what amounted to a superstitious desire to leave the witch's grave undisturbed.

She'd briefly considered trying to talk to Nicholas, but after seeing his performance in the tearoom that morning she'd decided to put it off. She certainly hadn't wanted to find herself alone with the man and his wandering hands. And so she'd looked up Thomas Abbott's telephone number online, and made the call.

He had seemed a little reluctant at first, but she'd promised to hear him out about his campaign to buy back the manor, assuring him that she would put his cause across in her article in a fair and neutral way. That had been enough to persuade him, and now here she was, wandering up the block-paved driveway.

She wondered how Thomas had reacted to the news of his cousin's death. They'd clearly not been on the best of terms, and now there was no chance of any reparations. Perhaps Thomas would be relieved that it was all over, or even gleeful in his odious cousin's demise. Or perhaps he'd feel wretched with remorse, wishing he'd taken the time to put things right. She decided not to mention it, as she trudged up to the doorbell and pushed the button. She'd soon know if she was no longer welcome.

She was surprised when he answered the door almost immediately. He peered out at her for a moment, and then something seemed to click, and he smiled. He was a handsome man, with thinning brown hair swept back from his forehead, blue eyes and a charming smile. He was full in the face, but looked healthy and trim, and was wearing a blue shirt tucked into a pair of what looked to be expensive jeans.

"Elspeth, I presume?" His voice was low and smooth, his accent public school.

"Yes, here for our meeting, if that's still all right?"

"Of course," he said, standing to one side so she could enter. "Come on in."

She started to kick off her shoes.

"Oh, don't worry about that. We're not precious here." He ushered her towards the kitchen. "Susan's just put the kettle on. Tea or coffee?"

"Coffee, please," she said, wondering at his cheerful demeanour. Hadn't he heard about Nicholas? She couldn't very well be the one to tell him if not. Surely that was better coming from another relation, or the police. She followed him into the kitchen. There was no sign of Susan, presumably his wife, although the kettle was churning away in the background.

Inside, the house was as polished and modern as it was outside. Sweeping granite worktops, spotlights, gloss cupboard doors, a big American fridge with an ice dispenser… not to mention the dining area, the two sofas and widescreen TV, and the glass wall looking out over the garden, to the woodland beyond.

"Oh, this is lovely," she said, walking over to peer out at the view. "My mum's house backs onto the woods, too. I used to sneak over the wall to play in them as a kid."

Thomas came over to join her, laughing. "That's what I love about being up here. We've got all the mod cons, but we're living next door to *that*. There's something about it, isn't there? That feeling of being close to the wild spaces."

"Yes, I think there is," said Elspeth. She understood exactly what he meant, even if he did sound a little pretentious. It was what she'd missed when she'd been down in London, where even the parkland was manicured, well tended. Up here, you really felt the changing of the seasons, saw the landscape adapting around you. You felt the passing of time. In the city, it all became a blur, one finite continuum that never really let you stop or pause for breath. She hadn't thought of it in quite those terms before, but that was the crux of it, right there. It was also what was so tempting about that sort of life, the way you could disappear into it and let yourself be carried along. It was like taking a trip that never ended, so that you never really had to face up to what you'd left behind.

The kettle clicked.

"I don't know where Susan's got to," mumbled Thomas, heading over to the kitchen counter. He held up a shiny little capsule. "We've got one of those machines, if you'd rather?"

"No, no. Instant's fine. Thanks."

"Well, don't let Susan know I gave you instant coffee. I'll never hear the end of it." He laughed, spooning granules into a red mug. He poured the water and put the mug on the counter top. "I'll let you see to your own milk and sugar."

"Oh, black's fine," said Elspeth. She retrieved the mug and took a grateful sip. Whatever he'd said, it was *good* instant coffee.

"So, you've got some questions for me?"

"Yes, for my article. I'm writing a piece about the excavations and the Hallowdene Witch." She paused. "But first, I have to ask – what's the attraction of the old manor when you've got all of *this*?"

Thomas laughed. "I must sound terribly greedy. Look, I never expected to inherit the old house. Not for a minute. But I'd always thought Nicholas and I had an understanding – that whenever the time came to sell up, there'd be no question of it going on the open market." He looked wistful. "And I suppose it never did. If it had,

I might have stood a chance. He just sold it out from under us to that Walsey chap."

"Yes, but why do you even want it? I mean, this place is *stunning*."

"I suppose it's a question of legacy, really. That house has been the seat of our family since it was built, hundreds of years ago. Nicholas knew that. There was even a time when he appreciated it, too. I just want to preserve that legacy. To keep that history alive, I suppose. It doesn't feel right to think of someone else living in that house, making changes, disregarding everything my family worked for."

Nicholas knew that. So he *does* know. It was unsettling how calm and collected he was; how little his cousin's death appeared to affect him.

"What happened between the two of you to drive such a wedge?" said Elspeth, wondering if this, at least, might elicit some emotion. He looked thoughtful, and she quickly added: "I'm sorry, I don't mean to pry. This isn't for the article."

Thomas shrugged. "Prying is your job. And I've nothing to hide. Nicholas was always difficult. A bully, really. He used to prey on us younger boys, my friend Arthur and me. He'd shoot stones at us from catapults, tell tall tales to try to get us into trouble, steal food from the pantry and claim it was me, that sort of thing. We used to go up there a lot when I was a boy, and I grew to hate those visits. Then one day I decided I wasn't going to put up with it any longer. We were out in the field, jumping off that old rock – the so-called witch stone – when Nicholas came sneaking through the long grass. He'd fashioned himself a bow and arrow, sharpening sticks with his penknife, and he barraged us with them. They weren't sharp enough to break the skin, but they didn't half hurt, and by the time he'd finished, Arthur was on the ground in tears, and I was smarting from half a dozen bruises.

"I lost it. I grabbed him and punched him in the jaw, and he fell back and banged his head on the rock. There was blood everywhere. At first I thought I'd killed him. Arthur ran off to fetch our parents, and they carried him back to the house and sent for an ambulance." He sighed. "It was nothing, of course. A concussion and a couple of stitches, but from that day things were never right between us, and we stopped going up to the old house. I tried to make peace with him in later life, but he was having none of it. He always had been one to hold grudges. And now he's dead."

"I'm sorry," said Elspeth.

Thomas shrugged. "I hope they catch whoever's responsible, but when they do, I'd bet my house on the fact that he brought it on himself, somehow. He was an expert at making enemies, and he'd developed a bit of a reputation in the village. Rumour has it he got a little... inappropriate with the ladies. Nothing that could ever be proven, but there were stories. Shameful, really, but there was very little I could do."

Elspeth decided not to mention what she'd witnessed

in the tearooms yesterday. This man already had a low enough opinion of Nicholas. There was nothing to be gained by making matters worse. "So now you're petitioning Hugh Walsey to let you buy the house back for the family? To restore that legacy for your own children?"

"I'm trying. I suppose in some ways it's about laying demons to rest. It feels as if I have unfinished business there, I suppose."

"And the witch stone…?"

"Ah, yes. The reason you're here. Well, I don't suppose there's much I can add, really. After what happened with Nicholas, we were told to keep away from the old rock. My aunt Jane – Nicholas's mother – became rather superstitious about the whole thing. She said that Nicholas's 'accident' had been a warning, that we all knew the stone was cursed, and that no one was to go anywhere near it ever again. All very melodramatic. Whenever someone petitioned to come and excavate, she was the one who always stepped in to block it, and I suppose the others just went along with it, even after she'd died. I'm not sure Nicholas really believed that the stone was cursed, but I imagine he felt he was honouring his mother's wishes to leave it be. Not that he'd ever admit anything like that to me."

"And you don't buy into it all? That the stone is cursed?" Elspeth sipped some more of her coffee.

"Of course not," said Thomas. "The only warning was from me – that Nicholas's bullying had to stop.

Besides, Aunt Jane had it all wrong. That's not how the story goes."

"What do you mean?"

"The stone isn't cursed. The *village* is. Or so the story goes. When Agnes Levett was taken to the gallows, her last words were to proclaim to the villagers that she wouldn't rest until she'd had her revenge. Or something along those lines, anyway. Then, in the days following her execution and burial, things started to happen to some of the people who'd accused her. Dying in mysterious circumstances, that sort of thing." He gave her an apologetic look. "I'm not very good at storytelling, I'm afraid. Haven't got the brain for details. But the villagers got spooked, and decided it was Agnes's unsettled spirit, living up to her promise. So they moved her grave and buried her beneath that witch stone as a way of keeping her spirit at bay."

This chimed closely with what Lee Stroud had told her, and what she'd read in the book the night before. He was right – everyone was talking about the witch stone, but that's not what the old legend said. It was the village that was supposedly cursed. "So now that she's free?" said Elspeth.

"I suppose we'll find out," said Thomas, thoughtfully.

And there's already been one mysterious death, added Elspeth, keeping the thought to herself.

She heard voices out in the hall.

"Ah, there she is," said Thomas, as Susan appeared in the doorway. She was a tall woman, a little older than Thomas, with red hair scraped back in a taut ponytail and high cheekbones. She was wearing black leggings beneath a grey woollen jumper-dress, and her expression was austere, concerned. Behind her stood Peter, looking smart in his charcoal-grey suit, his hair unkempt and ruffled by the wind. He locked eyes with Elspeth, but didn't say anything.

"Tom, this is Detective Sergeant Shaw. He's come to talk to you about poor Nicholas."

Thomas visibly bristled. He pushed himself away from the counter he'd been leaning against, drawing himself up to his full height. "To question me, you mean. We've already had one of your lot down here, breaking the bad news."

Peter stepped around Susan, hands outstretched in a placating gesture. "It's just a few questions, Mr Abbott. I assure you, it won't take long."

"It certainly won't. I resent the implication that I might do anything to harm my family, DS Shaw. And for the record, I was at home all night with my wife. So whatever you think you know about what happened, I can assure you, I wasn't involved."

Peter glanced at Susan, who nodded in agreement with her husband.

Elspeth was taken aback by the sudden, fiery change that had come over the man. He'd seemed so placid, so mild-mannered, she'd have sworn he couldn't have hurt a fly. And then to watch him suddenly transform into this... she wondered if this was what had revealed itself all those years ago, at the witch stone. Perhaps this was the side of him that Nicholas had seen, and the real reason for the rift between them.

"And besides," went on Thomas, "I'm not stupid. I'm petitioning Walsey to let me buy the manor house back for the family. Yes, I was furious at Nicholas for selling it in the first place, but I can hardly put that right from a prison cell, can I?"

Elspeth felt a pang of sympathy for Peter. He was only trying to do his job.

"Look, Mr Abbott," he said. "I'm sure you understand, I need to explore all lines of inquiry, even just to rule them out. I'm as anxious as you are to catch whoever's committed this awful crime against your family. Answering a few questions now could help us to identify the real culprit."

Thomas seemed to have lapsed into a sullen silence. Elspeth took the opportunity to interject. "I think it's time I was making tracks," she said. She placed her half-empty mug on the counter. "Thanks for the coffee, and for taking the time to see me." She glanced at Susan. "I'll see myself out."

Peter caught her eye as she quit the kitchen, and she knew he'd speak to her about this later. She let herself out the front door, and set off back down the driveway towards the car.

Inside, she turned the ignition key. The radio stuttered to life. She'd left it tuned to an eighties channel, and was greeted with a sudden blast of Morten Harket.

She drummed along on the steering wheel until the song had finished, and then switched modes, scrolling through her phone until she found the latest EP from Gabrielle Aplin. She'd had this on a constant loop since downloading it a couple of months ago. Aplin singing dreamily about lost love seemed to speak to her recent mood. She pulled away along the slip road.

The first song was just coming to an end when it cut off abruptly, replaced by the shrill trilling of her ringtone. She glanced at the display on her dashboard: Mum Calling.

"Hi, Mum," she said.

"Ah, so you are still alive," said Dorothy, her voice blaring through the car speaker system. Elspeth hurriedly turned it down. Had her music really been that loud?

"Sorry, Mum, I'm on a new assignment. You know, about the dig at Hallowdene."

"You said. I just wanted to make sure you were all right, is all, and not mixed up in that business on the news. I heard something about it on the radio."

So the Nicholas Abbott murder had hit the news. Someone had obviously spoken to another journalist, although she'd not seen anyone around. She'd better hurry up and update her piece on the *Heighton Observer* website. She'd fired off a quick article that morning, suggesting that more news would be forthcoming soon. So far, she had very little to add.

"You mean the murder?" she said, turning the car onto the main road.

"Of course that's what I mean," said Dorothy, with an exasperated sigh.

"Not really, no. I'm covering the news for the paper, but it's nothing to do with the dig or the fayre. At least, there's no obvious connection. Probably more to do with money and inheritance and all that sort of thing."

"All right, love. Well, keep safe, and say hi to Peter for me."

"I will, Mum. See you tonight. You haven't forgotten I'm bringing Abi round, have you?"

"No, no. It's all under control. I'll see you then."

"Thanks, Mum. Love you."

Elspeth ended the call. The music started up again.

Five minutes later the phone trilled again. This time it was Peter.

"That went well," she said, by way of greeting.

"Yeah. Talk about passive-aggressive."

"Less of the passive," said Elspeth. "He seemed so nice and calm beforehand, too. To just flip like that, as if someone's tripped a switch."

"Clearly a sore subject," said Peter.

"He'd hinted as much," she said. "Before you arrived. He was telling me about Nicholas, and how they'd fought as kids, and he'd got the blame for Nicholas having an accident. It sounded as if he's never really forgiven him for it."

"What were you doing there, anyway?" said Peter. "You haven't taken it upon yourself to investigate without me, have you? He could have been dangerous."

"No, it wasn't like that," said Elspeth. "I already had an appointment to see him. I was there about the dig, trying to get to the bottom of why the Abbotts would never let anyone in to excavate. That's why he told me the story about Nicholas. Or at least, I think that's why. He was explaining how Nicholas's mother, Jane, had forbidden any of them going near the place after that. She said the stone was cursed and that it was responsible for Nicholas cracking his head on it."

"Right. Because that makes perfect sense," said Peter.

"I'm starting to think that, to that family, it was all relatively normal."

Peter laughed. "Where are you? Fancy a coffee?"

"All right. I'm on the road back to Heighton. Where to?"

"Where do you think?"

CHAPTER TWELVE

They met back at Lenny's in Heighton twenty minutes later. It was almost eleven and the place was filled with the familiar bustle, mostly comprised of office workers who'd sneaked out for 'meetings with colleagues', mums who were making the most of the fact their kids had been safely deposited at school, or shoppers taking a short break while they took stock of their purchases.

Elspeth was first to arrive – unusual, given Peter's typical driving style, which tended to veer towards the 'heroic', hurtling down country lanes, swinging the car around bends at the last minute, all as if he was constantly chasing a villain from an American TV show. She supposed he'd gone to drop off the car at the station up the road.

She ordered him a latte with an extra shot, and a black Americano for herself, and then installed herself at a small table by the window, plugging her phone into the wall socket to boost the charge. Lately, she'd been having trouble with the battery life, and couldn't quite afford a replacement.

She watched the other patrons for a while, sipping at her coffee and tapping her foot to the tune playing in her head. The people in Lenny's were a different breed to the clientele she'd seen in Richmond's. Much more cosmopolitan, which was laughable, really, considering it was still just a small town on the outskirts of Oxford. Nevertheless, she supposed Heighton was at least three or four times the size of Hallowdene, and a destination for people from the surrounding villages. Richmond's, on the other hand, traded on its parochial nature, packaging up that perfect ideal of a quaint, picture-postcard village and selling it to tourists in droves. She imagined Richmond's would be heaving with tourists, come the fayre.

"No cake?"

She looked up to see Peter standing over her, a look of mock disappointment on his face. "I won't lie. I thought about it, but then figured I'd be having lunch with Abi shortly, once I've picked her up from the station…"

Peter shook his head. "You suffer, I suffer."

"Something like that."

Peter sat down, sipped his coffee and leant back in his chair. "I met with Daisy," he said.

"I don't know why I told you about that, really. She seems like a nice girl. I can't imagine she had anything to do with the murder."

Peter looked thoughtful. "And yet, there's something not right. I got the sense she was hiding something from me. When you saw her that morning, was she wearing a bandage on her hand?"

Elspeth tried to cast her mind back. "No, I don't think so. I certainly didn't notice anything." He nodded, as if she'd somehow confirmed his suspicion. "Did she tell you what happened?"

"She said she'd cut herself opening a tin of beans."

"But you don't believe her."

"Like I said, she was keeping something from me. When I asked her about Nicholas Abbott, she confirmed your story. She didn't have a good word to say about the man." He was playing with the rim of his empty cup, peeling the cardboard away from the plastic lining.

"Would *you*, about someone who'd repeatedly groped you and made disgusting comments?" said Elspeth. "Perhaps she's just embarrassed about it."

"Embarrassed?" He glanced up at her, perplexed.

"Embarrassed, ashamed, uncomfortable," she said. "We're talking about repeated sexual assault here, Peter. Can you imagine what that does to a woman? How it makes her feel?"

"No. You're right. I can't imagine, and I wish I could prosecute the bastard for doing it. I just wish she'd reported it while he was alive, because now I'm forced to ask the question – what *did* it do to her? Was there more to it than what she's let on?" He'd finished peeling the cup, and he dropped the remains of it onto the table. "She doesn't have an alibi."

"And she *does* have a slight motive," said Elspeth. "I understand. Look, I'm heading back there later. I'll keep an eye on her, see if I can find out what it is she's so afraid of."

"All right. But be careful."

She offered him a beaming smile. "I always am."

He laughed. "Now you're lying to me as well."

She slapped his arm. "Busy afternoon?"

"Paperwork. And waiting for forensics to come in from Abbott's house. And trying to work out who else might have had cause to choke the old man to death in his living room."

"Nothing much, then." She glanced at her watch. "Listen, I've got to run. Don't forget about Abi coming tonight." She stood, gathering up her coat and bag.

"I doubt I can make dinner," he said. "Sorry – I'll probably end up working late. You know how it is. Maybe see you in the pub later?"

She stooped and gave him a kiss on the cheek. "Yeah, perfect."

CHAPTER THIRTEEN

"It's so good to see you!" Abigail dropped her bag and came running across the concourse to bundle Elspeth up into a huge bear hug. Her friend had always been like this – unafraid to show her emotions, larger than life. Elspeth somewhat envied her that. She gave her an affectionate peck on the cheek, all while attempting valiantly to breathe.

"Let's have a look at you, then." Abigail stood back, holding Elspeth by her shoulders, looking her up and down appraisingly. "Well, I have to admit, Oxfordshire does seem to suit you. There's even a little bit of colour in those cheeks."

"God, you sound like my mum," said Elspeth.

"Heaven forbid!" countered Abigail. She rolled her eyes. They both laughed.

"Still, you're not looking bad yourself," said Elspeth.

Abigail always had a way of making Elspeth feel underdressed. Standing there in her jeans and baggy sweater, she felt completely self-conscious. Abigail just seemed able to exude confidence in a way that Elspeth had never been able to. Not that Elspeth held it against her – Abigail was probably her oldest friend, Peter aside, and during her split with Andrew and everything that had happened with her job, she'd been the only thing that had kept Elspeth sane. Yet she'd always felt she suffered somewhat by comparison, often coming up short in terms of men, and dating, and glamour.

"How's work?" said Elspeth.

"Oh, you know," said Abigail, with a shrug. "I've brought my laptop, just to finish a few things." Abigail worked for a London publishing firm as the editor of an imprint, and she was always harried with deadlines. Elspeth knew the feeling.

The station was buzzing with people. A young mother was attempting to get past with her buggy, looking harassed. Her child had abandoned its perch and was halfway across the concourse to WHSmith, attracted by the colourful display of bagged sweets by the side of the counter, giggling and waving his arms. Elspeth pulled Abigail to one side so the woman could pass. She smiled gratefully and charged after her wayward toddler, calling his name in exasperation. "No, Charlie, leave those alone."

"Come on, I've made plans for lunch," said Elspeth. She stooped to retrieve Abigail's bag. "The car's just out there."

They wandered out towards the car park. "I thought I'd treat you to a takeaway tonight," said Abigail. "What do you reckon? Girls' night in?"

"Ahhh," said Elspeth, ducking into the car and starting the engine. "I might have promised my mum I'd take you round there for dinner. And then on to meet Peter for a drink afterwards…?"

"Oh, now that *is* interesting," said Abigail. "The mysterious policeman. I've been looking forward to meeting him."

They pulled away, the satnav chattering on in the background as Elspeth attempted to find her way back to the main road.

"He's hardly mysterious," she said.

"Oh, I don't know. Tall, handsome stranger turns out to be childhood sweetheart, and walks back into your life after nearly twenty years. I'd say that was pretty mysterious. I mean, what's he been doing all this time? Waiting for you to come back?"

"Don't be daft. Anyway, it's not like that."

"Then what is it like, Ellie?" There was the hint of a playful tease in Abigail's voice, but an undercurrent of concern, too. After everything that had happened in London with Andrew and her job, and then the Carrion King case, Abigail was worried that Elspeth was getting involved with Peter on the rebound. She'd said as much on the phone.

"Oh, I don't know. There's clearly something there. I guess in some ways there always has been, even if we were too young to know it. But I don't know. Something seems to be holding him back, and I suppose I've started to wonder, did we miss our chance? Stupid, really, but I can't help overthinking it all."

"It's not stupid," said Abigail. "It's natural. All I'll say is that you shouldn't rush into anything. Perhaps it's a good thing that he's holding back a little. It'll give you time to decide what you really want." She paused for a moment. "Look, don't be mad at me…"

"What have you done?" said Elspeth, her heart sinking.

Abigail laughed. "Don't worry so much! There's a job going, at my place. An editorial position. Non-fiction. Just your sort of thing."

"And…?"

"And I had a word with my boss. Recommended you for the position."

"You did *what*?" Elspeth was more surprised than angry. "What did they say? Do they think I've applied for it now, or something?"

"The editorial director wants to meet you. Nothing formal. I've made it clear you don't know anything about it, that I was the one who put you forward. But you're *perfect* for it, Ellie. And it would get you back to London again. We'll set you up with a new place. It's just what you need."

"I have a new place here," said Elspeth. "A lovely little flat. And besides, I'm practically living at Peter's these days." Although she had to admit, there was a certain appeal to the idea. An editorial job. London. Abi and her other friends.

"You've gone quiet. Have I done the wrong thing?

I'm sorry if I have, I was only trying to help. I wanted you to have options."

"No, you've done nothing wrong. I appreciate it, Abi. I really do. It's just... there's so much going on here. My freelance work is taking off, there's Mum, the new flat, Peter... I'm starting to feel settled." Could she really consider giving all of that up, going back to London, where everything had gone wrong? She did miss the convenience of it all, how easy it was to get about, to see friends and visit new places. But the thought of all the stress of a London-based job, with the terrible pay, the late nights and the lack of prospects wasn't particularly appealing. She hadn't even really considered it... until now.

"Like I said, it's just an option," said Abigail. "I've told Simon – that's my boss – that we'll be going to a launch party later in the week. You can meet him there. No strings, no interview. Just a chat and a drink at a nice little do."

"A launch party, in London?"

"Yeah, you know, one of those things I've dragged you to before. Some new thriller."

Elspeth shook her head. "All right, if it means we don't speak about it again until then, I'll go."

Abigail gave a little triumphant snort. "I knew it!"

"Don't start."

"I'm saying nothing. Not a jot. Quiet as a mouse, me." She paused. "Anyway, you still haven't told me how you and Peter got together. I want all the details."

"There's hardly anything to tell," said Elspeth. "It just sort of... happened."

"Oh, come on! You can do better than that."

Elspeth laughed. "I suppose it was everything that had happened to us during the Carrion King case. We'd been thrown back together after all these years, and were in each other's pockets, and in danger together, too."

"But there has to be more than that," said Abigail. "The way you talk about him."

"Well, I mean, he's very attractive," said Elspeth, feeling her cheeks redden. "The thing is, we just kind of carried on after the case had finished. Living in each other's pockets, I mean. Neither of us wanted to stop. We were seeing each other most nights, just chatting, meeting in the pub, going back to his place to watch films..."

"And?"

"And when I moved into my new place I invited him over."

"You pounced on him?" said Abigail, her tone full of mock scandal.

"I'd hardly put it like that," said Elspeth. "But I decided I didn't want to wait for him to make the first move. I grabbed him as he was sitting at the dinner table and didn't let go."

Abigail laughed. "Good for you! I'm looking forward to meeting him, now."

"You'd better not tell him I told you," said Elspeth.

"Brownie's honour."

Elspeth pulled the car to a stop by the side of the

road and cranked the handbrake. "Come on, then. There's a pub around the corner. Let's grab some food and you can tell me about what you've been up to."

"I'm sorry," said Elspeth. "I thought it looked cosy from the outside. I should have checked with Mum; she'd have probably told us to avoid the place. We can drink up and go somewhere else if you like?"

"No, no, it's fine," said Abigail, accepting her large glass of white wine. "We're here now, and I'm sure it'll be all right. Plus, there's wine."

She was putting on a brave face. Elspeth could tell. Abigail was used to trendy London restaurants and pizza places, not country pubs out in the wilds of Oxfordshire. Even Elspeth, who'd grown used to such places, felt this had a particularly rustic feel. Two large men in ill-fitting football shirts were sitting behind the bar, mumbling to one another while one of them was attempting to complete the crossword in a tabloid newspaper. A further two were sitting at the bar, nursing half-empty pints. An open fire blazed in the grate, but it was still cold, with the rear door propped open, allowing the chill air to gust in. The carpets were faded, the bar needed a good clean, and she had a sneaking suspicion that her food order was going to be prepared out the back by one of the two men, just as soon as they'd finished their conversation.

"I like the décor," said Abigail, indicating a leering

fox head mounted on a wooden plaque behind Elspeth's head. "Very authentic."

They both spluttered in laughter. She'd seen the place as she'd driven by the previous day, and had been attracted by the setting: beside a low stream, the apple trees in the front garden, the ivy growing carefree over the brickwork and around the windows. As they'd got closer, though, they'd realised almost immediately that whatever the Rowan Tree had in roadside appeal, it was severely lacking inside.

Still, like Abigail had said, they were here now. How bad could it really be?

The bar area was spacious, giving the impression that the place was more sparsely populated than it was. She regarded the two men sitting at the bar, a few feet apart from one another. One was an old man with nicotine-stained fingers, grey hair and glasses, and few, if any teeth. He was wearing a shiny two-tone tracksuit in red and blue, and looked half asleep over his pint of lager. The other was Christian Jameson, Sally Jameson's son, whom she'd seen confronting Lee Stroud the previous day before disappearing into the kitchen to argue loudly with his mother. Today he looked thoroughly dejected, sitting alone with a pint of beer, flicking idly through whatever he was looking at on his phone screen. He'd seen her come in, and she thought she'd caught a glimpse of recognition in his eye, but he hadn't acknowledged her.

The only others in the bar that lunchtime were the

television crew she'd seen at the dig. She knew the woman to be Robyn Baxter, the presenter of *Countrywide*, a rural-affairs programme that aired on Sunday evenings on BBC 2. She'd watched it on occasion, mostly to see the weekly weather forecast, but she recognised the woman, who was usually seen talking to camera as she walked across a field or shoreline, hair rippling in the wind, still somehow managing to look fabulous despite whatever inclement environment she found herself in. She looked the same now, digging into a plate of chips. Elspeth had no idea how she managed to pull it off.

The two men with her were silently munching on burgers. One was the tall, burly chap she'd seen handling the camera at the dig. The other was an Asian man in his mid-thirties, who she'd gathered was some sort of producer or showrunner.

He glanced up and saw her looking. "Hello," he said, after swallowing a mouthful of burger, "don't I recognise you from the dig yesterday?"

Elspeth smiled, embarrassed. "Yes. Hi, I'm Elspeth Reeves, a local journalist. I'm sorry, I didn't mean to stare. It's our first time in here and I was wondering what the food was like."

"Pretty good, actually," said the other man. "Considering."

Robyn beckoned them over. "Come on, join us." She lowered her voice. "If you're local, maybe you can recommend somewhere a little more salubrious for dinner later."

Elspeth glanced at Abigail, who smiled indulgently and picked up her wine glass. They moved over, pulling up a second table and properly introducing themselves.

"So, we're here until the fayre is over, and we've eaten in all of the two places in Hallowdene – here and the tearooms. You have to rescue me. Where can I get something that hasn't been deep fried?" said Robyn.

Elspeth laughed. "I'd take a drive over to Heighton. It's a town about twenty minutes from here, and you'll find pretty much all the major food groups – Thai, Indian, Mexican, fish and chips. Failing that, if you're after proper fine dining, Oxford itself is your best bet."

"Heighton. Right." Robyn looked from Avi to Steve. "Tonight, we're getting out of here."

"I do empathise," said Elspeth. "I suppose I'm used to it now, but when I lived in London I used to love being able to get whatever I wanted to eat, whenever I wanted it. Me and my ex made a pact never to eat from the same place more than once per month – we'd catch a tube into town and find somewhere new every time. We must have spent half our wages eating out, but it was worth it. You miss that in a place like this."

"Especially when you're confronted with a menu of cheap burgers and deep-fried everything," said Robyn.

"You don't think much of the place, then?" said Elspeth.

"Oh, it's not that. It's just, when you're used to basically living on the road, it can drive you a bit stir crazy to stay in one place for too long, if you see what I mean? Especially a little village like this, where everyone knows each other and you can't help but feel you're getting in the way of something."

"Still, it's anything but quiet," said Avi. "I mean, we hadn't been here five minutes before there was a bloody murder!"

Elspeth laughed. "How's the programme going? You getting everything you need?"

Steve rocked his hand back and forth. "I think so. The stuff at the dig was good. And we've been interviewing all the people involved in the fayre. Now we're really just waiting for the main event."

"Twenty-five years this year," said Abigail. "That's how long it's been running. The fayre, I mean. I read something about it on a flyer, earlier."

"Twenty-five years since it was *reinstated*," corrected Avi. "It's a tradition that dates back a few hundred years, first recorded about five years after Agnes Levett's death. It petered out in the nineteenth century when people started to acknowledge that the whole era of witch trials and executions was an embarrassment from a more unenlightened time. Then Sally Jameson and Iain Hardwick started it up again in 1993 as a way of trying to bring the villagers together, and they've run it every year since. That's what they told us, anyway."

Elspeth had met Sally at the tearooms, but she'd yet to speak to Iain in person, having exchanged only a handful of emails with him to arrange an interview. He worked in IT, apparently, a systems analyst, which seemed to Elspeth like an odd occupation for someone so engaged in the revival of a pagan festival. She was seeing him tomorrow for a more detailed interview about the origins of the fayre.

"Yeah, I feel sorry for those two," said Steve. "The amount of crap they have to put up with."

"How do you mean?"

"Well, you know, everyone's got an opinion. Just this morning, a fella was kicking off while we were trying to film an interview segment on the village green. Kept shouting about how the fayre was disrespecting the true history of the village, that they were dabbling in dangerous things they couldn't understand. You wouldn't believe how many takes we had to do, and we're still going to have to piece it all together in editing."

"That'll be Lee Stroud," said Elspeth. "I met him yesterday. I gather he's a bit of a local character, but he seemed all right when I talked to him. He's got it into his head that we're putting everyone in danger by allowing the excavation to go ahead."

"Pfft," said Robyn. "Really? In this day and age?"

"He's not the only one," said Elspeth. "I think a few people around here are nervous about what it means."

"Fascinating, isn't it," said Avi, "how superstitions manage to persist and pervade. Although I think most folk see it for what it is – a chance for their village to get a bit of national attention." He was grinning again. "Although I suppose it's a little different in Agnes's case. She was accused of murder, too…" It was clear to Elspeth that he was the one with the real interest in the subject, here. The others were nice enough, but they were here to do a job. To Avi, this sort of stuff was his lifeblood.

"Scampi and chips and a burger," came the dulcet tones of one of the barmen. Elspeth and Abigail turned, taking their plates from the man and sending him away to fetch ketchup. She'd ordered the scampi and was now regretting it; it looked far from appetising.

She pushed a bit of scampi around with her fork. "Help yourselves if you're still hungry," she said.

Robyn laughed. "So we'll be seeing you in Heighton later, then?"

"Probably," said Elspeth, with a chuckle.

CHAPTER FOURTEEN

Elspeth felt guilty for leaving Abigail in the Rowan
Tree, especially after the others had finished lunch
and gone back to their rooms to prepare for the next
shoot – it turned out they were actually *staying* at the
pub, too – but she'd assured Elspeth she had plenty of
work to do. Elspeth had left her to it, meandering up
through the winding roads of the village to Richmond's
in the hope of both catching Daisy and finding something
more palatable to eat.

She found the place near-deserted after the lunchtime
rush, and chose a table in the bay window at the front,
with a nice view out along the lane. The cottages here
were all stone, dating back centuries, and they listed
and leaned against one another like dominoes that
hadn't quite gathered enough momentum to fall.
Thatched roofs and smoking chimneys, bulging walls
and leaded windows completed the picturesque scene.
No wonder the tourists loved it here. It was a slice of
'olde worlde England', perfectly preserved – even down
to its summer rituals and parades.

There were only two other people in the café with her, aside from Daisy, Christian and Sally – an elderly man and woman; a couple, she presumed. The man sat with a stooped posture, hunched over the table. His skin was yellowed and liver-spotted with age, and his eyes were rheumy. Patches of silver whiskers erupted unevenly from his chin, and just under his nose. When he smiled at Elspeth, she saw he was missing two teeth. He looked happy, though. She could only see the woman's back, but she watched as she fussed over the man, dabbing at his chin with a serviette and holding his hand across the table top.

"I hope I can find someone like that to grow old with," said Daisy, wandering over with her order pad, smiling in amusement at the old pair. "Gives you hope for the future, doesn't it?"

"I suppose it does," said Elspeth, not adding the rejoinder that went through her mind: *and fear for the present, too*. "Hello again."

Daisy grinned. She looked absolutely exhausted, with dark rings beneath her eyes. Her hand was bandaged, just like Peter had said. "Have you decided what you want? Only, once I've seen to this, I can knock off for the rest of the day."

Elspeth nodded. "Just a pot of tea, and a piece of that lemon cake," she said, pointing to the glass cabinet by the door where the cakes were on display. "And if you're knocking off, how about you take the weight off for a bit and join me?"

Daisy looked a little taken aback, but then she smiled again, and this time there was something more genuine about it. "Okay, you're on." She set about sorting out the tea and cake.

Elspeth checked the messages on her phone. There was nothing from Peter. She wondered how he was getting on with the Abbott case. She'd call him later; let him know how the chat with Daisy worked out.

Nearby, Christian was also busying himself on his phone. He was standing by the till, leaning with his elbows on the countertop, his phone held up before him. At first Elspeth thought he was pointing it at Daisy as if taking a photo, but then she saw his thumbs dancing back and forth on the screen and the intense look on his face, and she decided he had to be playing a game. She supposed it was hardly busy.

Daisy returned a couple of minutes later carrying a wooden tray, bearing a large pot of tea, two cups and saucers, and two slices of lemon cake. She placed them down on the table, untied her apron and sank into the chair opposite Elspeth. She issued a long, heartfelt sigh.

"Been a hard day?"

"You could say that," said Daisy. She rocked forward, placing her elbows on the table. "Look, I wanted to say thanks for yesterday. You were a real lifesaver, standing up to the old man like that. I really appreciate it."

"No problem at all," said Elspeth. "I've never understood what drives men to behave that way."

"I've never understood what drives men, full stop,"

said Daisy. She laughed, and reached for the teapot. "It wasn't the first time he'd done something like that. It was starting to become a real problem. He even followed me home one night. I'm appalled by what's happened to him, but he won't be missed." She poured the tea and then sat back in her chair, rubbing absently at her bandaged hand.

"You okay?" said Elspeth.

"What? Oh, yeah, fine," said Daisy. "It's nothing really. Cut it opening a can of beans."

"Ouch."

"Yeah, I know. Been giving me gyp all day. Stupid really. It'll be gone in a couple of days."

"So, what do you do when you're not working here," said Elspeth. "Aside from inexpertly opening cans of beans?"

Daisy laughed. "I paint."

"Oh, you're an artist?" said Elspeth. She splashed some milk into her cup.

"I try," said Daisy. "I'm not sure I'm very good."

"I'm sure you're being too hard on yourself. What sort of thing do you do?"

Daisy thought about it for a moment. "Well, there are the watercolours. Landscapes, mainly; views of the village and surrounding area. But those are just for money, really. Sally helps me out, stocking a few in the shop." She waved at the shelves. "But my real passion is portraiture and mixed media."

"Mixed media?"

"Art and music," said Daisy. She seemed to have forgotten all about her hand, and was leaning forward, enjoying the opportunity to talk about her passions. "I'm working on a new sequence at the moment. Portraits of women in different guises, each of them set to a different soundtrack."

"Interesting. So what comes first, the music or the painting?" said Elspeth.

"It depends. I take my inspiration from the subject. Sometimes there's a little refrain that grows like a seed while I'm painting. Other times it's as if the painting is silent, right up until the end, and then something clicks and it all comes alive. I think there's something fundamental about the link between music and art. One inspires the other in a kind of constantly repeating circle." She was watching Elspeth intently, waiting to gauge her reaction.

"I think I can understand that," Elspeth said, after taking a sip of her tea. "I think it's the same with music and words. They both inspire a tone, a mood."

"Exactly!" said Daisy. She broke off a piece of cake and nibbled on it thoughtfully. All Elspeth wanted to do was take the whole piece down in one bite. She cut it in half and tried not to reveal how hungry she was as she took an enormous mouthful.

"I'd love to see some of your art, sometime," she said, once she'd wolfed down the other half. "Do you ever exhibit?"

Daisy laughed. "God, no. Nothing like that. But

you're welcome to come by the cottage. I've got a little studio set up inside. Maybe you could even pose for one of the portraits, if you like?"

Elspeth felt suddenly embarrassed. "Oh, well, I don't know about that. I'm sure you've got specific things in mind. But I'd definitely love to come by, thanks."

"Great. How about tomorrow night, once I get off here?" She looked at Elspeth hopefully, and Elspeth couldn't help but notice there was an undercurrent to the question, a subtext that spoke of loneliness. It wasn't desperation – Daisy was too smart, too *cool* for that – but Elspeth sensed that she was looking for something, even if it was simply an opportunity to share her art.

Abigail would be on her way back to London in the morning, and Elspeth had made no specific arrangements with Peter, who would likely still be tied up in the Abbott case. She knew what *he'd* say about her visiting the home of a potential suspect. And this after she'd just assured him that she'd stay safe. Still, she didn't sense any danger from Daisy – more just a young woman who needed a friend.

"Count me in," said Elspeth.

"Great," said Daisy, dabbing at the crumbs on her plate with her thumb. "I'd be interested to see what you make of it all."

"Maybe I could even do a piece for the paper," ventured Elspeth. "A local spotlight, or something."

"The paper? Oh, God. Listen to me going on. I've just talked at you about me, and haven't asked about you at all. I'm so sorry."

Elspeth laughed. "Don't be. It's kind of my job, after all, getting people to talk." She told Daisy about her work for the *Heighton Observer*, and the reason she was there in Hallowdene in the first place.

"Oh, you must talk to Sally," said Daisy. "She's one of the organisers of the fayre."

"I will." She glanced over, but Sally was nowhere to be seen, and the elderly couple were putting their coats on. Christian was watching them from his perch by the till, his brow furrowed. He looked away when he saw Elspeth looking. "Well, I suppose I'd best be off," she said, downing the last of her tea. "But it's been lovely to chat."

Daisy smiled. "See you tomorrow, then, about six?"

"I'll be here." She stood, reaching for her bag. "Oh, and what do I owe you?"

Daisy waved her away. "I think this one can come out of my tips."

"Well, thanks," said Elspeth. "I'll bring a bottle tomorrow or something."

"Perfect."

CHAPTER FIFTEEN

There was something reassuring about being back in Wilsby-under-Wychwood. There was stillness here, a sense of calm. Everything seemed to slow down to a more reasonable pace of life.

Maybe it had something to do with the trees, the gentle sighing of their branches in the evening breeze, the distant chattering of the birds. Maybe they had a soporific effect, relaxing her. Or maybe it was just the same feeling that everyone had when they felt truly at home. Elspeth had grown up here, after all, and the place had left an indelible impression on her. For a while, the Carrion King case had confused all of that, leaving her feeling unsettled, all those homely emotions intermingled with fear and treachery and doubt. But that was gone now, and those complicated feelings had passed with the killer's sentencing. Now, she was pleased to find her memories of galumphing through the woods as a gleeful child remained largely untainted.

She still thought of Rose, from time to time – her would-be friend from the *Heighton Observer*, the agony aunt who'd been so brutally murdered. Elspeth wished she'd had time to get to know the woman better. More than that, she wished she'd been able to act, to stop her killer from doing what he did to her, while she had sat in the audience of a play with Peter, unsuspecting.

Images of Rose's body still haunted her, permeating her dreams. She hadn't spoken to Peter about it, or her mum. What would they say? That perhaps she wasn't really cut out for reporting on murders? That she'd have to keep away from such things in future?

She knew it wasn't that. This was more personal. With most of the victims, she hadn't known them, so she had been able to assume some level of cool detachment, but with Rose, the killer had reached into her own life, and broken something.

Still, all of that was over and done with now. She only hoped that Daisy really hadn't been involved in Nicholas Abbott's murder. She'd really taken to the young woman, and if she turned out to be responsible for his murder – however much he'd provoked her – Elspeth didn't know how well she'd cope with the blow. That said, having met Thomas Abbott, she had a sense that he was a far more likely candidate – the way his mood had suddenly flipped, right before her eyes... Anger such as that could be dangerous.

"This really is lovely," said Abigail, shaking Elspeth out of her reverie. "You made it sound as if you'd grown up in *The Waltons* or something."

Elspeth laughed. "You haven't met my mum, yet." She led Abigail to the door.

Inside, it was quiet, with just the ticking of the grandfather clock in the hall, and the creaking of the old house. Elspeth had always found something familiar in that groaning, like an old man, yawning and stretching as he welcomed her home. She could smell something spicy wafting from the kitchen, and led the way through the study to find her mum, Dorothy, standing over the stove, stirring a pot of what she presumed to be curry.

"Hi, Mum," she said, dropping her bag on the table. "This is Abi."

Dorothy beamed and came over to shake Abi's hand, then gave Elspeth a peck on the cheek. "Hi, love. Nice to meet you, Abigail. Hope you're hungry."

"Famished," said Abigail, slipping off her coat and handing it to Elspeth, who hung it up carefully, rather than tossing it over the back of a chair like she usually would.

"We had lunch in the Rowan Tree," said Elspeth, coming back through from the hall. "It wasn't up to much."

"Well I hope this curry fares better," said Dorothy, peering at the cookbook she'd propped up on the countertop. "I'm trying something new. You're guinea pigs." She sounded dubious.

"You shouldn't have gone to any trouble," said Abigail. "Not on my account."

"Well, to be truthful, there's this fella at work who keeps going on about curries, and I thought if this worked out, I might invite him over next week."

"Mum!"

Dorothy shrugged. "Well, why not?" She tested the curry from the edge of her wooden spoon, and looked slightly taken aback at its ferocity.

Elspeth rolled her eyes. Abigail laughed.

"So – tell me, how's the story coming along?" said Dorothy. "I haven't been over to Hallowdene for years. Not since you were a little girl. Do you remember—"

"Yes, I remember, Mum," said Elspeth, cutting her off.

"Remember what?" asked Abigail, her voice dripping with innocence.

"Oh, I took Elspeth to the fayre one year, and she was *terrified*. She spent most of the day clutching my leg and refusing to look at anything."

"I was six! And they were all wearing those horrible masks and carrying an effigy through the streets."

"You were seven," corrected Dorothy. "But yes, I suppose you're right. Looking back, it's not really in very good taste, is it? I shouldn't have dragged you along."

"Oh, I don't know," said Abigail. "It's just a bit of fun. Like Guy Fawkes or something. People celebrating tradition, coming together for a party."

"I suppose that's what I used to think, too. We all did. It was just a bit of fun. But now, I can't help thinking about that poor woman, lynched for being a witch. Perhaps it's time to let go of tradition," said Dorothy. This was the first time Elspeth had heard her give an opinion on the subject, and she was surprised to find herself in agreement.

"It does seem a little macabre," said Elspeth.

"Especially now they're digging up her grave, too."

"I meant to ask you about that," said Abigail. "Was it terribly grisly?"

"Not really," said Elspeth. "Not compared to some of the other things I've seen. It was just a skeleton, really, with a few trinkets. Nothing to get worked up about."

"It would give me the creeps," said Abigail. "And I edit books about murderers."

"Me too," said Dorothy, fishing plates out of the cupboard. "If you're ready, I'll get this dished up."

They chatted as they ate, about Abigail's job in London, about the nights out she and Elspeth had enjoyed, about Andrew and everything that had gone on when Elspeth had discovered he'd been cheating on her.

Elspeth found herself wanting to change the subject. She took another swig of water. The curry was *hot*. "This is lovely, Mum."

"Yes, thank you," said Abigail.

Dorothy looked a little red in the face. "I think I might try to tone it down a little bit if I make it for Nigel," she said.

"Might be a good idea," said Abigail, fanning herself, and smiling. "Unless you want to scare him off."

Dorothy laughed, and Elspeth sighed, grinning despite herself.

After dinner, Elspeth helped Dorothy with the washing-up, while Abigail made a few calls from the other room, catching up with her other friends from London.

"What do you know about the story of the Hallowdene Witch, Mum?" said Elspeth, slotting plates back into the rack in the cupboard.

"Just what everyone else knows, I guess," said Dorothy. "Why?"

"I was just wondering if you had any insight, that's all. I was thinking about what you said, about it all being in bad taste."

"Some things should be left buried," said Dorothy.

"That's odd. That's exactly what I overheard someone else say at the tearoom. That no good ever comes from digging up the past."

"Wise words, if you ask me," said Dorothy.

"So you think there's something to all this talk of a curse, then?"

Dorothy shook her head. "No. That's just silly superstition. I know all that business with Carrion King might have made it seem as if there was something supernatural going on – and for all I know, there might have been – but this really is just a bunch of daft folk wearing masks. I can't believe in witch's curses."

"Then why are you so hesitant about them excavating?" said Elspeth.

"Because whatever else people say about her, that woman was a murderer. They dressed it up as witchcraft but if all the stories are true, she brutally murdered another woman in the woods. That's why I don't think we should be digging her up, or making her into a tourist attraction. It's in such bad taste." She drained the soapy water from the sink. "I used to think it was all just a laugh, like your friend Abigail. But after all that business with the Carrion King… I just think she should stay buried and forgotten."

Elspeth screwed the tea towel up into a ball and dropped it on the work surface, and then bundled her mum up into a big hug. "I'm all right, you know. You don't have to worry about me."

"Of course I have to worry about you, Ellie. That's my job."

Elspeth came out of the hug to see Abigail standing on the kitchen threshold, looking a little awkward. "Just wanted to let you know we're all set for the day after tomorrow." She waved her mobile phone.

"What's happening the day after tomorrow?" said Dorothy.

"Oh, it's just a party that Abi's got us invited to in London."

Dorothy looked surprised. "London? Well, don't you go giving her ideas," she said to Abigail. "I won't have you stealing her away again." She smiled. "You off to the pub?"

"Yeah, off to meet Peter," said Elspeth. She grabbed her bag. "Thanks for dinner, Mum."

"See you, love. Don't be a stranger."

As they walked through the quiet streets, Abigail seemed unusually quiet. "You really love it here, don't you?" she said.

"I suppose I do," said Elspeth.

"I'm not trying to steal you away, you know, with all that talk of jobs and stuff. It's just, I miss you, Ellie, and I want what's best for you. You upped and left so quickly after Andrew…" She trailed off. "Well, look, I'm not trying to persuade you. That's what I'm trying to say. It's just another option to consider."

Elspeth smiled. "I know, you silly sod. But thank you."

The rap at the door was loud and insistent. Frowning, Daisy tossed the tea towel onto the work surface and hurried to answer it. She had no idea who it could be. She wasn't expecting anyone. Her stomach churned at the thought it might be the police. Had someone come forward to say they'd seen her in the vicinity of Nicholas Abbott's house the previous night?

Steeling herself, she opened the door to find, to her surprise, Christian Jameson standing in the front garden, kicking the bottom step with the edge of his shoe. She heaved an audible sigh of relief. "Christian! I, um, wasn't expecting to see you." He'd never been to call on her before, except to run errands for his mum. "Is everything okay? Does Sally need something?"

He looked up, meeting her eye. "No, no. Nothing like that. I was just passing and I, well, I wondered if you fancied going for a drink. I'm headed to the Rowan Tree." He swallowed, looking increasingly uncomfortable.

Daisy didn't know what to say. She leaned against the doorframe. "Oh, sorry, I'm expecting a call from a friend shortly. Maybe another time."

He looked crestfallen. "Okay. Yeah. Another time." He started to turn away.

Daisy felt as though she'd kicked a puppy. She really didn't want to get into this now, but she supposed she owed it to him – or to Sally, at least – to see if she could get to the bottom of it. "Look, something's clearly on your mind. Is everything okay?"

Christian nodded. "Yeah, everything's fine. It's just... I suppose I've been thinking a lot about things, recently, that's all."

"What things?"

He sighed. "About my dad. About the fact he's never been around. I guess – I know it's different, but I thought you might understand, that's all. You've been through so much, and look at you – you're so strong. I don't know how you do it."

So *that's* what all of this had been about – what he'd been trying to get off his chest. Daisy stepped out and wrapped him in a tight hug. For a moment he didn't seem to know how to react, sucking in his breath as if he'd just been dunked in freezing cold water, and then slowly he brought his arm up around her shoulders and held her for a moment. Then, as if embarrassed, he gently pushed her away.

"I'm all right. Really. It can wait. You're busy."

"I'm sorry, Christian. I mean it, though. Another

time, we can talk. And for what it's worth, I miss my parents too."

He smiled. "Thanks, Daisy."

Peter was waiting for Elspeth and Abigail when they arrived at the White Hart a short while later, nursing a pint by the snug. He stood to greet them – an oddly formal gesture that betrayed his nerves at meeting Abigail. Elspeth leaned in and kissed him.

"Nice to meet you," he said, shaking Abigail's hand. "Drink?"

"What's good?"

Peter looked perplexed by the question. "They do a good pint of Landlord," he said, with a shrug.

"Get her a G&T," said Elspeth, laughing. "And I'll have an orange juice."

He nodded sombrely and headed for the bar.

"So, this was your local while you were growing up?" said Abigail.

"Yeah, they couldn't keep us out of the pub. They started us drinking at the age of four. That's what it's like out here in the outback."

Abigail laughed. "And Peter lives here, too?"

Elspeth nodded. "Yeah. Peter's just over the road. It's just convenient, that's all. And cosy. We could go into Oxford, but..."

Abigail nodded. "Students."

"Something like that."

Peter returned with the drinks.

"I read Ellie's piece on the Carrion King case. She did make it sound exciting around here," said Abigail. "You've lived here all your life?"

Peter laughed. "I have. Although I'm not sure exciting is the word for it. The Carrion King case was a bit of an exception. Out here in the sticks, it's usually nothing but robberies and car crime, really. At least ninety per cent of the time. I'm pretty busy at the moment, though."

"You make it sound as if you're bored," said Elspeth.

"Not bored. Just that I think I could do more," said Peter.

"That's what I was saying to Ellie earlier, in the car," said Abigail. "There's so much more opportunity in London for someone with her skills."

"So you're thinking of going back?" said Peter, warily.

"No. Nothing like that. I'm going to a party with Abi, that's all. A launch for a book she's been involved in." She glowered at Abigail, warning her not to contradict her. Abigail took a sip of her drink. "But this is new – this talk of doing more?"

"It's nothing," said Peter, waving his hand in a dismissive gesture. "Someone brought up the idea of a transfer, a quicker way to get a promotion, but I'm not going to pursue it."

"A promotion?" said Abigail.

"Yeah. But it would mean transferring to another district."

"You mean like Oxford?"

"No. One of the big suburban cities. Birmingham or Manchester. Newcastle, maybe. Somewhere like that." He took a swig of his pint. "As I say, it's not worth talking about."

Elspeth glanced at Abigail, who gave her a pointed look, as if to say: *that's what he's been holding back, Ellie. That's what's giving him pause.*

Elspeth wished she'd ordered something stronger. What was he saying? That she was holding him back? That what he really wanted to do was up sticks and move on, and the only reason he was hanging on in a place where he was bored, in a job that wasn't going anywhere, was because of her?

She thought again about the conversation with Abigail in the car, about her hesitation, the tug that she'd felt when Abigail had mentioned the job. Was she doing the same? Were they just two people, clinging onto one another through familiarity, unable to push forward for the worry of what it might mean for the other person?

She felt suddenly nauseous. "Excuse me for a minute." She pushed her chair back and practically ran to the loo. She locked herself in a cubicle and sat for a moment, trying to straighten it all out in her head.

What she really wanted to do was talk to him about it. To ask him what he wanted. But with Abigail there, it was impossible. And besides, she wasn't sure she was going to like the answer. She wasn't even sure what she'd be able to say in return.

She heard the door to the ladies creak open and someone come in. "Ellie, are you okay?"

Abigail, ever the trooper, come to make sure she was okay.

"Yeah, fine. Be with you in a minute."

She stood, took a deep breath, and then flushed the loo, painting on her best winning smile.

Abigail was waiting for her by the hand dryers. "Oh, Ellie, you do pick them."

Elspeth rinsed her hands. "Don't I just."

"Look, you can dump me here for the evening, if you want. Go and talk to him. Get it off your chest."

"No, no. It's fine. You've come all this way, and we've *all* had enough of my ridiculous love life."

CHAPTER SIXTEEN

Lee Stroud tramped over the uneven ground, his shoes sinking into the mud with every step. He cursed as he almost turned his ankle on an unexpected molehill, stumbling and throwing out his arms to maintain his balance. His raincoat rustled in the darkness.

Up ahead, he could see the silhouette of the crane, stark against the moonlight, unwelcome and unwanted by the landscape. Beside it was a large, dark shadow, squat and uneven and seeming to absorb all the light: the witch stone. He felt his stomach constrict. The open grave was only a hundred yards away.

Why had they wanted to meet out here? Perhaps they were going to do something to disrupt the dig, and thought he might be a good ally for their endeavours? He'd certainly been loud enough in recent days, making his feelings known. He'd never been one for taking real action like that, though. Protesting, yes – trying to get his point across – but he'd never resorted to sabotage.

The problem was, no one around here seemed to care. No one except that woman from the newspaper who he'd talked to yesterday. She'd listened to what he had to say, and she hadn't thought he was mad, either. At least, she hadn't given that impression, and he could usually tell. Why couldn't they all be a bit more open-minded, like her? Instead, they'd just forged ahead blindly, merrily opening up the grave. Well, they'd have to suffer the consequences, wouldn't they?

He circled around a large cowpat on the field, and carried on his way. He'd brought a small torch along with him, but hadn't used it yet, navigating instead by moonlight. He didn't want to draw any attention to the fact he was up at the dig site late at night.

He knew they'd removed the bones now, so there was little chance he'd encounter any security – apart from the crane there was nothing left to be stolen – but the manor house was only a short distance away, and there were lights on in the facing windows. He'd already seen the girl, Lucy, looking down from one of the upper-storey rooms, her face clear and bright in the artificial light.

He rarely saw her about the village. Perhaps she was just busy being young and carefree. He'd added her name carefully alongside the others on his genealogy charts, and knew that the Polish woman, Petra, wasn't really her mother. He wondered what that must be like, to have a stepmother who was only a few years older than her. It must be a difficult thing for a young woman to deal with.

The Polish connection had been difficult to trace, so

he'd only gone back one or two generations. The Walseys themselves had already featured, of course, having been in the village for generations – at least until a few years ago, when Hugh had upped and left – but now he was back, and he'd done well for himself, bringing his wife and nineteen-year-old daughter in tow.

It was a difficult job, keeping track of all the comings and goings amongst the villagers, but he'd started nearly forty years ago, and now saw it as a kind of duty. If he didn't keep it up, who would?

He knew there was a tendency for people to look down on those interested in the minutiae of local history, to see them as lacking the imagination to look beyond their own boundaries. He'd fallen in love with this village, though, growing up here as a child, with its crooked buildings and even more crooked history. The remnants of the ancient Wychwood provided a deep, mythical backdrop, and his imagination *had* been fired. He'd dreamed of fauns and secret hollows, of Carrion Kings and Herne the Hunter. He'd read books about folklore and lost himself in tall tales.

Then, as he'd grown older, he'd realised all of those stories he'd loved – they had their roots in something *real*. Something tangible. And so he'd set to work, digging deeper into the past like Jenny Wren and her spade, excavating the stories. In doing so, he had constructed a history of the village like no other he had seen. He'd mapped a woven web of people's lives, drawing it out on his charts. That was the thing that so many missed.

History wasn't about *events*: it was about *people*.

That's why they should have listened to him about Agnes. He knew what she was capable of. The deaths that had followed her execution should have served as a warning to them all. And now, they'd gone and dug her up, and he was too late to stop them.

He'd reached the graveside. He looked around, but there was no sign of anyone else. He hesitated, but then positioned himself with his back to the manor, withdrawing the torch from his coat pocket. Surely they wouldn't notice if he just took a little look? He'd keep himself between the manor and the torch beam. There wasn't much of a risk.

He twisted the head on the little metal torch and it flickered to life. Cupping his hand around the end of it, so as to narrow the beam, he passed it back and forth across the grave.

He could see where the ground had been disturbed, and little white, numbered markers had been pinned into the soil. There were some discoloured patches, too. Nothing to suggest a person had even been buried here. Nevertheless, he felt a chill running up along his spine.

This is where she'd lain for centuries. Trapped beneath the stone.

He felt suddenly claustrophobic, and clicked the torch off. Better to stand there in darkness, he decided.

Across the grave from him, he could see a little red light, hovering in the darkness in the shadow of the witch stone. He narrowed his eyes, wondering what it could be. Some kind of insect? It was tiny, just a pinprick, and he hadn't even noticed it on his way up here. He sidestepped around the edge of the grave, careful not to lose his footing. He was just about to lean in to peer more closely at the light, when he heard the scuff of a boot from behind him.

"Ah, so you made it," he said, his head turning just as something hard struck him across the side of the skull. He heard something break, and dropped unsteadily to his knees. The vision in his left eye was foggy, and he could feel hot blood coursing down the side of his face.

He sensed someone hovering over him, scrabbled with both hands before him, still down on his knees, begging for help, but his only reply was a clear and sombre whisper, right in his ear.

"*Without grace or remorse.*"

"Agnes?" he mumbled unintelligibly, just as the metal bar struck him again and again, battering his face and hands, splitting his flesh and breaking his bones.

CHAPTER SEVENTEEN

Daisy's phone vibrated again to alert her to another message. She looked down at the screen, and sighed. "Oh, *come* on," she said, reading the message back. "Really?" She thumbed a quick reply and hit send.

She was pacing back and forth in the darkness, growing increasingly impatient. She understood things were difficult, but to leave her standing out here, alone, in the dark… there had to be something better, or easier, than this. She kicked at a stone in frustration, sending it hurtling down the path towards the rear wall of the courtyard, where it skittered to rest amongst some overgrown weeds.

She looked up at the big house. There were lights still on inside. She walked along the boundary wall, careful to keep to the shadows. She didn't want to be seen. That would give everything away.

What was she going to do now? Had she really traipsed all the way up here for nothing?

Her hand was still throbbing, and she adjusted the bandage absent-mindedly. She still wasn't clear what had happened to her the previous night. She'd spent the entire afternoon in bed after leaving Richmond's, and felt a whole heap better for it – but running back through the events in her mind, she still felt deeply unsettled.

Two missing hours, in which she'd wandered, without memory, deep into Raisonby Wood.

Perhaps it was all the stress. She'd been putting herself under a lot of pressure recently. Maybe she needed a holiday, a break from all of… *this*. She'd thought twice about coming out again tonight, but at least it would have given her the opportunity to talk to someone about it all. Now, here she was in the middle of the night, skulking about, alone.

Again.

Well, screw that. At least she could get a decent night's sleep before her shift tomorrow. And that pretty woman from the newspaper was coming around tomorrow, too, so she'd have something to take her mind off it all. She wondered whether Elspeth would let her paint her, in the end. She hadn't seemed keen on the idea. Perhaps when she'd seen the other stuff Daisy had been working on. It was the best work she'd done. She was sure of that. She'd not been lying, though, when she'd told Elspeth she wasn't sure if she was any good. She could feel the doubt creeping in again. It was an ever-present spectre, making her question everything she was doing.

The trouble was, she didn't really understand her own process. It was something primal, instinctive – but that made it sound pretentious, and she was anything but that. It was as if the sounds and the colours built up inside her like a tidal wave, and she had to find a way to let it all out, or else she would burst. She painted in stuttering bursts of hyperactivity, unable to do anything else but work while the inspiration was flowing, an almost ritualistic purge that went on until the piece was done. Then she'd be left floundering again, unsure how she'd managed to get through it, how the piece had even come together in the end.

She wondered if that was what last night had been about: a sudden burst of insanity, a brief, un-channelled flare in the darkness. The thought scared her. Maybe she *should* go to see the doctor. But what if they told her that's exactly what it was? That there was something wrong with her, and she needed medication, or counselling, or both – something to take the edge off. Would she still be able to paint in the same way, dosed up on drugs?

Her phone thrummed again in her palm. She looked down, then shook her head and slid it back into her jacket pocket. "Fine." She wasn't even disappointed. She'd grown so used to it now that she just felt mildly irked. And what did that even say about the whole situation?

Shaking her head, she struck out in the direction of home, skirting round the side of the manor to the dig site. The light was wan, but she could just make out the wide depression in the ground where the witch's remains had been uncovered. She had to admit she felt a grisly fascination when it came to the bones. She knew they'd been moved now, but she hoped they'd be put on display at some point. Just the thought of all that history and mythology wrapped up in them intrigued her. Perhaps she'd paint them, too. That would add another dimension to her sequence of portraits – a study of what comes after, what awaits us all. She liked the notion of that: a theme to bring her sequence to completion.

Well, perhaps her trip out here hadn't been a complete waste of time after all.

She turned at the sound of a man's voice, coming from the direction of the manor house behind her. Someone was coming out.

Hurriedly she looked for somewhere to hide, ducking behind the arm of the crane. She peered out, careful not to reveal herself. Had someone spotted her? Was it Hugh Walsey, coming out to confront her, or worse, a security guard making his rounds? She'd never seen one up here before, but then, they'd never had a high-profile archaeological dig on site, either.

The figure emerged. He was wearing a white shirt, and seemed to be surrounded by an odd, diffuse glow. Daisy felt the hairs prickle on the back of her neck. Something here wasn't right. She crouched lower, trying to keep herself out of view.

The man was carrying another person in his arms, a woman. She was limp, her head hanging loose, hair trailing over the side of his arm, billowing in an absent wind. She was wearing a nightgown. Was it Petra? And was that *blood* on her nightie? Daisy felt her heart lurch. She felt sick. What the hell was going on? What if it were Lucy?

Daisy tried to focus, but somehow she was struggling to see clearly, as if a fog had suddenly descended, muting everything with that same soft, diffuse glow that she'd noted around the figure of the man.

He was whimpering, repeating something over and over as he ran across the lawn. The sound made her skin crawl, like the mewling of a wounded animal. He was heading for Raisonby Wood. Daisy wondered if she should call the police. Had Hugh done something? Was someone hurt? Something about the scene caused her to think twice. If Hugh had suddenly flipped and done something to Petra, perhaps he'd try to hurt her, too. But why was he running for the woods? Why not send for an ambulance? She didn't know what to do.

Daisy pulled out her phone, but the icons on the screen were swimming. She felt a sudden flash of pain in her head, and gasped, a stream of bile dribbling from her mouth. She hunched over until it had passed. She clutched for the crane, leaning upon its neck for support. It was cold and clammy to the touch. Her breath was coming in short, shallow gasps, and her head was swimming. Was she having another episode? It felt just like it had the previous night.

She steadied herself, searching the garden for any sign of the man. He was getting away, nearing the treeline that bordered the estate. Without thinking, she stepped out from behind the crane and lurched after him, one hand to her head, rubbing her throbbing temple.

As she ran, she felt the world shift, and she pitched forward, throwing her hands out to catch herself as she went down. Her palms skidded on the damp earth. She tried to push herself back up, but everything was spinning, and she slumped over again, unable to find her balance.

"*Without grace or remorse.*"

She felt herself mouthing in time with the whispered words, felt panic bloom. The world swam up to meet her, and blinked out.

Daisy tried to move, but something had snagged her tights, and she felt them tear as she kicked at whatever it was, trying to get free. Thorns scraped at her calf, and she opened her eyes, suddenly alert.

It was still dark. She was on the ground. Slowly, she placed her hands palm down by her sides and levered herself up. The ground was hard and cold, and gritty. When she'd fallen, it had been in the field close to the manor house. Where was she now, then?

She moistened her dry lips, spitting frantically at the mouthful of dust and grit she was rewarded with for her efforts. She wiped her face in the crook of her arm. Her sore hand was stinging.

It was darker here than it had been before. She looked up, but she couldn't see the moon through the dense foliage. She pulled herself into a sitting position, tucking her legs beneath her. She was sitting on a packed dirt floor. Around her, the jagged shapes of crumbling walls loomed out of the trees.

She was in a building. But why were there plants?

A cold finger of dread seemed to run along her spine. Had someone taken her? Had they put her in this place, a makeshift cell or outbuilding? Was she trapped?

Quickly, she got to her feet, feeling a little woozy. She stepped forward, arms outstretched, fingers encountering nothing but leaves. She pushed forward, one more step, then another. The foliage grew increasingly dense, and then, behind it, an old stone wall. It was slick with moss and grime.

She searched her pockets for her phone. For a moment she thought she'd lost it, but it was there, in her pocket, as before. She pulled it out and thumbed the torch on, turning on the spot. The weak light revealed a small room with no roof. The walls around her had mostly crumbled to stumps, one of them collapsing outwards, disturbed by tree roots that had crept inside, rupturing the packed earth, causing little eruptions of green and brown in places they should never have been. Trees, she realised, were growing *inside* the shell of the small building. The whole place stank of earth and decay.

The building, she realised, was a little one-room house or hovel that had been long abandoned.

A hovel out in the woods.

The thought struck her with a certainty she couldn't

ignore. This was Agnes Levett's house. She was standing in the ruins of the witch's old home.

She'd known this place as a kid. They all had. The creepy old witch's house in the woods. Their parents had told them to stay away from it, but they'd come here to look at it, once even creeping inside, terrified of what they might find. Then Bill Clemens had gone missing, and everyone at school had claimed it was the witch, taking him back to her house in the woods to eat him. He'd turned up safely, of course, two days later after trying to run away to London – but she'd never gone near the witch's house again after that, too afraid of what might be lurking inside.

And now she was here, in the dead of night, and she had no recollection of how she'd arrived.

Daisy swallowed. All she could taste was bile.

It had happened again. She'd blacked out, up at the manor, and wandered back into the woods. But why here? Had it just been unconscious, because she'd been standing near Agnes's grave before she passed out? Perhaps it had been on her mind, and her unconscious brain had brought her here on autopilot.

Whatever the case, she needed to get home.

She pushed her way through the vegetation, flinching as the branches scratched at her face.

She emerged a moment later into the clearing around the front of the house, onto the path that would lead her back up towards the manor. It was only then she remembered the figure she'd seen fleeing into the woods, carrying the woman. What had happened? Where had he been taking her?

She looked at her phone screen. No messages. It was late, but surely Lucy would still be awake. She dashed off a quick message:

Everything okay at your place?

The answer was almost instantaneous:

> **Fine. Boring. Dad and Petra watching a film. Sorry I couldn't get away. Are you home yet?**

Daisy paused for a moment, and then typed:

Just got back. About to turn in.

She hit send.

So, whatever she'd seen, it was either a figment of her imagination, or the Walseys simply weren't aware of it, the latter of which seemed highly unlikely.

So… she was seeing things now, too. *Great.*

CHAPTER EIGHTEEN

Jenny Wren was feeling buoyant as she pulled her beat-up Land Rover to a stop in the small car park they'd been using to service the dig. There was only one other vehicle parked there at this hour – a black BMW, presumably belonging to one of the fishermen who'd risen at the crack of dawn to secure his choice of vantage point around the perimeter of the lake. It seemed such a lonely occupation to Jenny, but she presumed that was entirely the point – that catching fish wasn't so much the object of the exercise, but to absent oneself from everyday life, to find some solitude away from the bustle of other people. That, she could understand. It was one of the reasons she liked to arrive early at her dig sites – to take a few moments alone to prepare for the day ahead, without having to think about organising everyone else.

Today would be a relatively easy day, however. The TV crew had everything they needed, and the bones and other associated finds had been securely transferred to her lab in Oxford. All that remained was for the stone to be replaced and the site to be handed back to the Walseys.

She knew, of course, that the stone wasn't going to remain there for long, not when the foundations for the new cottages were due to be dug in a few weeks' time – but she liked to leave things as she found them, so there could be no finger-pointing at a later date. That, too, was a lesson she'd learned the hard way over the years.

She hopped down from the Land Rover and slammed the door. She never bothered to lock it, not unless she was transporting one of her finds; the chances of anyone choosing to steal her ratty old thing over a shiny BMW, or anything else for that matter, were negligible. It was one of the reasons she loved it.

The march up to the house was brisk, following the long gravel approach up the small incline. She'd thought about tramping up over the field, but it was still dewy and the soft earth made it hard going. This way, she got to revel in the beauty of the manor house as she walked. It looked palatial, sitting there at the end of the long drive, fronted by formal lawns, with twin topiary bushes to either side, sculpted into peacocks. In many ways it was akin to hundreds of similar properties throughout the country, but the fortifications made this one special, at least to her mind. It was as if the Walseys had moved in and gone to ground, awaiting the oncoming siege.

Perhaps that's how it felt, as interlopers, taking over the manor after hundreds of years of the Abbott family: a war of attrition between the gentry and the villagers, who valiantly fought against progress whenever it dared rear its head.

She knew she was being unfair – the people here
were hardly yokels – but there was an overwhelming
sense that tradition had been broken, a mourning, of
sorts, for what had passed.

Now, of course, Nicholas Abbott was dead.
There'd been all sorts of talk about that at the dig
yesterday, people claiming that the spirit of Agnes
Levett had returned to claim his scalp. More likely,
she considered, some enterprising scoundrel had taken
advantage of the timing to see him off. By all accounts
he'd been an odious toad, with any number of people
bearing grudges. She couldn't imagine the police were
having any difficulty whatsoever identifying suspects,
and the long-dead Agnes Levett certainly wasn't
amongst them.

Still, people were going to talk, and she supposed
it only helped to raise awareness of the find. Then she
cursed herself for being heartless. A man was dead. No
matter who he was, or what people said he'd been like,
he'd been murdered in his own home in cold blood.
That wasn't a matter to be taken lightly.

She reached the courtyard at the foot of the house
and veered right, across one of the formal lawns –
treading carefully so as not to leave any boot marks
with her wellingtons – and into the field that housed
the dig.

The weathervane atop the church spire was spinning
in the wind, and now she was up here, exposed against
the elements, it felt colder, too.

She popped into the tent and unpacked her case, setting out the paperwork she'd need to get signed when they were finished. She checked her phone, but it was too early for messages, and then ducked back outside, filling her lungs with bracing fresh air.

Re-emerging, she glanced into the grave.

And screamed.

It was a hoarse, primal, anguished sound, utterly involuntary, and she didn't stop until she ran out of breath, panting, her throat raging and sore.

A man's body lay in the depression, his face so beaten and broken that he was completely unrecognisable. He was lying on his back, one leg folded over the other, an arm twisted and broken behind him. His bloodied face peered up at her accusingly. One eye orbit had been smashed, the eye itself pulped. His jaw had been broken, and his lips were bloodied, the jagged remains of teeth embedded in the soft tissue of his upper lip.

She thought she could see where whatever blunt object had been used to batter him had entered the skull, and dark fluid had seeped from inside the cavity, staining the soil beneath him. He was wearing a raincoat that seemed familiar, but she couldn't place it, not least because the bloody mess of the corpse looked somehow less than human. Even the bones that had previously occupied the grave had seemed more familiar, more recognisable.

Dazed, Jenny stumbled back, away from the grave, pulling her phone from her pocket.

CHAPTER NINETEEN

The timing could have been better. Another murder, and Peter still didn't have anyone properly in the frame for the first one. It just went to prove the old adage that you get what you wish for – he'd been desperate to sink his teeth into a more serious investigation, and now he was juggling two. The modus operandi was completely different, too. Where Nicholas Abbott had been throttled, Lee Stroud – he'd been forced to fish the man's wallet from his trouser pocket to identify him – had been beaten to death with a metal marker post, taken from inside the archaeologists' tent.

They'd found the weapon in the adjacent field, after DS Patel and PC Chambers had given the area an initial, cursory search. It looked as though the killer had casually discarded it after his crime, probably as he or she was fleeing the scene. Peter had had it bagged, ready to go to the lab for analysis. The SOCOs were on their way, and they'd do a more thorough job of interpreting the scene.

In the meantime, that left him with two murders to

solve, both with different MOs, both where victims had enough people bearing grudges against them to create a veritable queue of candidates. And the first two were Jennifer Wren and Hugh Walsey.

He was standing in Walsey's sitting room with them now – a room that was impressive by any standards, and probably larger than the ground-floor footprint of Peter's entire house. A large window looked out onto the formal gardens at the rear, with well-stocked flowerbeds and a smattering of fruit trees. Portraits lined the walls, and a large gilt-framed mirror hung over a baroque plaster fireplace. A leather Chesterfield suite had been neatly arranged around the centre of the large space.

He peered up at the portrait of a grave-looking man in an extravagant white wig, who appeared to be looking disapprovingly at Peter down the length of his nose.

"One of the Abbotts, I think," said Walsey, quietly. "Nicholas included most of them in the sale. Said he had no need for them any more, and that they wouldn't fit in his new cottage."

"I suppose not," said Peter, recalling the three paintings he'd seen on the wall of Abbott's cottage. "May I?" He indicated a chair opposite Jenny Wren, who looked as white as a sheet, and was nursing what Walsey had told him was her third brandy of the morning.

"Of course," said Walsey. "Look, do you want a drink? I'm afraid my manners have gone out the window. This is all a bit of a shock."

Peter shook his head. "No, thanks. Bit early for me."

"Coffee, then?" said Walsey.

"I had one on the way over," said Peter. He could hear two women shouting at one another in the background, elsewhere in the house. He couldn't make out what they were saying, but the shrill sounds were excruciating.

Walsey looked pained. "Excuse me for a moment," he said, leaving the room and pulling the door shut behind him.

"So, Ms Wren, I need to ask you a few questions. DS Patel will be along shortly to escort you to the station, where you'll be asked to make a formal statement, and the officers will take your fingerprints."

She looked up, suddenly more alert than she'd seemed. "My fingerprints?"

"Yes," said Peter. "We'll be taking fingerprints and DNA samples from all of your team, just so we can rule out any incidental imprints from the scene. They'll want to take a look at your footwear, too."

Jenny shrugged and took another swig of her brandy, shuddering slightly as the alcohol hit her palate. "I suppose you need to do whatever's necessary," she said, by way of agreement.

"Ms Wren, we're awaiting formal identification, but we believe the person you found to be a local man by the name of Mr Lee Stroud."

"Lee Stroud? That's who it was in the grave? That's awful."

"We're waiting for confirmation, but that seems to be the case. Tell me, did you know Mr Stroud?"

She nodded. "Not well, by any means. I'd only met him a couple of times."

"He'd been quite disruptive, I believe, coming out to the dig to protest?" said Peter.

She gave him a hard look. "I know what you're getting at, and you're wildly off the mark, DS Shaw. I'm used to dealing with that sort of thing. I've seen it all, in my time – developers who want to pay you off to pretend you haven't really found something of archaeological value, protestors arguing against the removal of ancient monuments, people angry because a Roman wall has prevented them from getting fibre optic broadband. It comes with the territory, and you learn to deal with it. You certainly don't murder people and contaminate your dig site with their corpses."

"All right," said Peter, levelly.

"Look, I didn't murder him," said Jenny. "The man's been a bit of an inconvenience, but that's hardly cause to kill him, is it?" She looked at her glass, and then downed the last of the brandy. "Lee Stroud was, in my opinion, a very lonely man, looking for a cause, and he believed he'd found it in trying to 'protect' everyone from the consequences of the dig. I hear he'd been stirring up trouble down in the village, too, and posting letters through the Walseys' door."

"Yes, I'll be exploring all avenues," he said. "Tell me, what did he say to you when he first came up to the dig site?"

"He was very quiet, that first time," said Jenny.

"Thoughtful. He asked if he could speak with me, took me to one side and explained very calmly that he was a concerned citizen and wanted to warn me about the dangers of exhuming Agnes Levett's remains. He seemed to take it all very seriously. Truly believed that people would start dying if we lifted that stone."

"People have started to die," said Peter.

She seemed to consider this for a moment, as if realising it for the first time. "Yes, I suppose you're right. But not in the sense that Lee Stroud meant. He talked about supernatural phenomena, about unquiet spirits and ancient curses. Surely you can't consider any of that a lead?"

"Lee Stroud was killed by something very corporeal, Ms Wren," he said. "I can assure you of that." He scratched at his chin. He hadn't had a chance to shave that morning, and his stubble was irritating where it rubbed against his shirt collar. "So these 'dangers' he mentioned – they were all stories about the risen dead, and historic curses?"

"Exactly that," said Jenny. "He said that Agnes's body had originally been buried closer to the church, in an unmarked grave away from hallowed ground, but that her body had been moved after a series of unexplained deaths throughout the village and placed beneath the witch stone to protect the remaining villagers."

"Is there any evidence to support that story?"

"Archaeologically speaking, no, just stories repeated by the villagers, folklore and received wisdom passed down through the years," said Jenny. "I did my research before commencing with the dig. It seems to be the accepted story of what happened."

"And the deaths?"

"It was the 1640s, DS Shaw. People died from the cures, let alone the sickness. A few unexplained deaths would be more sensibly ascribed to the pox, or a nasty strain of dysentery or tuberculosis. Look, I'm not sure what any of this has to do with Lee Stroud," she said.

"I'm trying to establish his motives, Ms Wren, to understand what drove him to act the way he did. In doing so, it might help to unlock why he was killed," said Peter.

She nodded, but didn't say anything.

"Finally, then, could you tell me your whereabouts between 9 pm and 1 am last night?"

Jenny laughed. "Oh, how I wish I could tell you some salacious story about my love life, but I was at the Rowan Tree, down in the village. I've been staying there for the duration of the dig. The TV lot are usually there too, although they were out in Heighton for dinner. I had a steak-and-ale pie in the bar, and a couple of glasses while I read my book, before heading to bed about eleven. Alone."

Peter made a note in his police notebook. "All right. Is there anything else you can think of to tell me?" he said. "Anything at all, no matter how small or insignificant it seems."

"No," she said, rolling the brandy glass around in her

fingers. "No, I can't think of anything. Except – you might want to talk to that journalist, Elspeth Reeves. She talked to Lee Stroud at the dig the other day, if you remember?"

"I remember," said Peter, smiling inwardly. "All right, DS Patel will be along shortly to escort you to the station."

"Will it take long? Down at the station?"

"A couple of hours," said Peter, "but you won't be able to get back on site for a day or two, I'm afraid. Forensics have to do their thing."

"I'm pretty much done here anyway," she said. "I'll be examining the bones back at my lab in Oxford. The organisers of the fayre have requested they be displayed for the weekend at the village hall as part of an exhibition they've been putting together about the Hallowdene Witch, so I've got my work cut out preparing them for the public."

"I can't see that being a problem," said Peter. "They're not connected to the murder. At least, not directly."

"I wasn't asking," said Jenny, "but thanks all the same."

Peter put it down to the shock and the booze. He left her in the sitting room and went to find Walsey, who was sitting on the stairs next to his daughter, who'd clearly been crying.

She looked up when Peter approached, then rose, turned around and hurried back up the stairs, trailing streamer-like earphones in her wake.

"I'm sorry," said Walsey. "Lucy's finding it hard. The move, the house… my marriage." Peter noticed he had a large wet patch on his shoulder, where her tears had soaked into his shirt.

"It's a difficult age," said Peter. "I know how I felt. Everything and everyone was against me."

"Sometimes I feel like they still are," said Walsey. "Here I am in the house of my dreams, enough money in the bank to retire, and the only thing I can't do is keep the important people in my life happy."

Peter supposed it was true what they said about money and happiness. "I'm sorry, Mr Walsey, but I do have to ask you a few questions."

Walsey nodded.

"Lee Stroud. Did you have much to do with him?"

Walsey frowned. "Only in as much as he's been a constant thorn in my side since I filed plans to develop the land down by the church."

"In what way?"

"Constant objections. He seemed to have nothing else to do with his time except write letters to the council insisting that they refuse planning permission because of the important local landmark of the witch stone." Walsey looked annoyed, even at the thought. "I really thought at one point I was going to have to rethink all of my plans. But it turns out the councillors were a little more understanding than Mr Stroud. That's why the dig went ahead – to ensure anything of historic or archaeological interest was preserved before the diggers move in."

"So it's fair to say he cost you time and money," said Peter.

Walsey looked hesitant. "Yes... but... Oh, I see what's going on here. That's Lee Stroud out there, isn't it, in the ditch, and you're trying to establish whether I had a motive to kill him."

Peter looked at him expectantly.

"Well, yes, he did cost me time and money, but that doesn't equate to me wanting him dead. The council granted my planning permission and the dig's practically done and dusted. If I'd wanted Lee Stroud out of the way, DS Shaw, I'd have seen to it a lot earlier. I can assure you, his death has nothing to do with me."

"Except it was carried out on your land, just yards away from your house," said Peter.

Walsey nodded, conceding the point. "Apart from that," he said. "But I can assure you, none of us are involved. Lucy and Petra were both here, at each other's throats as usual, and when they finally stopped arguing, Lucy went to her room and Petra and I watched a movie. We didn't hear anything, we didn't see anything. If we had, we'd have called for you immediately."

"All right," said Peter. "Thank you." He wasn't surprised that none of them had heard anything, what with the noise the two women had been making earlier. He wondered what it was all about.

"What about the dig site?" said Walsey, as Peter was turning to leave.

"DS Patel will explain everything," said Peter, "but no one's to go down there for the time being, and the forensics team will need constant access for a few days. I trust that won't be a problem?"

"Not at all. And the body...?"

"We'll be moving that presently, sir," said Peter. He hesitated. "Oh, and one last thing – Nicholas Abbott. He was also murdered, two days ago, as I imagine you'll have heard. Have you any reason to suspect the two murders might be related?"

Walsey looked baffled. "Surely that's your job, not mine, Detective?"

"Can you think of any reason that anyone would have to want him dead?"

"I'd suggest you talk to his family. Thomas Abbott. Feelings were certainly running high. Other than that, no. I have no idea," said Walsey. "My business transaction with Mr Abbott was smooth and straightforward. I understand that people found him to be a... difficult man, shall we say, but most of my interactions with him were pleasant enough. He seemed to like the colour of my money."

"All right, that'll be all for now. Thank you." He glanced up at the stairwell to see Lucy resting against the banister, peering down at him. She was wearing her earphones, but Peter had the distinct impression she'd been listening to everything he'd said.

CHAPTER TWENTY

With Abigail safely deposited at the train station in Charlbury – and promises made to meet at Paddington the following night for the party – Elspeth had struck out for Hallowdene and her appointment with the co-organiser of the Hallowdene Summer Fayre, Iain Hardwick.

That had been an hour ago, and she was still trying desperately to find a route through the traffic. She'd already put a quick call in to Iain via her hands-free system – which she absolutely abhorred – and he'd seemed very understanding, telling her to get to him when she could. Nevertheless, she could feel herself getting wound up, the muscles in her neck and shoulders tightening with every incremental tick of the clock. It was an essential dichotomy of Elspeth's life that she *hated* being late, but was, inevitably, always the last to arrive. She could never explain why this was. She always set out to be on time, but then something would happen, and by the time she arrived at her destination she'd be running behind schedule and feeling fraught. Today was no exception.

She willed herself to breathe steadily as she threw the Mini around another corner, saw an opportunity to make a break for it, and put her foot down. *Peter would approve*, she thought. She finally left the city behind and sped off down the back lanes towards Hallowdene, nudging seventy miles per hour on a road that was capped at sixty, Wolf Alice blaring on her stereo.

She arrived a short while later, parking outside the front of Iain's house, having successfully negotiated the winding lanes of the village. It was bigger than she'd realised, the houses spreading back from the main thoroughfare to form a number of small estates she'd never seen before – although none of the houses appeared to be younger than a hundred years old. Iain's house was no exception; a beautiful thatched cottage with brightly coloured hanging baskets, a front garden filled with wondrous-smelling flowers, thick, whitewashed walls and an irregularly shaped front window.

He met her at the door, a broad grin on his face. He was a tall, balding man in his forties, with a ruddy complexion and an appealing, friendly manner. He wore wire-rimmed glasses and a tweed jacket over a black T-shirt and jeans. "I'm so sorry you've had such a nightmare journey over," he said, ushering her inside. "I've got the kettle on, and I've got cake."

"You're a man after my own heart," said Elspeth, with feeling. She followed him towards the living room where another man was sitting on the sofa, reading a book. He looked up and smiled, folding his book on his lap.

"This is Carl, my husband," said Iain. "Carl, this is Elspeth Reeves, from the *Heighton Observer*."

Carl shook her hand and looked at her with renewed interest. "Ms Reeves of Carrion King fame," he said. "You're most welcome."

She'd had this occasionally in the months following the coverage of the Carrion King case – people who'd been fascinated to follow all the details of the story, reading along with her articles and blog posts. "The very same," said Elspeth, smiling. "Mind if I…?" She gestured to the chair.

"No, no, you make yourself at home," said Iain, as she plonked herself down in an armchair. "Now, you look to me like a coffee drinker…?"

Elspeth laughed. "I don't know what that says about me, but yes, thank you, you're right."

"And cake, of course," said Iain. "I shan't forget that. Back in a mo."

Carl had found a scrap of paper to mark his place in his book – a history of Roman Oxfordshire, she noted – and popped it on the side table by the sofa. "So, you're interested in our local witch," he said, leaning forward and resting his arms on his knees. He was younger than Iain, in his late thirties, she guessed, with short hair, coffee-coloured skin and startling green eyes.

"Yes, I suppose I am," said Elspeth. "I'm writing a piece on the fayre for the paper."

"And no doubt the murder of our former lord and master, too?"

Elspeth nodded. "I'm afraid so. Man on the ground and all that."

"He was an utter bastard," said Carl, "but he didn't deserve that. No one does."

"I saw what he was like," said Elspeth. "Couldn't keep his hands to himself."

"Or his vile opinions," said Iain, carrying a tray back into the room. "You should have heard the things he'd say to us whenever he saw us together."

Elspeth could imagine.

"But like Carl says," he went on, pouring the coffee into mismatched mugs from a bright red pot, "it's terrible what happened to him. Do the police think they know who's responsible?"

"I'm afraid I don't have any inside track," said Elspeth, offering them an apologetic smile. It wasn't far from the truth, either. She knew that Peter had spoken to both Thomas Abbott and Daisy, but wasn't sure who else he had in his sights. She hoped to glean a bit more from him later. "Anyway," she said. "Tell me more about the fayre."

"Well, I presume you're aware of the history? The story of Agnes Levett? That's the reason the fayre even exists."

"I've been reading up," said Elspeth, "and talking to people up at the dig, but I'll be honest, there's not much detail to the accounts. As far as I know, Agnes was found performing a ritual with the body of Lady Grace Abbott in Raisonby Wood, and was executed for witchcraft by the villagers. Ever since, subsequent generations have 'celebrated' her passing with an annual parade."

Iain looked at Carl and grinned.

"Well, that's a grave oversimplification," said Carl, "but essentially right." He accepted the mug that Iain had proffered him and sat back in his seat.

"I'm afraid Carl is something of an expert on such matters," said Iain. "He'll bore your socks off if you're not careful."

Elspeth laughed. "No, please, go on. I'm interested to hear more."

"Well, since you've twisted my arm," said Carl, grinning. "What do you know about Agnes herself?"

"Only what I've read in the guide book I picked up in Richmond's, or the pictures I've seen. She seems to be portrayed more as a caricature than a real person, as if the myth has overtaken the history, and there's very little of the real Agnes left."

Carl glanced at Iain. "She's clever, this one." They all laughed. "You're spot on, of course. The Agnes you hear about today bears little resemblance to the historical figure, or at least what we know of her. Just like the parade, really – it's all a bit of fun, but doesn't really reflect what happened."

"So who *was* Agnes, then?" she said.

"Well, that's the trouble. It's all become rather distorted over time. As far as I can tell she was a spinster, living in a small cottage close to the woods. Her brother-in-law had been a woodcutter, but he and her sister, Ruth, moved away during the onset of the Civil War and left her to fend for herself. She's quite a melancholy figure, really. The Levett family had lived around these parts for years, but were almost obliterated due to a nasty dose of scarlet fever, from which only Agnes and her sister survived. Ruth was the younger of the two, and soon found a husband, and Agnes, it seems, never really recovered from the loss. She never married, and in many ways became the last of her line, survived only by her sister's children."

"That's awful," said Elspeth. "So what happened to turn her into the evil character we see today?"

"It seems she got a bit of a reputation amongst the villagers," said Carl, "as a healer, a wise woman. They would come to her for traditional treatments when their Christian prayers let them down."

"Herbal medicine, that sort of thing?"

"Yes, but probably dressed in the guise of pagan rites and healing spells. You can see where this is going – it's what happened to a lot of these women, during the witch hunts. People whose lives had been saved by these women turned on them, decrying witchcraft, and pointing to their remedies and rituals as evidence."

"You think that's what happened to Agnes? What about the murder?"

"Ah, well, that's where it gets interesting," said Carl. "Cuthbert Abbott claimed to have discovered Agnes in the woods, performing a ritual with his wife's corpse. She'd apparently been stabbed in the belly, and had pagan symbols inscribed all over her flesh. He claimed that Agnes had murdered Lady Grace as a means of attempting to commune with the other side."

"The other side? In that she was trying to commune with the spirit world?" said Elspeth.

Carl shrugged. "Perhaps. It's all just supposition. The most interesting elements, as far as I'm concerned, are the specifics of the stories used to justify Agnes being lynched. She was accused of practising 'rites that violated the true laws of nature' and 'attempting to commune with the spirits of the dead'. That's not your typical, off-the-shelf witchcraft."

"What do you think she was up to, then?" said Elspeth, fascinated now.

"It's almost impossible to tell," said Carl. "I've tried to marry what brief account there is of the ritual with other contemporary references to occult practices, but there's very little that bears comparison. There's one ritual to do with directing the spirits of the dead, and another that appears to be a sort of resurrection spell, but neither of them quite fit. Whatever ancient art she was attempting to harness is lost to us now."

"But whatever it was, it sounds as if she'd taken Lady Grace as some kind of sacrificial victim," said Elspeth.

"Unlikely," said Carl. "Human sacrifice doesn't usually play a part in the traditions of English witchcraft."

Elspeth nodded. "So Agnes was lynched, and I know there are stories about a curse, and her body being moved…"

"That's right. It's all very melodramatic. Agnes swore

as she was dying that vengeance would be forthcoming. No one believed it, of course. How *could* she do them any harm? She'd been hanged. But then, soon after she'd been put in the ground, three villagers died in quick succession, one in a fire at his home, another trampled by a spooked horse, the third of apparent fright. It might well have been a coincidence. Yet… it's recorded that people from around the village claimed to hear Agnes speaking to them in those days immediately following her death, and in one case she was said to whisper to the victim right before he died." Carl grinned. "To help silence her unquiet spirit, the vicar had the body moved and sealed beneath the witch stone, along with a score of fetishes, one for each family in the village."

"Do you put any stock in it all?" said Elspeth. "The curse, and Agnes's unquiet spirit?"

Carl shrugged. "It's just an old story, told to scare children at bedtime. But it *is* interesting, isn't it? Agnes was apparently dabbling with practices involving the spirits of the dead, and then, days after being buried, she was said to have found a way to speak to people, before driving them to their deaths."

Elspeth shuddered.

"And now the witch stone has been disturbed," said Iain, "and the killings have started again."

"You can't really believe that Nicholas Abbott's death is related to the excavation?" said Elspeth. "You said yourself, he was a difficult man with lots of enemies in the village. Surely it's just a coincidence?"

Carl was smiling again, his grin lopsided, knowing. "Just like the unusual deaths in the 1640s, you mean?" He laughed. "Yes, of course you're right. It's nothing more than a coincidence. What else could it be?"

Elspeth sipped at her coffee.

"Right, cake," said Iain, sensing a change in the tone of the conversation. He handed her a little side plate bearing an enormous slice of Victoria sponge. "Here you go."

Elspeth dug in. "So, the fayre," she said, between mouthfuls, "how did that all start?"

"Well, Sally and I were both members of the parish council, back in 1993, and there was talk about trying to put on a fete or gala to try to bring the villagers together. I had a vague recollection of seeing photographs of the parade from the Victorian era, and when I started digging, it turned out it had once been quite an event, before it was shut down by the puritans, who didn't appreciate the more pagan elements. It seemed like an obvious thing to do to bring it back, as the centrepiece of the new village fayre."

"So you and Sally worked together to resurrect it?" said Elspeth.

"Precisely that," said Iain. "We dug out all the old photographs and accounts, and using those we were able to put on the best approximation we could of the original parade, or at least how it had been in Victorian times. It proved so popular that we did it again the following year, and it's been going ever since, with the rest of the fayre sort of growing up around it."

"And you see it as a sort of celebration of the village's history and tradition?" asked Elspeth.

"Yes, I suppose that's exactly what it is," said Iain.

"Of course, there's always been fayres and parades around these parts," said Carl. "It's likely that the villagers simply incorporated the witch into their existing festivities, dating back years before Agnes Levett's time. That's why Iain's always encouraged the villagers to dress up and join in, and why you'll see all sorts of different masks and mythical figures amongst the crowds."

"To me it's always just been an excuse to dress up and have fun," said Iain.

"I imagine most people see it that way," said Elspeth, but she couldn't shake the image of the terrifying effigy of Agnes Levett she'd seen all those years ago as a child.

She finished her coffee. "You must be pleased about the attention you're getting this year, too, with the crew from *Countrywide* here to film everything?"

"Oh, yeah. It's brilliant, isn't it? Hallowdene on national TV!" Iain looked genuinely thrilled. "I just hope all that business with Nicholas Abbott isn't going to cause any problems. I'd hate for everyone to miss out if we had to cancel the fayre."

"I don't imagine so," said Elspeth. "Have you spoken to the police?"

"Not yet. I'm kind of working to the principle that if I don't hear anything, I can just plough on with the arrangements," said Iain. "Sally's a little more circumspect, but then she knew Nicholas a little better than me. Had done for years."

That was interesting. "As a customer at Richmond's, you mean?"

"I think they must have been friends, once. I'm not really sure – you'll have to ask her, I'm afraid." So Sally knew Nicholas outside of his shenanigans in the tearooms. Elspeth made a mental note to follow up on that.

"Well, I suppose I'd better leave you to your preparations," said Elspeth. She was thinking about the mountain of work she had to do, updating news articles on the Abbott investigation, and making a proper start on her piece about the fayre and the dig. "Thanks for your time. It was really fascinating."

CHAPTER TWENTY-ONE

The day had run away with Peter, seeing to all of that business up at the manor. After a brief spell back at the station briefing DCI Griffiths on his findings, he was on his way back to Hallowdene to talk to Sally Jameson about Lee Stroud.

He'd intended to try to catch Elspeth over lunch again today, to see if he could straighten things out with her a bit. He didn't like how they'd left things in Lenny's the day before, with neither of them entirely clear about what the other was thinking. Ellie was too important to him for all that. In the last few months they'd grown closer, and he'd started to think that things had a chance of becoming serious between them. He'd certainly *hoped* that was the case.

Now, though, there was talk of London, and new jobs, and Abigail, and he had to wonder – was he putting his own life on hold for something that wasn't real? They'd been thrown together in a moment of crisis, rekindling old childhood affection. Was that enough to base a relationship on? He certainly fancied her, there was no doubt about that, and they really did seem to connect on an intellectual level, too. The thought of her going back to London caused his guts to twist uncomfortably. What did *that* mean?

Then there was the promotion. If he managed to sort out either one of these murder cases, he'd be a shoo-in. There was no doubt about it. He could make DCI, be running his own small team, dealing with important matters like these every day. Wasn't that what he wanted?

One thing was certain – he'd have to make a decision soon, and he had to do what was best for him in the long run. But did it really have to come down to a choice between Elspeth and his career? The thought of it made him nauseated.

In the end, all he'd managed was a brief phone call and a flurry of text messages with her during the course of the afternoon. She'd spent the day in Hallowdene, working from the pub, writing bulletins for the *Heighton Observer*'s website about the investigation into Nicholas Abbott's murder, and the discovery of Lee Stroud's body that morning. She'd seen the news go out and had called him immediately to make sure he was okay. She'd barely mentioned the details of the case – the call had been about *him*, and how he was holding up. That had told him something, too.

The worst thing was, now he needed to talk to her in a professional capacity. Not that she was a suspect – she had no reason to be involved in any of this – only that she'd talked to Stroud at the dig site, and seen the way he'd behaved at Richmond's, and might have some insight to share.

For now, though, he'd settle for a chat with Sally Jameson regarding Stroud's ongoing campaign against her exploitation of the Hallowdene Witch. Then he'd have to head back to the station to read through Jenny Wren's official statement.

It was close to six when he pulled up outside Richmond's, although the sun was still high in the sky, finally hinting at the coming change in seasons and the onset of summer. He swung the car into a space and trudged up the path to the door. Through the window, he could see it was empty, and the staff were cleaning up, ready to close. He walked in, and the bell trilled.

"I'm sorry, we're closed for the day," said Sally, without looking up.

He cleared his throat. "Ms Jameson? DS Shaw, Heighton police. I wonder if I might have a word?" He held up his warrant card.

The woman looked up, surprised, but then nodded meekly and closed the open till. "Yes, of course. Um, I suppose we could go through to the office."

Peter nodded, and followed her through the kitchen, retracing the route he'd taken with Daisy the previous day.

"I'm sorry it's such a mess," she said, squeezing in and taking a seat on one of the chairs. She was wearing the same black-and-white uniform as Daisy, and she crossed her legs in a protective gesture, placing her hands on her knees.

Peter remained standing, his back to the door. "I'd like to talk to you about Lee Stroud," he said.

"Poor Lee," said Sally, hanging her head. "I can't imagine what drove someone to do such a thing." So she'd obviously heard the news.

"I understand he could be a little... difficult, from time to time?" said Peter.

Sally looked pained. "He had his troubles, but he never meant any harm by it all. He was a lonely man, and he'd developed something of an obsession with local history. Sometimes that obsession got the better of him, is all."

"You mean the Hallowdene Witch?"

"Yes, amongst other things. He'd spent most of his life researching the history of Hallowdene and the surrounding area."

"So you knew him well?"

"Not really, no, but he's always been there, a fixture, if you like. Nicholas Abbott used to call him the village idiot, but he was always unkind to people who were different. The thing is, Lee really believed in the story of the witch, and her curse, and he was trying to warn us about it. He was a caring man. Just a bit confused."

"When did he start causing trouble for you in the café?" said Peter.

"Like I said, he's a bit of a permanent fixture. He's always objected to the way we've turned Agnes into a commercial enterprise, both in the shop and through the fayre. But then it's not just us, is it? It's the whole village. We all capitalise on the old stories. It brings the tourists in, and without them, we're just another tiny village in Oxfordshire with nothing to set us apart." Sally rapped her fingernails on the desktop. "It got worse in recent weeks. He'd started coming in every couple of days, ever since the archaeological dig was started. At first he'd seemed quite level-headed, quite rational, and took me aside for a quiet word about his concerns. When it became clear that I wasn't going to act on those concerns, though – well, he started to get a little frustrated."

"And how did that frustration manifest itself?" said Peter. "Was he ever violent towards you?"

"Oh, no!" said Sally, abruptly. "Never that. There was a bit of shouting, that's all. Christian was usually on hand to help out, though, and would usher him back out the door before the other customers started to complain."

"It seems you've had your fair share of disruptive customers, Ms Jameson," said Peter. "What with Nicholas Abbott making passes at your waiting staff."

Sally went as white as a sheet. She pursed her lips, trembling with repressed emotion. He couldn't tell if it was raging anger or harrowing fear. "He was a difficult man," she said, after a moment. "In his own way, as troubled as Lee."

"So everyone keeps saying," said Peter. "Do you

think the stories about him are true?"

"The stories…" started Sally. "You mean about the woman." She sighed. "Yes, I think they were probably true. Nicholas was an arrogant man, Detective, but he was clever, too. There was never any proof. Just stories about wandering hands, and filthy words whispered in ears. But yes, I think he probably did deserve his reputation."

"Why didn't you bar him?"

"He… he…" Sally hung her head again. "It's difficult. He wasn't always like that. I'd known him for a long time."

Peter felt a sudden flood of compassion for the woman. She looked on the verge of tears. Had Abbott been pestering her, too? "Are you okay, Ms Jameson? Do you need a minute?"

She waved her hand. "No, no. I'm fine. It's just been a bit of a shock, is all. Two murders in as many days. Here, in Hallowdene. It's enough to make you wonder if Lee was right all along, and we are all cursed."

"What about Daisy?" said Peter. "Do you think she might have been involved in Nicholas Abbott's murder? She was overheard threatening him that day when he assaulted her."

"She was? I wasn't aware of that, Detective, but I can't think of anyone less likely to carry out cold-blooded murder. Daisy's had a difficult life, but I think of her as a daughter, and she's a wonderful human being. There's no way she could be involved in any of this."

"But you weren't aware of the incident that day,

out there in your tearoom?" pressed Peter.

"Well, no…"

"Where were you when it happened?"

"I must have been back here, in the office or the kitchen," said Sally. Her eyes darted nervously to the door, and Peter knew immediately she was hiding something.

"It's a small place, Ms Jameson. I find it difficult to believe that you wouldn't hear a commotion out there on the floor, particularly as there were raised voices… Unless there's something you're not telling me?"

Sally sighed. She looked utterly defeated. "I was having an argument with my son, Christian."

"Regarding what?"

She looked up at him, her eyes pleading. "About how he'd treated Lee Stroud when he'd thrown him out. I thought that he'd been too hard on Lee, calling him names and manhandling him out of the door. But he was only trying to defend his mum. It's understandable, really, when you consider Lee kept on coming back and wouldn't get the message."

"Where were you and Christian last night?"

"Here, together. We live in the flat above the tearoom. We had dinner, and then he went into his room to watch TV. I know he didn't come out, because it was blaring on into the small hours, and I struggled to get to sleep until he switched it off, about 2 am."

"Can I speak with him?"

"Yes, of course. He's just out there helping close up for the day."

Peter opened the door.

"Is that it?" said Sally, hopefully.

"For now," said Peter. "We may need to talk to you again."

Out in the main room, Christian had continued cashing up the till for his mother while Daisy was perched on the edge of a table talking to Elspeth, who looked as though she'd just arrived. She looked surprised to see Peter – perhaps even a little sheepish.

"Hello," she said. "I wasn't expecting to see you here."

"You weren't?"

"No. I'm here to collect Daisy. She's going to show me some of her paintings."

"I'll just go and fetch my coat," said Daisy, eyeing Peter with trepidation. She hurried off out the back.

"Are you sure that's a good idea?" said Peter, lowering his voice so that Christian wouldn't overhear. "You said you were going to keep an eye on her, not become best chums."

"I know what I'm doing," said Elspeth, as if that answered all of his questions. "I'll call you later. It'll probably be too late to come over." She brushed the back of his hand. "What are you doing here, anyway?"

"I came to talk to Sally Jameson about Lee Stroud," he said.

"Anything useful?"

He glanced over his shoulder, but Christian was lost in his counting, and neither of the two women had re-emerged from the back rooms. "Only that I need to have a word with our friend here, too."

Elspeth nodded. Her face was close to his, and he could smell her floral perfume. "He did lose his rag a bit the other day."

They stepped apart at the sound of the kitchen door swinging open. Daisy made a beeline for them. She was wearing a denim jacket over her uniform. One of the cuffs, Peter noted, was dirty with mud. She put her hand on Elspeth's shoulder. "Ready?"

"Lead on," said Elspeth cheerily, and they bundled out of the place, laughing at some unheard joke. She didn't look back.

Peter turned to Christian, who was watching the girls through the window as they marched off towards the village, a wistful look in his eye. "I don't suppose you get much chance to socialise, helping your mum out here all the time?"

Christian gave a somewhat belligerent shrug. "Doesn't really bother me, to be honest," he said. "There's nothing much to do round here anyway."

"Where were you last night?" said Peter.

Christian gave him a fierce look. "I was in my room, watching TV."

"What were you watching?"

"I was streaming the first season of *Agents of S.H.I.E.L.D.*, if you must know."

Peter knew the show, but he'd never managed to make it through the first season, despite being a massive comic-book fan. It was guaranteed to send him to sleep on the sofa. "What can you tell me about Lee Stroud, Christian?"

"The man was an imbecile," said Christian. He shovelled a handful of counted notes into a red cloth bag and closed up the till. "Always going on about the witch, and how we were disrespecting her and her story. It was rubbish, and he knew it. I reckon he had a thing for Mum, and was using it as an excuse."

"Your mum said he'd been around here a lot lately," said Peter.

Christian nodded. "We're all sick of him, customers included. And he never stood a chance with Mum. A man like that? She'd have to be mad."

"I heard you got a bit handy with your fists the other day when you threw him out."

Christian shook his head. "No. That's not what happened. I grabbed his arm, pushed him out the door, told him he wasn't welcome here. I never hit him. There are witnesses, too. The place was packed."

"But your mum thought you'd been a little tough on him, didn't she? There was an argument…" said Peter.

"She's too soft, that's all. She lets people walk all over her, and then forgives them for it. I was standing up for her, but she didn't see it that way. Said it was bad for business for me to be going off on one like that in front of the customers. But that's not how it works. You know that, being a copper. When someone starts making a fuss, you shut it down. That's what I was trained to do."

"Trained?"

"I used to be a bouncer, in Oxford. I've seen all sorts. And I know how to handle someone like Lee Stroud."

"Did you want him dead?"

"Of course not. I just wanted him to leave us alone. And the other day, I think he finally got the message."

"All right," said Peter. "Thanks for your time." Christian followed him to the door, saw him out, and then turned the sign on the door to 'CLOSED' before pulling the blinds.

Sitting out in the car, Peter ran through it all again in his mind. There were so many plates spinning. Christian's alibi was hardly watertight, but then, neither was Sally's. He didn't think it was Jenny Wren – she had no real cause to kill Stroud. But Hugh Walsey? Peter didn't think Walsey was the type to get his own hands dirty, but would he put it past the man to hire someone to do the job? It was still a possibility, despite what Walsey had said about planning permission and the fact that Stroud's objections had gone nowhere. He'd have to get Patel to take a closer look at the man's business affairs.

Then there was the Nicholas Abbott case. Were they connected? It didn't seem that way, at least at the moment, despite their proximity. There were two people still in the frame for that: Thomas Abbott and Daisy Heddle.

Thomas Abbott clearly had a temper. Could he have finally snapped? And was there any reason why he might have wanted Lee Stroud dead, too? The way that Stroud had been bludgeoned – the sheer, brutal violence of the act – seemed like something Thomas was capable of, but there was no reason to believe he had anything to do with Stroud. He'd have to see what the forensic report revealed about the murder weapon, but it was another line of enquiry to pursue.

That left the enigma that was Daisy Heddle. There was something going on with her, and he hadn't yet been able to put his finger on it. She was definitely holding something back. He needed to get to the bottom of that, peel back the layers to find out what was underneath. Perhaps Elspeth would be able to help. He'd wait to see what she had to say about their evening.

He glanced down the lane in the direction the two women had taken. The scene was picturesque, tranquil. It was hard to believe that two violent murders had taken place in the village within the last seventy-two hours.

It wasn't just witches who were buried here. There were secrets, too. Secrets that were now starting to reveal themselves, in dark and terrible ways. Secrets that had festered for too long. Just like Jenny Wren, he was going to have to dig them out and expose them to the light.

CHAPTER TWENTY-TWO

"This is me. Come on in."

Daisy pushed open the door to the little cottage and flicked on the lights. They were eco-bulbs, and took a moment to warm up to full brightness. Elspeth had to duck her head under the lintel as she stepped inside. Immediately, she could see it was a pretty little place, built from old stone, with walls as thick as her forearm. Daisy had retained many of the original features but she'd decorated in a modern style, posters and paintings covering the walls, vibrant rugs on the tiled floors, local pottery and stacks of books and art materials wherever she looked.

She kicked off her boots in the narrow hallway, placing them beside a pair of Daisy's Dr Martens, which were plastered thick with dry mud. "Been out walking in the fields?" said Elspeth.

Daisy frowned, and then smiled. "Oh, the boots. Yeah, it gets so muddy round here. I really must invest in some wellies. Tea? Wine?"

"Oh, go on then," said Elspeth. "I can have one."

Daisy led her through to the kitchen. She fetched two glasses and poured them both a large measure. "So that policeman," she said, with a knowing smile. "You two seemed quite cosy."

Elspeth gave her best 'caught me' expression. "We've been seeing each other for a little while now. He's an old friend, and we reconnected when I moved back to the area. You know how it is."

"Is he always so serious?" said Daisy, sipping her wine.

"Don't you believe it," said Elspeth. "We have a right laugh together when he's not on a case, and I'm not on a story – which, it turns out, are often one and the same thing."

"How often is that, then?"

"Not often enough, admittedly," said Elspeth. "How about you? Anyone special?"

Daisy seemed to be weighing up her response. "I thought there might have been, but now I'm not so sure."

"Rough patch?"

"Something like that," said Daisy.

"So how long have you lived here?" said Elspeth, looking around. The kitchen was small but perfectly formed, with a modern electric cooker, a Belfast sink, a window looking out onto the small garden, and two overhead racks, from which dangled cooking pots and bunches of drying herbs. "It all seems very idyllic."

"It took me long enough to get to this point," said Daisy, leaning her hip against the sink. "I've been at the cottage for about three years. Before that I spent two years living in Sally's spare room, after she took me in."

"What happened? No family?"

"Long story," said Daisy, "but Mum and Dad were killed in a car accident when I was seventeen. I kind of went to pieces. I'd only recently come out, and was still figuring out who I was." She shrugged. "Turns out Dad hadn't renewed the life insurance, and I lost the house. They left me with a little bit of cash, but I wasn't in much of a state to look after myself. I'd just started working weekends at Sally's place, and she took pity on me." She took a gulp of her wine. "I stayed there until I was back on my feet, and then rented this place. The waitressing allows me to pay the rent, and buys me time to keep going with my art."

"I'm sorry," said Elspeth. "That must have been so difficult."

"I miss them. A lot. But I'm grateful to Sally, and to my parents for bringing me up to be the person I am. They always taught me to be true to myself, and I try to stick by that." Daisy's phone buzzed, and she glanced at it, and then turned it over on the worktop, placing it screen down. "Look, give me a minute to get changed, will you? I hate wearing this thing." She tugged at the front of her work uniform and pulled a face.

"Of course."

"Go on through to the lounge. It's the second door on the left, back along the hall. I'll only be a minute."

"Then you can show me some of your art," said Elspeth.

The lounge was, like the rest of the house, an eclectic mix of the old and the new. It reminded her of Richmond's in the way that the wonky windows and wooden beams sat hand-in-hand with purple walls and psychedelic posters, featuring bands from an era before Daisy had even been born. Before Elspeth had been born too, for that matter.

One of the alcoves beside the fireplace was filled with racks of old vinyl records, mostly from the 1980s – Human League, Stevie Wonder, Kate Bush, Peter Gabriel – albums that Elspeth still had on her phone, and that she presumed Daisy must have inherited from her parents. The other alcove was filled with books of all shapes and sizes – paperback classics, philosophical tracts, cheap thrillers and beach reads, all propped up by a towering stack of coffee-table art books, with subjects ranging from the works of Vermeer to Elizabethan architectural design.

Daisy arrived a moment later, holding the wine bottle by its neck. She'd already topped herself up.

Elspeth held out her glass. "Looks like I'm getting a taxi home, then." She grinned.

Daisy indicated the room with a wave of her arm. "I'm sorry, I know it's a bit of a mess. I'd meant to tidy up, but things just ran away with me last night," she said.

"I love it," said Elspeth. "Really. It feels lived in."

Daisy cocked her head, and grinned. She'd changed into a pair of skinny jeans and a plaid shirt, and looked more relaxed than Elspeth had seen her so far.

"How's your hand, by the way?"

"Oh, it's on the mend. Still painful, but I'll live." She glanced at the door. "Come on, I'll show you the studio."

She led Elspeth up the stone steps to the first floor, each of them so smooth and worn that Elspeth felt as if she were navigating an assault course.

"You get used to them," said Daisy, laughing.

The studio had taken over what had originally been the spare room. The view out over the rear garden was obscured by a bolt of white cloth which muted the harsh light. An easel was set up in the centre of the room, containing a canvas that had been blocked out in reds and greens, in preparation for a new work. All around the room were paintings stacked against the walls. There must have been forty or fifty of them, their surfaces turned away so that only the backs were exposed. A guitar was propped against the radiator on the back wall, and a laptop sat open on a desk, cables trailing to what looked to be a small mixing desk. The floorboards were bare and spattered with paint, and the entire room smelled of turpentine.

"Well, it's certainly a proper studio," said Elspeth. She supposed she'd been expecting a few paintings in a spare room or shed out the back, but this was a room that had seen serious use. "Did you do *all* of these?" she said, wandering over to one of the stacks.

Daisy shrugged. "Yeah, but most of them aren't up to much. Feel free to take a look."

Elspeth picked up the nearest canvas, turning it over

in her hands. It showed the ghostly face of a woman, painted in white on a murky blue background. She was beautiful, ethereal, as if she had been born from the very light itself, swimming out from the canvas to greet Elspeth with her knowing smile. "Aren't up to much? Daisy, this is outstanding."

She picked up another. It depicted a woman reclining on a rock, somewhere by a lake or pool, half covering her naked body with a towel. Her hair was startlingly red, flowing over her pale shoulder. She was looking straight at the viewer, her coy smile captured perfectly. A third showed a young woman reading a book, hair tucked behind one ear, legs folded beneath her. She'd just looked up, as if caught by surprise, and the curve of her lips caught an attitude that was somewhere between innocent and expectant.

"I recognise her," said Elspeth, "but I can't place her. Is she from the village?"

"Yeah, I think so," said Daisy. "I've painted so many I lose track. They're mostly just people I get talking to, and want to capture their story."

"You have a wonderful eye," said Elspeth. "I'm very impressed."

"You'll let me paint *you*, then?"

Elspeth thought about it for a moment. "All right, yeah, go on."

"I was hoping you'd say that." She put her wine glass down by the computer and grabbed her phone from her back pocket. "Let's get some pictures, then."

"What, *now*?"

"Why not?"

"Because I don't know what I'm supposed to do," said Elspeth, feeling suddenly embarrassed.

"Do nothing," said Daisy. She started moving around, and the phone camera flashed. Elspeth laughed. "There. See, that was easy."

"That's it?"

"Yup. Got everything I need."

"Well, I look forward to seeing it," said Elspeth. "With some trepidation."

"Well, you've got an important decision to make before then," said Daisy.

Elspeth looked at her quizzically.

"Whether you want pasta or take-out."

"Take-out. My treat," said Elspeth. "On the condition that you place the order. This wine's already going to my head."

They settled on Chinese food, and ate it cross-legged on the floor in Daisy's lounge, finishing a second bottle of wine and playing old records that had them both singing at the top of their lungs.

This is what I've been missing, Elspeth realised. London was all well and good, but Abigail and the others – they were all too caught up in the social scene for a night like this. She loved Abi to bits, but when was the last time they'd really let their hair down and just had a laugh with some junk food and a couple of bottles of cheap plonk? There was always a party, always a reason to make an effort, a man to impress or something to get out of it all. Maybe this was what Abigail needed, too, and she just didn't know it. Maybe Elspeth didn't need London, but Abigail needed Oxford. She'd think on that.

Daisy scooped up the last forkful of sweet and sour chicken. "Tonight was just what I needed. What with everything going on, I've been feeling a bit out of sorts recently."

"Anything you want to talk about?"

"No... I..." She hesitated. "You ever just feel like you're not yourself?"

"Under the weather, you mean? A bit run down?"

"I suppose so. It's just, the last couple of nights I've felt a bit *odd*, that's all. But you're right, I'm probably just coming down with something."

"Or fighting it off," said Elspeth. "Just look at you tonight."

Daisy laughed. "Yeah. I'd best keep up my vitamins," she said, downing the last of her wine. Her phone was rumbling again, but she ignored it. She glanced at the clock on the mantel. "Oh, God, have you seen the time?"

Elspeth peered at the clock face. It took her a moment to work it out. It was nearly 2 am. She groaned.

"I've got a shift in the morning", said Daisy. "I'd better turn in. Do you want the sofa?"

Elspeth looked at the cosy pit of cushions, and considered the wait for a taxi, the ride back to Heighton, the trip back in the morning to fetch her car. "I was going to get a taxi, but yeah, if you don't mind."

"I really don't," said Daisy. "But I'll tell you if you snore."

Elspeth practically snorted her last mouthful of wine.

She helped Daisy pile the dishes into the kitchen – abandoning them on the work surface for the morning – and then fired Peter a quick text:

Great night. Staying over at Daisy's. Breakfast in the morning at Lenny's? X

And then fell promptly asleep on the sofa.

CHAPTER TWENTY-THREE

Hugh Walsey slammed the phone down on his desk and rocked back in his chair, grinding his teeth. The morning sun was streaming in through his office window, picking out the swirling dust motes in the air.

This was the last thing he needed. He'd staked everything on this house and his development of the grounds, and now, weeks away from commencing work, there was a problem with the funds.

Well, he wasn't about to be held to ransom by his contractors. He'd call the bank, see about extending his loan against the house. A few thousand more shouldn't hurt, and he'd make it back tenfold when the business was up and running. He'd just have to tighten his belt in the meantime; see if he could curtail Petra's spending a little.

He just hoped he hadn't pushed things too far. Buying Hallowdene Manor had been *his* dream, not hers, or Lucy's, and now here he was, juggling bills and trying to find a way to keep it all afloat. Everything relied on getting those cottages built. Once he was renting them out he'd have everything covered, and he could get on with all the other projects he'd planned. But first he had to get them built, and that was proving far more difficult than it should have been.

At least there'd be no more interference from Lee Stroud now. That man had got everything he deserved. What right did he have to climb up there on his high horse and tell Walsey what he could and couldn't do on his own land? That policeman had been right, Stroud *had* cost him both time and money, and Walsey hated him for it. If it hadn't been for that interfering idiot, he might not be in the position he was now, being forced to retain builders at extra expense, just because of the delay.

Even in death, Stroud had still found a way to be bloody awkward, holding up the dig while the police finished going through everything with a fine-tooth comb. It was a damned inconvenience.

In the other room, he could hear Petra going off on one again. When would they bloody well learn to get on? He'd had just about enough of it. He pushed his chair back from the desk and stood, marching through to the sitting room, where Lucy was sitting on one of the sofas, hunched over her phone, while Petra was striding back and forth like some Roman orator, giving forth about why Lucy was such an inconsiderate daughter. For once, Lucy didn't seem to have the energy to respond, tapping away on her screen with her thumbs and tartly ignoring her stepmother. At this precise moment, Walsey couldn't say that he blamed her.

"What's all this racket about?" he snapped, glaring at Petra. "I'm trying to work."

Petra ceased her pacing and returned his glare, face like thunder. "She's been sneaking out," she said, jabbing her finger melodramatically at Lucy. "I caught her coming back in last night at one in the morning."

Walsey looked at Lucy. "Look, don't you think you'd better take a bit more care? With everything that's happened… you don't want people asking questions. Not to mention that the killer is still out there, somewhere. Why take any silly risks?"

"I didn't take any risks, Dad. None of that's got anything to do with me. I was just meeting a friend, that's all," said Lucy.

Walsey shrugged. "Petra, the girl's nineteen years old. We can't stop her from seeing her friends."

Lucy looked up at him, and smiled. It was a move precisely designed to send Petra into apoplexy. "Oh, I might have thought you'd take her side in this. I'm worried about her, Hugh. We don't know *what* she's getting up to. Two people have been murdered, she's out there alone, and you don't think it's a problem?"

He sighed. "Petra has a point, just while this business is cleared up by the police. Maybe if you're going to be out you could do us the courtesy of letting us know?"

"Okay, Dad. No problem," said Lucy.

"There. No need for all that shouting, was there?" he said. He didn't care if he sounded patronising. There was a time when he would have done anything for

Petra, when he would have practically fallen at her feet for a single kind word. Now, he had to admit, all the drama was growing tiresome. Couldn't they just start avoiding one another?

"Right," he said, "I need to place a call to the bank. It would be nice if I could hear myself think."

He stepped aside to allow Petra to barge past him and out into the hall. He heard her footsteps thundering on the stairs. "And Lucy – please try to get along with her. For my sake. I'm not asking you to act like best buddies or anything. Just a bit of toleration."

"*She's* the intolerant one, Dad," said Lucy, finally lowering her phone. "It's that bloody Catholic upbringing. It's wound her as tight as a gnat's arse."

Despite himself, Walsey laughed. "I suppose you're not wrong. Come here, kiddo." He plonked himself down on the sofa beside her, wrapping her in a tight embrace. "We doing okay?"

"*We're* fine, Dad. Always will be."

CHAPTER TWENTY-FOUR

Elspeth knew she shouldn't really be driving, but a strong coffee at Daisy's had helped to drown out the buzzing headache, and the bottle of water she was sipping as she sat in traffic was helping to rid her of the carpet mouth she'd woken up with.

Daisy had been up and out at the crack of dawn, trilling away in the kitchen as she made coffee as if she hadn't even sniffed a glass of wine. She'd popped into the lounge with a mug and a set of keys for Elspeth, laughing gleefully at Elspeth's bleary-eyed greeting, and asking her to lock up behind her and post the keys back through the door.

Elspeth had cocooned herself in the blanket and buried her head in the cushions, managing another half-hour's sleep before the constant beeping of her phone had finally forced her to get up. She'd zapped the coffee in the microwave, freshened up in the bathroom and stumbled out to her car, having read the five messages from Peter interrogating her about her evening.

She turned onto Heighton High Street and then

swung in by the shops, relieved to find a spot for the Mini on the hill. She fed coins into the machine and pinned the ticket to the windscreen, then hurried over to Lenny's.

Peter was waiting for her inside, a smug look on his face. She bent down to kiss him, and then dropped heavily into the chair opposite. Thankfully, he'd already bought her a coffee.

"You smell like a vineyard," he said, laughing.

"I feel like one too," she said, not even sure what she meant.

"Good night, then?"

"Great night, actually," said Elspeth. "Daisy's a lot of fun, and an amazing artist. You should see some of her portraits. I really think she could make a go of it."

"And good wine, too?"

"Well, there was that. And singing."

"Oh God, save me," mocked Peter. "Seriously, though, I was worried about you. She's still a prime suspect in Nicholas Abbott's murder, and you weren't supposed to go getting that closely involved. I thought they taught you this at journalism school, or something."

"This wasn't about journalism, or the story, or even really about the investigation," said Elspeth. "It was about me, and a young woman who needs a friend. She's been through a lot. She told me about her upbringing, how her parents had both been killed in a car crash when she was seventeen."

"Christ," said Peter. "That's tough."

"There's definitely something going on with her. She said she'd been feeling not quite herself the last few nights, and her boots in the hallway were covered in mud… but I don't know, my opinion might not count for much, but I just can't see it. I think it's more that she's a bit alone in the world, and it's getting to her, is all."

"You do have a tendency to see the best in people," said Peter. "It's one of your defining qualities."

Elspeth grinned. "You say the nicest things." She sipped her coffee. It was like liquid bliss. "How was your evening?"

"Just what you'd imagine. I spent most of it at the station, working with the team to plot out all the possible leads, seeing what connections, if any, we could draw between the two deaths."

"And?"

"There's very little to tell. Patel's off to speak to Thomas Abbott again today, to see if he can get a sense of the man's movements over the last few days. As far as we know he had no connection to Stroud, but that temper…"

"You didn't tell me how he'd been killed," said Elspeth.

Peter lowered his voice. "It's not for public consumption, all right, but he was battered to death with a marker pole from the dig. Whoever it was made a right mess of him."

Elspeth pulled a face. She could imagine. "Do you have any idea who you're looking for?"

Peter rocked his hand back and forth in a tentative

gesture. "It's an open book at the moment. We've been trying to get prints off the weapon, but the killer must have worn gloves, and it's such an isolated spot up there that no one saw them. The TV crew had left a time-lapse camera set up on the site, but the killer must have seen it and taken it with them. We've got people looking for that, too."

"What about the Walseys?"

"Arguing amongst themselves as usual," he said.

"Any luck with Sally and Christian Jameson?"

"No. Not really. There's nothing to place either of them at the scene, although their alibis are pretty thin. It's clear that Christian thought the man was a pain in the arse, but without any evidence it's a big leap to put him in the frame for the guy's murder. I suppose they might have been working together, but again, there's nothing to suggest it." Peter shook his head. "Sally did seem rather cut up about the Abbott murder, but I'm not sure what the connection is yet. It still feels like a hell of a coincidence that two people would be murdered, a day apart, in an otherwise quiet village with one of the lowest crime rates in the area. It can't just be a coincidence."

"Three unexplained deaths," said Elspeth, quietly.

"What's that?" said Peter.

"Three deaths in unusual circumstances. I saw Iain and Carl Hardwick yesterday, about the fayre, and it's just something that Carl said." She poked an errant strand of hair back behind her ear as she leaned forward. "Back in the 1640s, when they first buried Agnes Levett.

Soon after, there followed three unexplained deaths, and people said they'd been hearing Agnes's voice. What you just said, about it not being a coincidence. Carl said something similar about those historical deaths. I can't help wondering – both of these murders have happened within a couple of days of the witch stone being moved and Agnes Levett's grave exposed."

"You're not suggesting her spirit has returned to wreak vengeance, are you? I can't very well take that to Griffiths as my working theory," said Peter.

"Maybe not," said Elspeth, "but you know as well as I do that there are more things in this world than can be easily understood by the likes of us."

Peter looked thoughtful, as if her words had struck home. "Is that a quote?"

"I'm paraphrasing Shakespeare. Badly. But okay, let's say these deaths have got nothing to do with Agnes Levett. What if someone's trying to make it seem like they do?" She drained her coffee and looked over at the queue, then felt crestfallen when she saw the length of it. She'd have to get another coffee at home, before setting out for her train to London. She had no idea how she was going to get through another night out. Not to mention the work she still had to do en route.

"All right, so someone who's aware of the old story is using the excavation as a trigger to murder people. They'd still need a motive," said Peter. "It makes no sense that they'd just randomly select people to die."

"Who's to say that they are random, in the mind of

the killer?" said Elspeth. "All I'm saying is that *could* be your link. The story. And if it is, it suggests another person is going to die."

"Great," said Peter. "Just what I need."

"I'm sorry, just trying to help." She reached over for his coffee cup and took a long swig.

He watched her with amusement. "No, you are helping. It's just, if that's true, it means we could be looking at anyone. It doesn't necessarily allow us to narrow the field."

"And nothing at Abbott's or Stroud's houses has suggested anything useful?"

"Not yet. The SOCOs are still analysing fibres from Abbott's house, but I'm not holding up much hope." He sighed. "Even the Carrion King case seemed simple compared to this one."

They lapsed into thoughtful silence.

"Look, let's get out of here for a minute. Take a walk," said Elspeth.

"All right," said Peter, frowning. "Is everything okay?" He got to his feet.

"I think so," said Elspeth. "It's just, this doesn't seem the right place to talk, you know?"

He nodded. "I know just the place. Come on." He took her by the hand and led her out onto the High Street. She followed as he led her down a narrow passage between two buildings – a bank and a chemist – which opened up onto a small area that had once been the back yard of the bank, but had now been converted into a small public garden.

"I had no idea this was here!" said Elspeth.

"It's new. The council have just finished renovating it. It was too small for a car park, and too out of the way for an office, so they decided to create a few flower beds and a seating area for the public. I've been waiting for a chance to show it to you."

"I love it," said Elspeth, taking a seat on one of the benches. Peter sat down beside her, and Elspeth took his hand in hers. She gave it a gentle squeeze. "Talk to me about the promotion," she said. There, she'd said it. She studied his face carefully, looking for some sort of sign, some giveaway as to his true thoughts.

Peter rubbed his other hand over his chin. "Ah. So that's what this is about." He sighed. "There's really nothing to tell. It's just something that's been mentioned, is all. And really, is it for me? Big city life? You know what that's like. Would I really fit in?"

"Of course you would. If you wanted to." She felt something flip in her stomach. The thought that he might actually be considering going…

"That's just it," he said. "I'm not sure that I do want to." He looked at her, holding her gaze in silence for a moment.

"But you're unhappy here?" she asked. She swallowed, her throat dry.

"No, no. It's not that. Look, I've lived here all my life. You've been out there, seen the world for what it is. I'm just a local boy who chose to stick around.

It's just... the Carrion King case. It gave me a taste of something bigger, I suppose. And it felt good. I don't mean all the death, all the *horror* of it, I mean putting an end to it. Helping people. Saving lives. Seeing justice done. I just... I think I can do more."

"I'm sure of it," she said. How could she say anything else? He was right. He did have more to offer than chasing after burglars and car thieves. "But isn't that what you're doing now? Griffiths isn't breathing down your neck, is she, about the Abbott murder?"

"No, you're right. Not yet. She's letting me get on with it for now." He took his hand from hers, rubbing his chin. "I suppose it's a bit of a test. That's why I've got to be seen to play everything by the book. You understand, don't you?"

"Perfectly."

He looked at her again, and she could tell he was working himself up to another awkward subject. "What about you? Aren't you tempted by all that stuff that Abi was talking about? Launch parties and publishing jobs? The Carrion King case has done that for you, too, hasn't it? Opened up new possibilities?"

Elspeth couldn't meet his gaze. "I suppose so," she said. "I'd be lying if I said I hadn't thought about it. But I'm happy here. I'm finally starting to feel at home. I'm not looking for more, not at the moment." And yet, she was still going to the party with Abigail that night, and was still going to meet with Simon, the editorial director. She didn't want to tell him about the meeting, though, because she didn't want to scare him into making a different decision of his own. If he thought she was going, would that push him into taking a transfer? And if so, what did that mean for the two of them? They'd barely been together for three months – what right did she have to expect him to stay for her if he wasn't happy?

"Then we're both worrying about nothing," said Peter. He didn't sound convinced.

"All right," said Elspeth. "But let's make sure we talk about it, okay?" He nodded. Her phone trilled, and she fumbled for a moment to find it in her bag. She looked at the screen: Abigail. Perfect timing.

"Hang on, it's Abi." She accepted the call. "Hi, Abi."

"Hiya. Just wondering what time you're getting in today? I've taken the afternoon off so I can meet you, and we can get glammed up at my place."

Elspeth wanted to groan. Just the thought of going out again seemed like torture. She'd promised, though, and she didn't want to let Abigail down. Plus she supposed she really should meet this Simon character that Abi kept talking about, just so she knew what she'd be turning down. "My train's due in at three."

"Okay, perfect. Bye!"

The line went dead.

She looked at Peter, feeling a little guilty.

"You go and enjoy yourself," he said. "I'm tied up here, anyway. Look, there's one last thing. It's about the case…"

"Go on."

"When you talked to Lee Stroud up at the dig, did he say anything that might be useful?"

Elspeth cast her mind back over the conversation. "No, I don't think so. He mentioned there'd been some deaths – that's the first time I was aware of that part of the story – and said that it was nice to have someone take him seriously for once. He said he only wanted to help, and that they shouldn't go stirring things up, that people like Agnes Levett don't rest easily. He talked about echoes of the past, and everything coming around again."

They stood, and kissed.

"If he wasn't one of the victims, I'd say he would have been our prime suspect," he said. "But nothing's ever that easy, is it?"

"Nothing is, no," she replied.

CHAPTER TWENTY-FIVE

It was mid-afternoon before Peter got away from the station again, having mooted Elspeth's idea about the killer being inspired by the exhumation of Agnes's bones to recreate the story from the legend. This had gained some traction amongst the team, although there was still the question of motive, and so they'd set to work researching the original legend online – as far as they could – and attempting to identify potential candidates from amongst the villagers and suspects.

The problem was, they kept coming up short. There was no one amongst the notable figures they'd identified in the village with more than a speeding ticket to their name, except Thomas Abbott, who had a previous for ABH after getting into a fight in the pub one night with another local man. It hardly identified him as a cold-blooded killer. Hugh Walsey, too, was thought to have been involved in some shady dealings, perhaps relating to tax fraud, but again there was nothing concrete, and he'd never been convicted of anything, related or otherwise. They'd even managed to get hold of someone from the Krakow police force to run a search on Petra Walsey, formerly Nowak, but they'd come back with an instant negative. She was as clean as they come.

So, while Patel went out to Thomas Abbott's place, Peter decided to have another word with Daisy Heddle to see if she had any connection to Lee Stroud, and whether she had an alibi for the night of his murder.

He was still concerned that Elspeth had put herself so completely into Daisy's orbit. Even she'd been forced to admit that there was something going on with the woman, and if Daisy *did* turn out to be a killer, Elspeth would have spent a drunken night on her sofa, completely exposed. He didn't even like to consider what might have happened.

Luckily, she'd had a good time, and she was fine. Maybe he was being overprotective, and maybe he should trust her judgement more. If he could only get to the bottom of what Daisy was hiding. Every instinct told him it would help to unpick the tangled morass of secrets and relationships that comprised the village of Hallowdene.

He'd called at Richmond's looking for her, drawing sour looks from both Sally and Christian. They'd told him that she'd already finished for the day, having done the early shift, and directed him to her cottage down the road. Daisy was at the door within moments, looking up brightly, although her face fell when she realised it was Peter.

"DS Shaw," she said, levelly. "What can I do for you?"

He wondered if she were expecting someone else.

"Just some follow-up questions, if you have a few minutes?"

She released her hold on the door and beckoned him in. Her hands were covered in paint, and she was wearing denim dungarees that clearly served as overalls; mandelbrots of various different colours were spattered down her front. Her hair was tied back from her face. She was wearing a small gold ring through her pierced eyebrow.

"Excuse me for a moment," she said, brandishing her hands. "I'd better just clean up."

She went through to the kitchen and ran the tap for a minute, leaving him hovering in the hallway feeling awkward. The house reminded him of a Hobbit hole – small and cosy and full of *things*. He felt too big inside, like a giant who'd accidentally wandered into the wrong children's story.

She reappeared a moment later, still drying her hands. He couldn't help but notice that the bandage had gone, and the wound on her palm looked like a ragged tear, as opposed to a cut she might have acquired from an open tin of beans. It had clearly started to heal, the skin puckered, red and scabrous, and it obviously hadn't been deep enough to require stitching.

"Working on a new piece?" he said.

"Yeah." She cocked her head. "Actually, you might like to see it," she said, with a shrug.

"I'd like that."

She led him up to the studio and indicated the canvas

on the easel. "Here. It's early days, but it's starting to take shape."

He took a step closer, trying to make sense of the gossamer shapes, the dancing of the white paint over the red and brown of the background. Then he noticed the eye, staring out at him, and the face seemed to resolve around it. It was Elspeth, looking intently up at him, a cheeky smile on her slightly parted lips.

He stepped back, unable to take his eyes from the picture. "That's incredible," he said. "How long have you been working on it?"

"Just a few hours," she said. "I took the reference pictures last night. You mustn't tell her you've seen it, though. She knows I'm doing it, but I still want it to be a surprise." Daisy looked pleased with herself.

And she has a right to be, thought Peter. "These are all yours?" he said, stooping to look at some of the other stacked canvases.

"Yeah. I'm hoping to try to exhibit some of them, some time."

He looked up, seriously impressed. "I'm as far from an expert as you can get, but Ellie was right – you've got a real talent."

She looked faintly embarrassed. "Ellie said she might do a piece for the local paper, try to get some attention."

"Then I'm sure she'll see it through, just as soon as the fayre is out of the way and all the excitement has died down."

"Ah, yeah. The 'excitement'. I heard about poor Lee."

"That's why I'm here," said Peter. "I just need to ask you a few questions."

Daisy looked a little deflated. "No problem. Shall we have a cup of tea?"

"That would be nice. Thank you."

They returned to the kitchen, and Daisy set about making the drinks. "So, what do you want to know?"

"Firstly, I'm interested in how well you knew Lee Stroud."

"I didn't," said Daisy. "Not beyond what I saw of him in Richmond's, or occasionally around the village. He never really spoke to me, unless it was to ask after Sally. Christian always said that he had a thing for her, but I don't think Lee was really wired that way."

"How do you mean?"

"I don't know. I don't really think he was that bothered about love, or sex. That's how he came across. I'd just never thought of him in that way. He always seemed more interested in his history and genealogy. I never saw him troubled by a pretty girl. Or a pretty man, for that matter."

"We've certainly found no evidence that he shared his life with anyone," said Peter.

Daisy nodded. "That's sad. Everyone deserves someone, don't you think?"

"I suppose I do," said Peter. He accepted the mug of tea she'd been making. It was hot, and he put it straight back down on the work surface. "So you'd never had a run-in with Stroud?"

"Not like I had with Nicholas Abbott, if that's what you mean. Lee just wanted to be heard, I think, and he'd fixated on Sally as someone he thought should be listening. I always tried to dissuade him when he started making a scene, and sometimes he'd listen to me and leave quietly. Other times he'd just keep shouting for Sally until she put in an appearance and tried to placate him."

"What about Christian? I've heard he took umbrage at Stroud's regular visits."

"That was only recently, really, since they'd started work on the dig. Christian was just trying to protect his mum, I think, and the business, too – we'd had a few customers complain about Lee's behaviour," she said.

"Anyone I should know about?"

"Nicholas Abbott for one," said Daisy, "but he'd complain about anything if he thought it might get a rise out of someone. Other than that, just the odd comment, really. A few of the older customers who like a bit of peace and quiet with their teacakes. And maybe Carl Hardwick, too. I seem to remember him saying something about the noise. Nothing untoward, though. They're generally a very friendly bunch."

It certainly didn't sound as if Daisy had any reason to go after Stroud.

"Can you tell me your whereabouts the night before last? Did you happen to go up to the manor?"

She frowned. "No. I've no reason to go up there," she said.

Peter nodded. It sounded like a practised response.

She'd been expecting that question. "I noticed your boots in the hall," he said. "It was muddy up at the dig site, that's all."

"I like to go walking in the woods, sometimes. I just haven't got round to cleaning them yet. Sometimes I don't even bother, to be honest, as they'll only get muddy again."

"Raisonby Wood?"

"Yeah. There's something about that place. It's almost like stepping back in time."

"So that's where you were the night before last, walking in Raisonby Wood?" he asked.

"What? No. I was here, painting. That's what I'm usually doing when I'm not at Richmond's. I don't have that much of a social life, out here in Hallowdene. Sometimes I head over to Oxford for a night out with old friends, but really, my life's here, with these people, and apart from the odd drink in the Rowan Tree, there's not a great deal to do." She sipped her tea. "I guess that's why I had such fun with Ellie last night."

"She did look a bit worse for wear this morning."

"Didn't she just!" Daisy laughed.

"So, just to confirm, you were here alone, and you saw no one between the hours of 9 pm and 2 am?"

"I suppose when you put it like that, I don't have much of an alibi. But when you live alone, and you have a solitary hobby…" She shrugged. "I'm sorry I can't be more help. And I'm sorry about what happened to Lee. I had no fondness for Nicholas Abbott, but I suspect he brought it on himself – and that's not an admission – but Lee seemed like a harmless soul. I can't imagine who'd want to hurt him."

Peter took a couple of gulps of his tea, then made his excuses and left. On the way out, he couldn't help but notice the flaking mud in the hallway, and remembered Daisy's jacket from the previous evening, with the muddy cuff. Had she done that in Raisonby Wood, too?

He walked slowly back to the car, if anything feeling increasingly uneasy about Daisy Heddle. To him, it was almost as if there were two Daisys – the artist and waitress who'd made such an impression on Elspeth, and the quieter, scared young woman who bristled at his innocuous questions and obfuscated when she had to explain herself.

There was something there, bubbling under the bright, cheerful surface, and whatever it was, she was deeply reluctant to reveal it.

Back in the car, he wondered how Elspeth was getting on. He pulled out his phone, but the only message was from PC Chambers, saying that Griffiths wanted to see him back at the station. He considered giving her a call, and then thought better of it, and tossed his phone onto the passenger seat as he drove off.

CHAPTER TWENTY-SIX

For a moment when Ellie walked into the bar, dressed in a smart little cocktail dress, she remembered what it was she loved about London – the fact she could go anywhere, at any time, find bars that weren't just another rustic country pub, stay out late and feel like she was at the beating heart of the world, where everything was happening, and everything was possible.

Of *course* she had missed it. How could she have forgotten *this*?

And then she stood at the bar for a moment and watched the people fawning over one another, the men in their Savile Row suits and the women in their designer dresses, and she remembered exactly why she'd left. None of this was real. Nobody really *existed* in this world. It looked glamorous enough, tricked you into falling for its illusion, but ultimately, that lifestyle of endless parties and empty shags amounted to nothing. Not to Elspeth. She'd never been interested in that.

Andrew had been a part of that world, and she was certain he'd been taken in by it. That's probably why

229

he did what he did – because, fired up on booze and parties, he'd felt as if he could do anything he wanted, and there was no one in the world who could stop him. That life – it chewed people up and spat them out, and she didn't think she wanted anything to do with it.

Of course, she knew full well that not all of London was like this, that this was only a small slice of what life here was like. But it was how Elspeth had come to see it and tonight, at a place like this, surrounded by people she didn't know and didn't want to know, it only reinforced her fears.

Move back to London and lose yourself. Take a new job, put on a party frock, and become someone else.

The thought of it left her feeling utterly exhausted.

She leaned against the bar, trying to catch the barman's eye. Perhaps she was still hungover from the night before. She wasn't as young as she'd once been. She'd had fun with Abigail, back at her apartment, chatting about men, trying on some of Abi's outfits, choosing what she was going to wear for the party. For a while she'd even started to think that perhaps it wouldn't be such a bad thing to come back, and that if this editorial position worked out it might be another step towards getting back on her feet.

That's when it had hit her. She already was back on her feet. She had been for months. She was making a go of her freelance career, she had a flat that she loved, she had family and friends, and she had Peter.

That's what this was really about, she realised. She

was building contingency plans. She was scared he was going to go, and that they'd never really live up to their potential. They'd been too coy, too reserved, too caught up in what was going on around them to notice that they'd not really talked, not made any plans. She'd have to do something about that, just as soon as she made it home.

She almost laughed at the irony. *Home*. Of course that's how she felt about it. Oxfordshire was her home, now, and she wasn't about to give it up. Still, it didn't stop her from having fun with her friend.

Abigail suddenly appeared by her side, pushing a drink into her hand. Elspeth took a sip, and shuddered at the hit of almost neat vodka.

"I know the barman," said Abigail, leaning in and raising her voice to be heard. "He'll see us right."

"He'll see us drunk and disorderly," said Elspeth, taking another sip. At least, she supposed, it might blow away the last of the previous night's cobwebs. "I thought we were going to a launch party?"

"Oh, yeah. This is just an aperitif," said Abigail. She clinked her glass against Elspeth's. "We'll have a couple here to loosen us up before we head to the party. It's just down the street."

"I don't know about loosen us up," said Elspeth, "so much as wipe us out." She put the drink on the bar. She'd better take it steady – she didn't want to be all over the place when Abigail introduced her to Simon.

Abigail seemed to notice her mood. "You okay?"

"Yeah. Of course. It's just a bit loud in here, that's all."

Abigail laughed. "You're getting too used to life in the country. Come on, then. Finish your drink and we'll head off."

The party was a relatively low-key affair in a hired room beneath a swanky bar, which was decorated with old distilling paraphernalia and towering brass vats, set amongst metal gantries and mezzanines. Thankfully the music was relatively low-key, too, and after all the speeches were done and everyone had congratulated the author on the book – a grisly thriller about people-trafficking from Eastern Europe – Abigail had walked her around, introducing her to everyone.

At least here she felt more at home amongst the crowd, surrounded by fellow book lovers. The publicity team were friendly, and asked her lots of questions, and the other editors seemed genuinely interested in her work. Simon, however, seemed more concerned with the length of her skirt.

"So, Abi tells me you're interested in applying for our new editorial position," he said, knocking back a small glass of red wine as if it were a shot of tequila. He looked her up and down. He was a handsome, smartly dressed man in his fifties, with a style that seemed a little anachronistic, evidenced by both his waistcoat and pocket watch and his apparent attitudes towards women. "I'd certainly be interested to hear more. We've been looking to extend our non-fiction range, and Abi tells me you're something of a hot property at the moment. Broke a big story about a murder, didn't you?"

Elspeth wasn't sure she liked being considered a 'hot property', particularly by a man who had so far been unable to make any form of eye contact. "You could say that, yes. I formed part of the investigative team working on the Carrion King case."

"Ah, right, of course," he said. "Well, there's a book in that, of course. Have you considered that? Writing a book?"

"I've thought about it," said Elspeth.

"You have?" said Abigail.

Elspeth nodded. "It's something I'd like to do, one day."

"You should," said Simon, fiddling with one of his cufflinks. "And when you're ready, talk to Abi. She's one of our star editors. I'm sure she'd be delighted to have you on her list." He made it sound as if he were introducing the two of them for the first time.

"Thanks," said Elspeth. "I'm sorry, you'll have to excuse me for a moment." She handed Abigail her glass, ignoring the woman's urgent eye-rolling, and ducked off in the direction of the loo.

At the last minute she veered left, slipping behind one of the tall brass vats, out of view of the rest of the party. She heaved a sigh of relief.

She pulled out a chair by a little round table and sat down, taking out her phone. She thumbed through her list of recent contacts and found Peter's name. She hit dial.

He answered almost immediately. "Ellie? Is everything okay?"

"Of course it is," she said, laughing. "I don't only phone in emergencies, you know."

"I know, but aren't you supposed to be down in London, attending some swanky party?"

"I'm here now, and it's deathly," she said. "I'd much rather be with you, having a drink in the Old Dun Cow." The pub had become her Heighton local, and she often went for a drink there on a Thursday evening with Meredith and the gang from the *Heighton Observer*.

"The feeling's mutual. I'm still at the station."

"Any developments?"

She heard him swap his phone to the other hand. "Only that Thomas Abbott has a cast-iron alibi for the night of Lee Stroud's murder," he said. "He was at the theatre in Oxford. Plenty of witnesses."

"So we're back to square one," she said.

"We?"

"Of course. We're in this together, aren't we?"

"Always. But I'm pleased to hear you say it." She had the sense that they were talking about more than just the investigation.

A pause.

"I spoke to Daisy again."

"And?"

"There's no obvious connection to Stroud, but I don't know... I still think she's hiding something, Ellie."

"I know. Perhaps she'll open up a bit, now she

knows she can trust me. But I don't want to betray that trust. Like I said, she needs a friend," said Elspeth.

"I just want you to be careful. That's all. I couldn't bear it if you got hurt."

"I know. Goes both ways, you know."

She heard another voice in the background, and thought she recognised DS Patel.

"All right, you'd better get back to the party," said Peter.

"Do I have to?"

"Yes, you do. Your friend is waiting for you. Go. You'll be home tomorrow, and we'll try to make a night of it. There's some grand unveiling of the witch's bones at the Hallowdene village hall, and then we could head back to my place?" he said.

"You're on." She looked up and saw Abigail heading for her table. "I'd better go. See you."

She cut the connection.

Abigail pulled out a chair and sat down. "All right, missus, are you going to tell me what's going on with you?" She pushed Elspeth's drink across the table.

"I just wanted to speak to Peter, that's all," she said. "Sorry to dash off like that." She put her phone back in the little clutch bag she'd been carrying around all night.

Abigail sighed. "Look, I was wrong, Ellie. Things have changed for you. This isn't your scene, not any more. I'm sorry – I thought I was doing the right thing, but I can see that all you want to do is go home." She looked a little crestfallen, but she reached out and put her hand on Elspeth's arm.

"I'm sorry," said Elspeth. "I really do appreciate it. It's not that I don't want to see *you*. It's just all of this," she waved her arm, encompassing the venue, the party. "I'm standing there talking to people and all I can think about is the story I'm supposed to be working on, and getting back to Peter."

"Love can do that to a girl," said Abigail.

"Love?"

"I've seen the way you look at him."

Elspeth shook her head. It was too early for talk like that. And besides, she still didn't know if he was planning to stick around. There'd be no talk of love. Not yet. "Look, I'm going to cut and run. You stay. I can make my own way back to your place, see you later when you're done here."

"Don't be daft. I'm coming with you."

"I don't want to spoil your evening," said Elspeth. "I feel bad enough as it is."

"You think I want to hang around here and get ogled by Simon any more than I need to? I can do that any day at the office. Let's head back to mine, crack open a bottle of wine and watch a crappy movie."

"Now you're talking," said Elspeth. They stood, looping arms. "Thanks, Abi."

CHAPTER TWENTY-SEVEN

The headstone felt cold against the backs of her legs. Daisy shifted position, glancing at her phone screen. The light from the device was the only source of illumination for miles around, encasing her in its warm orange glow – a protective shield, holding back the darkness.

In the distance, down the hill, she could see a few pinpricks of light in the village; the sodium glare of the street lamps and the occasional burst of a security light flickering on to snapshot the sudden movement of a bird or cat.

Behind her, the old church loomed, shrouded in shadow and surrounded by the looming headstones of its silent congregation, now resting here in permanent, rapt attention. The place gave Daisy the creeps. Why she'd want to meet here was beyond her.

She checked her phone again. It was nearly 1 am.

She heard the scuff of a boot on the wall, and looked up to see Lucy jumping down into the graveyard, running towards her, a beaming smile on her face. She was wearing a jumper dress and black leggings, with purple boots and a short denim jacket. She grabbed Daisy by the lapels, pushed her back against the headstone and kissed her deeply.

"Hi," she said, when she finally came up for air. "I've been waiting all day to do that."

"Trouble in paradise?" said Daisy.

"Petra caught me sneaking back in the other night and went apoplectic. Caused a right barney. Dad stood up for me, of course, but then backtracked a bit when Petra pointed out there was a murderer on the loose. Said he wanted a running commentary of my comings and goings until it was all over."

Daisy sighed. "You're going to have to tell them about us, Lucy. I'd never pressure you, you know that, but *I* worry about you too. And we can't keep doing this, skulking around graveyards and meeting in the dead of night. Can't you just stay over at mine?"

"I can't risk it. You know that. If someone were to see me, it might get back to Dad and Petra. At least here, we're not likely to be spotted."

"We can't go on like this, though. We're not kids any more," said Daisy.

"I know, I know," said Lucy. "And I'm sorry. It's Petra. She has this hold over Dad, and she's such a bitch. I think she already suspects something. She keeps going on about Iain and Carl, and how disgusted she is every time she sees them holding hands in the village. I know it's the way she was brought up, but it still hurts."

"I know," said Daisy. "I'm so sorry you have to put up with that." She pulled Lucy into a hug. "But remember, I'm here if you need me, and most people don't think like that any more."

"How are you doing, anyway?" said Lucy. "I saw you with that reporter woman the other day. Is she bothering you with lots of awkward questions?"

"Quite the opposite, actually," said Daisy. "She's great. I'll introduce you at some point, if you like. She's going to do a piece on my artwork for the local paper."

"That's good, isn't it?" said Lucy. "About time people saw what you were capable of."

"I suppose so," said Daisy. "I guess I'm just a bit nervous. Once it's out there in the world, it becomes real, you know?"

"It *is* real. And it's *great*," said Lucy. "People are going to love it."

They kissed again.

"So what about the murder enquiry?" said Lucy. She found a patch of dry earth and sat down, her back against a listing headstone. "People are saying you did it. Well, that you did for Nicholas Abbott, anyway. They're saying that you threatened him in the tearooms, and then later went round and throttled him to death in revenge for touching you up all the time."

Daisy stared at her. "Is that really what they're saying?"

"Well, that's what I've heard. Someone in the hairdresser's the other day was going on about it. Petra agreed with them of course. Silly cow." Lucy looked at her warily, as if expecting some sort of revelation. "I mean... you *didn't* do it, did you?"

"Of course not! How could you even ask that?"

"It's just that you're always so strong. You know exactly what you want, and you don't stand for any bullshit. I wish I could be like that. I just wondered – had you had enough of the old codger and decided to see him off?"

"I can't believe you'd even consider that," said Daisy. The image of Abbott's house on Hulston Lane came unbidden to her mind: the whispering voice, the dizziness. The fact that she'd found herself in the woods two hours later, with no recollection of where she'd been, what she'd done.

"It's a compliment!" said Lucy. She clambered back to her feet, coming over to tug on Daisy's jacket again. "I only meant to say that I think you have it in you to do anything you want, and damn the consequences. It's a very attractive quality."

"Well it doesn't feel that way," said Daisy. "And this isn't something to take lightly, Lucy. If people in the village think I did it, what do the police think? That detective was up at my house today, asking more questions. Do they think I'm responsible, too?"

"Look, I'm sorry," said Lucy. "I didn't mean to worry you."

"Well you did," said Daisy. Her heart was thumping in her chest. She kept going over it all in her mind – the blackouts, the whispered voice, the questions from the police. Nicholas Abbott's lascivious expression as she'd warned him off.

"I'm not feeling very well," said Daisy. "I think I'd better go."

"I've only just got here," said Lucy.

"I'm sorry, Lucy. I can't do this, not now. I need to go home."

"Are you okay?" She sounded genuinely concerned. She put her arm around Daisy's shoulders.

"I will be. I just need to think things over."

"What kind of things?"

"Everything," said Daisy. "I just… I don't know. I'll call you, okay?"

"Okay," said Lucy. "Tomorrow? Just to let me know you're all right."

Daisy nodded. She forced a smile. "Don't worry. It'll all be okay. I just… I'd better go." She cupped her hand around Lucy's cheek, and then turned and hurried off down the hill, leaving Lucy staring after her from amongst the headstones.

She was nearly home before the dizziness came again, striking her like a wave, carrying her along in its disorienting pull. She paused for breath, leaning one hand against a lamp-post, fighting the urge to vomit.

She issued a wretched, anguished moan. She'd hoped this was over with; there'd been no indication of anything untoward last night while she'd been at home with Elspeth. She staggered back from the main street, sinking into the shadows of a nearby lane. Whatever was going on, she didn't want anyone to see her. She didn't want to have to answer more questions.

She clenched her jaw, trying to hold back the fog that was threatening to close in on her mind.

To fight it off.

That's what Elspeth had said, that maybe she was fighting something off. It certainly felt that way. She could almost sense it, like a tangible thing. A force that was trying to enshroud her, to subsume her in its terrible embrace.

She coughed, buckling at a lancing pain in her head. Tears stung her eyes. She couldn't stop it. She was drowning. She gasped for breath.

The darkness swam in.

Her eyelids fluttered open.

It felt like only seconds had passed. She was standing before the ancient cross on the green, right at the heart of the village. The breeze was ruffling her hair.

This would become the centrepiece of the fayre, where the parade would culminate and the effigy of the witch would be placed on a temporary gallows and then burnt while all the villagers watched and cheered, feasting on marshmallows and burgers and sweets and beers. Now, though, it was utterly deserted. It seemed as if even the surrounding houses had somehow been pushed back, as if the entire world had shrunk to just this single point in space and time, right there at the heart of Hallowdene.

The sight filled Daisy with a deep sense of foreboding. She realised she was unconsciously rubbing her throat. She swallowed, but her mouth was dry, her tongue swollen in her mouth.

"*Without grace or remorse.*"

The whisper was a dry croak, like the breaking of twigs underfoot. It was close. Too close.

She turned on the spot, but there was no one there. Just the shifting of the shadows in the moonlight, the stirring of the trees in the wind.

Something had brought her here. There was no other explanation. She knew it with a horrific certainty. Something had wanted her to come here, to stand before the gallows, to feel the fear and trepidation that it had felt. To know what it was to be afraid.

Daisy turned, and ran.

CHAPTER TWENTY-EIGHT

Hallowdene village hall was, like many municipal buildings in the area, an old Victorian structure that had seen better days. Built from red brick with tall sash windows, it looked terribly dilapidated, with crumbling fascia boards, peeling paint and old metal guttering that was badly rusted. It stuck out like a sore thumb amongst the whitewashed stone cottages that comprised the remainder of the village, and despite being over a hundred years old, gave the impression of being a modern building that had somehow been displaced in time. A display board outside encouraged donations for a project to replace the roof, and listed the times and dates of a number of local clubs that took place inside – Weight Watchers, Pilates, a youth group and a film club. Elspeth wondered how well they were attended.

This particular Saturday afternoon, the hall was bustling with people, and she was surprised to find herself having to squeeze through a sizeable crowd to find a spot with a good view. She recognised many of the faces in attendance – Hugh and Lucy Walsey, Sally Jameson,

Iain and Carl Hardwick, Jenny Wren. Daisy was there too, dishing out cups of tea from a serving hatch by the side of the stage, wearing her uniform from Richmond's. She was too busy to look up, so didn't notice Elspeth as she sidled around the edge of the crowd.

Avi Dhiri and Robyn Baxter were standing close to the stage, sipping from paper cups and looking harassed. She wondered if they were going to film the whole thing, or just get some shots of the display afterwards. She glanced around, but there was no sign of Steve or his camera. The thought that she might get caught on film wasn't particularly appealing.

Up on the stage itself a display case had been arranged, covered for the moment by a blue velvet curtain, no doubt awaiting the big reveal. Behind it stood three blue display boards, with photographs and print-outs pinned to them, presumably relating the story of the Hallowdene Witch and how Jenny and her team had come to excavate her remains. Elspeth was impressed by how quickly they'd put the display together, given that the dig had only taken place earlier that week, but it nevertheless had something of the appearance of a school project about it.

She supposed she was being unkind. It was a good thing for the village, and the display would undoubtedly draw in even more folk from the surrounding area for the coming festivities. It was hardly as though Iain and Sally had been gifted with time to do anything more professional.

Elspeth couldn't talk. She was hardly feeling professional herself, still vaguely tired and hungover from the night before. She'd spent the morning in London with Abigail, taking her for brunch at a café near the train station before heading off, still apologising for the previous night. She felt as though she'd let her friend down, even though they'd ended up having a nice time back at the flat and Abigail hadn't seemed particularly bothered about the party. She was more concerned about Elspeth, keen to stress that she hadn't intended to exert any undue pressure about London, or Peter, or the job. She'd somehow got the impression that she was the one who'd made Elspeth feel uncomfortable.

Elspeth knew it would all blow over – that things would be back to normal between them in a few days... whatever 'normal' was. She'd been thinking about it on the train home, and she'd come to the conclusion that she and Abigail were simply on different paths, and while that didn't mean they couldn't be friends – and close ones at that – it did mean that they were less likely to fall into one another's natural orbit. She'd have to make more of an effort, that was all, and for her part, Abigail would need to try to understand that Elspeth simply wasn't interested in returning to her old life, or any of its trappings.

She felt someone nudge her arm, and turned to see Peter, smiling down at her. He was wearing his grey suit, his shirt open at the collar. He'd even brushed his hair. She felt a sudden rush of relief at seeing him, and she slipped her arm around him and gave him a squeeze.

"All right! I'm on duty, remember. At least until this is over with."

"I know. It's just… I'm pleased to see you."

"Glad to be home?"

"Yeah."

He gave her a squeeze back, and they gently parted. "There's been a right business here this morning," he said. "A few of the locals have signed a petition saying the fayre should be cancelled in light of the murders. They delivered it to the parish council earlier, and then set up a demonstration outside Richmond's. Sally Jameson called in the police to have the group disbanded."

"Understandable, I suppose, that people are nervous. It certainly doesn't feel like a time to be celebrating."

"Yeah. With a murderer – or two – at large, I know how they feel. Especially after what you said, that another death might be likely."

"Well, we don't know that for sure," said Elspeth. "It could all be unconnected."

"Hmmm," mumbled Peter, noncommittally. "Here we are. Looks like they're getting ready for the big moment." He nodded towards the stage, where Jenny Wren, Sally Jameson and Iain Hardwick had gathered before the covered display case. Close by, Avi was looking furious. He exchanged a few words with Robyn, and then pushed past her, cutting a swathe through the crowd towards the exit. Elspeth watched him go. Peter had seen it, too.

She turned back to the stage. Sally was waving for quiet. "Hello? Hello, everyone? Thanks for coming."

The cacophony of chatter died to a low murmur.

"Thank you, thank you. Welcome to what promises to be a very special event in the history of our village, and marks a spectacular opening for the annual Hallowdene Summer Fayre, starting here tomorrow!" She paused for a brief round of applause.

"Now, you all know me and my co-organiser, Iain Hardwick, but today I'd like to introduce to you Ms Jennifer Wren, the lead archaeologist from the team that's been busy working to bring us this historic find. Jenny?"

Jenny stepped forward, looking rather awkward. "Thanks, everyone. We're here today for the unveiling of a rather special exhibit, a rare chance for the local people who've been so supportive of our project to get a first look at the finds excavated from the grave of the so-called Hallowdene Witch."

A brief cheer went up. Jenny waited until it had died down.

"So without further ado, I'd like to introduce you all to one of Hallowdene's oldest residents, the remains of a person I believe to be Agnes Levett." She turned, and with a flourish, whipped the velvet drape from the display case, revealing the grisly treasure within.

A murmur passed through the audience, with everyone straining to see.

The case was horizontal, fronted with glass on all sides, and sitting atop four grey, metal legs. Inside, it had been laid out much like the grave, with Agnes's skeleton – now cleaned and free of soil and other remnants – positioned in repose, empty eye sockets staring up vacantly at the ceiling. Around her, the fetishes of the old villagers – or at least those that had survived intact – had also been positioned, exactly as they'd been found during the excavation.

Elspeth felt a shudder pass along her spine. She tried to look away, but it seemed to take a supernatural effort to drag her eyes from the woman's remains.

She glanced around the room, judging people's reactions. Hugh Walsey was peering at the display case hungrily, as if weighing up how he might somehow use this whole situation to his advantage. Sally and Iain were speaking in hushed tones, both beaming at the audience's response, while Jenny had retreated temporarily to one side of the stage, to allow people to see.

Daisy had come out from behind the tea stand and was peering up at the skeleton with something that looked like terrified fascination. She had one hand to her mouth, and was stock still, like a little island in the midst of the milling crowd.

Elspeth tugged Peter's sleeve. "I'm going to have a word with Daisy. I'll catch up with you in a bit, okay?"

He eyed her warily. "Just remember what I said."

"Yeah, and you too."

She hoisted her bag onto her shoulder, and then wove a path through the locals, trying not to bump people with her elbows. She saw mums and dads lifting their kids up onto their shoulders to get a better look, and wondered whether Dorothy would ever have brought her along to such a thing. She supposed it was no different, really, from a trip to the museum to look at the remains of Ancient Egyptian mummies, or bog people. Somehow, though, this seemed more personal. Perhaps it was because the skeleton had a name and a story, a deep connection to many of the people in the room, whose relations had been the ones to condemn the woman to her pitiful death. To that end it felt more like a wake.

Daisy was still standing by the side of the stage, transfixed by the skeletal remains.

"Seems sad somehow, doesn't it?" said Elspeth, coming to stand beside her. "All these people staring at her like she's some sort of celebrity, rather than a victim."

Daisy turned, her eyes settling on Elspeth. For a moment she looked at her vacantly, and then seemed to snap out of it, blinking as if having been lost in thought. "Oh, hi," she said, smiling. "Yes, I know what you mean. There's something a little exploitative about it all. I can't help thinking she deserves more dignity than this."

"I think that's exactly it, yes," said Elspeth, "although the dark, commercial side of my brain understands why they're doing it this way."

Daisy nodded. "I wonder what Lee Stroud would have made of it all."

"I dare say he'd be on the stage right now, trying to say his piece."

"Or as far away from here as he could get. He always seemed so scared of what the witch might do if she were set free."

"I wonder if she really has been set free? Or is this just a different sort of prison?" said Elspeth. "Stuck in a glass case, everyone peering down at her."

"I hadn't thought of it that way," said Daisy.

"How are you, anyway? Feeling any better?" asked Elspeth.

"I... not really, no. I had another funny turn last night. I was wondering, could you spare any time later for a chat? I feel like I'm going out of my mind at home alone, and I just want to get it all off my chest. I know it's an imposition, and we barely know each other..."

"Not at all," said Elspeth. "I'd be happy to. We had a good time the other night, didn't we?"

"Yeah, it was great," said Daisy. "Just what I needed."

"All right. Well, I can't do this evening, I'm sorry. I've been away so much, and I promised Peter – but what about tomorrow morning? What time's your shift?"

Daisy tried ineffectually to hide her disappointment. "I'm on lates tomorrow, so the morning's good. We could go for breakfast?"

"Perfect," said Elspeth. "I'll pick you up, and take you to my favourite place in Heighton. How does that sound?"

"Thanks, Ellie. I really appreciate it."

Elspeth was about to respond with another platitude, when she heard someone calling for quiet from the back of the room. People around her were turning to look.

She turned to see Avi Dhiri standing in the doorway, his face drawn.

"Is there anyone here from the police?" he said, quietly, although the words rang out in the sudden, eerie silence. "It's Steve. I think he's dead."

CHAPTER TWENTY-NINE

The dead man was slumped over the editing desk in the back of the TV crew's van, which was parked just a little way up the lane from the village hall, close to the village green.

The victim, Steve Marley, had been struck across the temple with something heavy and blunt, rupturing his skull and causing him to slump forward onto the electronics, blood oozing from the wound.

They'd been too late – while the body was still warm, there was no pulse, and Peter knew the paramedics would confirm his worst suspicions.

A third murder. Elspeth had warned him as much. But how could he have predicted *this*? There didn't seem to be any obvious connection between the victims. How could he protect people against a killer who seemed to choose their victims at random? Worse still, how could he identify who that killer was?

At least he knew who it *wasn't*, this time around. Hugh Walsey, Jenny Wren and Daisy Heddle had all been inside the village hall, watching the events on stage.

He looked again at the body. The poor bastard. He'd come here to Hallowdene to cover a country fayre, which should have been an idyllic, quiet job, and now this. It seemed particularly incongruous.

He wanted to reach forward and close the man's eyes, but he knew it was best to touch as little else as possible before the SOCOs arrived.

The dead man's head was turned to one side, a look of startled surprise on his face. Blood had pooled in his right ear, running down the side of his throat; a stark red line against the pale flesh, as if the killer had drawn a marker across the man's throat, picking him out for death.

He looked away.

The van was small, packed with technical equipment and monitors, forming a kind of makeshift studio for reviewing footage on the road. That way, they could check everything over to ensure they had everything they needed on site, before sending it back to the studio for editing.

They wouldn't be filming any such footage today, although he suspected there'd now be even more attention lavished on the Hallowdene Summer Fayre than even Sally and Iain were expecting.

Outside, he could hear that the crowd from the village hall had spilled out, gathering on the village green. Elspeth and the others were doing a good job of keeping everyone back. He'd told everyone to stay close, explaining that the police would want to talk to them all individually.

Well, they could bloody well stuff it.

He sighed. The smell in here was appalling; it was warm, and the dead man had soiled himself as the tension had abandoned his corpse and his muscles had relaxed.

He chewed his thumbnail. One of the monitors was still on. Marley had been watching something when he was killed – he appeared to be logged into some kind of online storage account. Peter would have to check with the rest of the crew to find out what he'd been watching – the storage box onscreen appeared to be empty, but he decided not to try clicking on anything until the experts had arrived.

Had Marley seen something that his killer wanted to remain hidden? The footage from the missing time-lapse camera by the dig, perhaps? *More secrets*, thought Peter. Soon enough, someone was going to have to give one of them up.

The distant wail of sirens made him jump. He placed the camera back exactly where he'd found it and stood, returning the handkerchief to his pocket. He opened the sliding panel in the back of the van, relieved by the sudden inrush of fresh air, and then climbed out, sliding it shut behind him.

Avi Dhiri was sitting on the kerb nearby, still looking completely shell-shocked. He'd have the paramedics take a look at him when they arrived. Daisy and another woman he didn't recognise were ferrying trays of tea and coffee back and forth from the village hall, dishing them out amongst grateful locals. The wooden gantry, with its makeshift gallows and surrounding pyre, made a gruesome centrepiece to proceedings on the village green, a reminder of the horror that had occurred in their midst. People had clumped together in small groups, and were giving it a wide berth.

He caught Elspeth's eye as she ushered back another group of young men who'd edged too close to the scene, and she looked weary, worried. He was glad she hadn't had to see the corpse. He thought the dead man's stare would haunt him for a very long time to come.

He wondered if this would be the end of it, now. Three deaths, just like the legends had said. Lee Stroud had said something to Elspeth about history being cyclical. Maybe he could hope that the worst of it was over? Whatever the case, he had to break that cycle. The deaths in the 1640s had been left unexplained. He resolved that the same thing wouldn't be true this time. He'd get to the bottom of what was going on. Whatever that was.

He glanced again at the gallows. Something told him that, despite all of that, there was something more to come.

He waved at the ambulance as it rumbled down the street towards him. The driver saw him and gave him a thumbs-up, before pulling up behind the TV van. He and his partner climbed down – a man who looked too young to be a qualified paramedic, and a woman in her forties – and collected medical kits from the back of the vehicle. They hurried over. Minutes later, three police cars came roaring up behind the ambulance, spilling an array of uniformed constables onto the scene. He recognised PC Chambers amongst them, and waved him over.

"All right, boss?"

"Not really, no," said Peter. "Another murder. It's as if the killer is just out to cause chaos. It makes no sense." He sighed. "Anyway, get the others to round up all these people, and try to corral them in the village hall. We'll have to see them all individually to take statements, just in case they saw anything useful. I want to speak to anyone who was on the village green. And see about getting a perimeter set up around the area."

Chambers nodded. "Right you are." He made his way back to the others, his high-vis jacket rustling as he walked.

Peter's phone trilled.

"Shaw."

"It's Patel. I'm on my way down. Just wanted to give you a heads-up – I'm bringing Griffiths."

"Thanks." He cut the call.

That was all he needed. Griffiths breathing down his neck. He supposed it was only to be expected. Things were spiralling out of control, and one thing was certain – he could use all the help he could get.

CHAPTER THIRTY

Somehow, the village hall seemed even more cramped now that the police had arrived and shepherded everyone back inside. It was growing stuffy, too – they'd opened the windows and left the door propped ajar, but with no air conditioning it was quickly growing uncomfortable, and people were beginning to get fractious. She'd already seen a spat between two boys, presumably siblings, who'd started with an argument over something stupid and ended up pulling each other's hair. The people nearby had showed a stoical level of toleration, but when one of the boys had kicked over a drink, soaking a woman's skirt, there'd been fiery looks and a few harsh words. Elspeth felt sympathy for the boys' parents, who looked as though the only thing they wanted to do was escape, but like everyone else, they were forced to remain here until the police were ready to see them. People had taken to sitting on the floor in small groups and helping themselves to drinks in the kitchen. Daisy had already been taken aside by Peter and questioned, and had presumably been allowed to go home.

Elspeth was sitting on the edge of the stage beside Avi and Robyn, tapping out a brief report of the situation on her phone to send to Meredith. Avi had been seen by the ambulance crew and given something to calm his nerves. He was currently wrapped in a foil blanket, despite the oppressive atmosphere in the hall, and the police had decided to give him a few moments before questioning him too.

"I just don't understand," said Robyn. She was balling her hands into fists in frustration, her brow furrowed in a deep frown. "Steve would never hurt a fly. He had nothing to do with this village, or the witch, or the people who live here. Why would anyone want to hurt him?"

"I don't know," said Elspeth. "Perhaps he was just in the wrong place at the wrong time."

"In the van? The killer must have known he was in there." She visibly paled. "Unless it was just bad luck, and it could have been any one of us."

"What was he doing in the van? I'd have thought you needed him here, filming the unveiling." Elspeth glanced over her shoulder at the display case. Someone had covered it up again with the velvet shroud, and she was pleased not to have to look at Agnes's eerie skull.

"That's why I went to find him," said Avi, quietly. "He was supposed to meet us here. He'd gone to the van after lunch to check out a hunch. He realised that the footage from the time-lapse camera he'd left up at the dig might have been automatically uploaded to his cloud storage box."

"A time-lapse camera?"

"You know whenever you see one of those shots of scudding clouds or blossoming flowers, sped up to look like it's happening in real time? That's filmed on a time-lapse camera," said Robyn.

"And Steve set one up at the dig?" said Elspeth.

"Yeah. He wanted a long shot of the sun rising and going down over the grave site," said Avi, "to accompany some narration about the passage of time."

"When was this?"

"A couple of nights ago. No, hang on. Today's Saturday, right?" said Robyn. Elspeth nodded. "So it was Wednesday night when the camera was stolen."

"So the camera was recording the night Lee Stroud was killed?"

Avi looked thoughtful. "Yes, I suppose it was."

Elspeth hopped down from the stage. "There's your motive, then," she said.

"What do you mean?" said Robyn.

"If the camera saw something that the killer didn't want to be seen, and Steve was reviewing the footage…"

"Oh God," said Avi.

"I'll find someone we can talk to," said Elspeth.

She wandered over to the door, where a female police constable was leaning against the brickwork, looking hot and tired. Outside, she could hear DCI Griffiths barking orders. "Excuse me, I wonder if you can get a message to DS Peter Shaw?"

The woman frowned. "Why do you want to speak to the detective?"

"I have some information that I think might be pertinent to the investigation."

"What is it?"

"I think I know why Steve Marley was killed."

The woman looked suspicious, but reached for her radio. "DS Shaw?"

Peter's voice crackled over the radio. "Here."

"There a woman here who says she's got information pertinent to the investigation. Name of..." The woman looked at her expectantly.

"Elspeth Reeves."

The PC repeated it into the receiver.

"I'll be along in a moment," said Peter.

It was ten minutes before he finally made it back to the village hall. Elspeth was waiting for him, sitting on a small wooden bench in a recess by the door.

"I haven't got long," he said. He looked exhausted. "What's up?"

She told him what Avi and Robyn had said about the camera.

"I *knew* it," he said. "He'd been watching something in the van, but the files look as though they're missing. I'll have to see if the tech boys can find a way to recover them."

"There you are, then," said Elspeth. "There's your connection."

"I could kiss you."

"Later," said Elspeth.

"Look, I'd better get back. I'll send Chambers over to take your statement so you can get away. See you back at mine?"

"All right. I'll stay over."

Peter smiled. "I'll call you when I get done here."

He squeezed her hand, briefly, and then ducked out again, immediately swept up in the chaos of the scene outside.

Elspeth took out her phone. The battery was looking decidedly low again, but she reckoned she could just about squeeze in a couple of thousand words for the *Heighton Observer* website before it gave up completely.

By the time PC Chambers came to get her, the article was already live.

CHAPTER THIRTY-ONE

Kate Bush was singing about gaffer tape and God on the stereo; about the desperate search to understand the unknown, and how it was eternally obscured from mortal understanding. Daisy wondered if that were really true. Was there a way to understand?

She'd never been a believer. Or rather, she'd given up on God when her parents had died and she'd been left on her own to cope. And all the while she'd begged that if there *was* a God, couldn't he just allow her one final moment with her mum and dad?

She'd soon given up, eschewing all notion of the supernatural. As far as she was concerned, life was short, and there was only one way to live it – to do what made you happy, and damn the consequences. Lucy was right about that. No regrets. That was her mantra.

So why, then, couldn't she shake the notion that whatever had been happening to her recently had something to do with Agnes Levett, and the fact that her grave had been disturbed, apparently for the first time in centuries? It couldn't really be a coincidence that the strange episodes had first coincided with the exhumation, could it? Especially when she considered the fact that, whatever it was, that dark presence she'd felt had seemed to pilot her like some mindless puppet, causing her to return again and again to locations relevant to Agnes Levett's life?

Or was it just because she didn't want to admit to herself that she was ill, and that her mind was somehow fracturing? She hadn't dared go to the doctor in the end, for fear that he'd confirm her doubts and worse, inform the police about her blackouts. She hadn't felt able to talk to Sally, either – the closest thing she had to family since her parents had died. It felt like too much of a burden to place on the woman. She was already dealing with so much – the shop, the fayre, the recent murders of people she might once have called friends... not to mention Christian and his objectionable attitude.

Then she'd gone and blurted out to Elspeth Reeves that she needed to talk. It was true, of course – she didn't think any of her friends would understand, and there was no point trying to discuss it with Lucy. The girl was fun, but immature, and she'd probably just dismiss it, especially after what she'd said up at the graveyard.

There was something about Elspeth, though. It felt as though she had Daisy's best interests at heart. It was odd, because she hardly knew the woman, but the other night they'd just clicked, and Elspeth genuinely didn't seem to want anything from her. Almost everyone she met had an agenda, and she'd grown cynical over the years, trying to work out everyone's angle. Even Lucy had an agenda, although she didn't know it yet; she was using Daisy for the excitement, for the thrill, as a voyage of discovery.

Elspeth just seemed to want a mate. It was refreshing, and Daisy found herself wanting to trust the woman. She'd talk to her in the morning over breakfast. Of course, she'd still have to be careful about what she said – Elspeth was sleeping with the detective, after all – but somehow she didn't think she had to worry.

The needle fell into the run-out groove on the record, and she got up to change it. As she did, she felt the now familiar blush of nausea, and the room spun. The floor came up to meet her, striking hard against her lip. She tried to push herself up, but the entire world seemed to be spinning.

"*Without grace or remorse.*"

She squeezed her eyes shut, willing the nightmare to end.

She sucked in a breath of cold air.

She was standing in the woods.

Around her, the trees were whispering, susurrating prayers to an ancient God. Beyond them, the world no longer existed, not as she knew it.

She heard a sound, and turned to see a small group of people enter the clearing. Agnes Levett led the way, dressed in an old, patched cloak. She was young, and not at all like the way in which she'd often been portrayed. In the books, she was ghastly and deformed, with a crooked back and claw-like fingers, a monster from beyond the veil, a murderess who killed with impunity. Here, she was perfectly normal, with high cheekbones and raven-black hair, which fell loosely around her shoulders as she hurried across the mossy carpet, her face drawn in concern.

Behind her was the man from the manor house, Cuthbert Abbott, his white shirt stained with blood. He was distraught, tears streaming down his face. The woman she'd seen earlier was still draped in his arms, her head lolling with his every step, and Daisy knew beyond doubt – as if someone else were guiding her thoughts – that this was Lady Grace Abbott.

Daisy knew all of this with a certainty that frightened her. The scene had the texture of a memory, well trodden and often recalled – but it was a memory that didn't belong to her.

She stood, transfixed, as events unspooled before her.

Directed by Agnes, Cuthbert laid the body of his wife upon the bed of moss, stepping back, his hands held together as if in prayer.

Grace was dead, or dying – she'd bled profusely from a wound in her side, her nightdress drenched in dark blood. Agnes stripped the prone woman of her nightdress, revealing a map of dark bruises across her milky white torso. Some had begun to fade, while others were ripe and fresh – the imprint of fists that had rained down upon her.

Agnes turned to glower at Cuthbert, who took a step towards the witch, brandishing a dagger he had pulled from his belt. He waved the tip of it inches from her face, encouraging her to go on.

Agnes returned to her ministrations, unfurling a roll of cloth, which she laid out upon the ground before her. The roll contained herbs and ointments, wooden tools and tiny bones, scraps of inscribed paper and sticks of charcoal. She took one of these blackened sticks and began making marks upon Lady Grace's flesh, drawing swirls and motifs, ancient wards and patterns she'd been taught by the old woman who'd brought her up after her mother had died in childbirth.

These symbols, Daisy knew, were part of the ritual that would reawaken Grace's spirit before it left this world, and heal her body so that she might yet live.

Agnes worked quickly, tearing the nightdress as she continued her work, swirling whorls of charcoal across the dying woman's belly. Then, when she had finished and the woman's body was thus complete – a canvas that had been worked into a letter for the gods – she returned to her roll and collected a bundle of herbs, which she pushed into the pink, ragged hole in the woman's flesh, packing it with salve. The woman – close to death, yet stirred by the horrific pain – bucked and screamed, her wail echoing through the trees, startling birds, which burst from cover, scattering into the night.

Rocking back on her knees, Agnes began to mumble a litany of foreign words, unspoken in this place for centuries. The trees seemed to respond in kind, whispering and rocking, until the litany became a song that built in a crescendo. Cuthbert Abbott watched in appalled fascination as the body of his wife seemed to jolt to life, twitching as if in violent spasm, writhing on the ground, foaming at the lips, eyes rolled back in their sockets to show only their milky undersides.

Daisy was crying out, now, telling Agnes to stop, but her words were silent and unheard; she was simply a spectator, a witness out of time. All of this had happened before, and would happen again as she watched, as sure as the changing of the seasons.

The ululating song came to an end. Everything was still. Agnes breathed, ragged and deep, rocking forward on her knees. Even the trees of the Wychwood seemed to know their place, and stood becalmed, silent and unmoving.

The man took a step forward, but halted at Agnes's raised hand. She shuffled forward on her knees, cradling the head of the other woman on her lap, using her sleeve to wipe away the spittle from Grace's chin.

She watched in silence for a moment, waiting for Grace's chest to rise and fall with the intake of her breath. It did not.

Gently, she laid the woman's head upon a pillow of leaves, and turned towards the man. The look in her eyes was answer enough, and enraged, he rushed forward, striking Agnes hard across the side of the head with his fist. She crumpled to the ground, crying out, but Cuthbert was incensed, and he struck her again, and again, and then kicked her in the stomach as she lay on the ground, weeping.

"*Without grace or remorse*," said the voice in Daisy's ear, and she finally understood what Agnes had been trying to tell her.

Cuthbert had killed his wife, and had gone to Agnes in search of help. When she'd been unable to save the woman's life, he had instead laid the blame at her door. The body had been covered in charcoal markings depicting strange symbols, and herbs had been stuffed inside her wounds, and so Cuthbert had argued that Agnes had used her craft to murder his beloved wife, and the villagers had found her wanting. She had been put to death for Cuthbert's crime.

He had abandoned her to die, and he'd continued to live his life unsuspected, without Grace, and without remorse.

"Help! Help me!" he called, bellowing at the top of his lungs. Daisy knew that Grace's screams of agony must have already drawn the attention of the villagers, and now Cuthbert was calling for them, ready to accuse Agnes of his crime. She heard voices amongst the trees. They were coming. There was nothing Agnes could do.

Daisy could feel Agnes's rage, her hatred, boiling up inside her.

She turned back to the clearing. Agnes was sitting up again now, clutching her midriff, her back to Daisy. Daisy wanted to go to her, to help, but there was nothing she could do.

And then Agnes turned and looked straight at her,

peering out across the centuries, and the look in her eyes was so vengeful, so demonic, that Daisy issued a wail of terror. She turned to flee, clawing at the branches that were suddenly closing in on her from all sides, crowding her, blocking her escape.

And then the whispering returned, and everything went black.

She came around screaming. She recognised the place immediately, from the scene she'd just witnessed. She was out in Raisonby Wood again. She had no idea of the time. She didn't even know if this was real or a dream. Her feet were bare, bleeding profusely from innumerable cuts, and she was still wearing her pyjamas. She'd torn the hem of both legs. Her left cuff was wet and muddy, and her lip had split and then healed, the dried blood gritty in her mouth. She dropped to her knees, whimpering in the darkness, and allowed the tears to stream down her cheeks.

CHAPTER THIRTY-TWO

"You look done in."

"Long day," said Peter, stepping aside to let her in. She stopped just inside the doorway, reached up on her tiptoes, and kissed him square on the lips. Then she tossed her handbag down in the hall and marched through to the kitchen, where she found two glasses and a bottle of brandy, and poured them both a large measure. She'd been over to visit her mum while Peter worked late on the case. Now, it was nearly midnight, and he still seemed to be at it.

"How was Griffiths in the end?" she called through to the other room.

"Oh, you know," replied Peter. "Her usual brusque self. But I must admit, with three murders on my plate, I could do with all the help I can get."

She carried the drinks through to the living room to find he'd returned to what he'd been doing when she arrived – squatting on the floor amidst a dizzying array of handwritten notes, drawings and what appeared to be genealogy charts.

"What's all this about, then?" She handed him his drink.

"Papers from Lee Stroud's house. I was thinking about what both you and Daisy said about him being obsessed with local history, and it got me thinking: could there be anything in his notes to help us understand what's going on?"

"About Agnes Levett, you mean?" She took a long draught from her glass, enjoying the warm sensation as the brandy hit the back of her throat.

"About *any* of it," said Peter. "Do you know he'd mapped the entire village?"

"As in the layout of the houses?"

"No, as in one massive, extended family tree. Every family, every individual, every single connection; it's all here, going back years." He reached for a fat lever-arch folder and passed it up to her. She flipped through the pages inside. Every chart was meticulous, drawn in fine black ink. Even his handwriting was perfect, each letter carefully inscribed. "And that's only one file. There are dozens of them."

"*Dozens?*"

"Yeah. They stretch right back to mediaeval times. And they're bang up to date, too. At least as far as the main Hallowdene families are concerned, the ones who've been there for centuries, such as the Abbotts and the Heddles."

"He must have spent his entire life compiling it all," said Elspeth. On one hand she was impressed at the scale of the achievement, on the other, saddened that a person could spend so much time concerning themselves with other people's lives that they allowed their own to pass them by. "Once you're finished with all this, we should do something with it," she said.

"Like what?"

"I don't know. Give it to a museum or a library? Anything that stops it ending up in a skip. I couldn't bear to think of it being destroyed."

"There's a distant cousin," said Peter, "at least according to this." He tapped his finger on another nearby file. "And there might yet be a will. But yeah, I'll make sure it goes to a good home if the family don't want it."

Elspeth found a perch on the arm of the sofa. There was nowhere else to sit. Peter's house had always been full of *stuff* even when it had belonged to his parents, but now, with his growing collection of comic books and paperback crime novels, it felt more compact than ever. *More homely*, thought Elspeth. More lived-in, a bit like Daisy Heddle's cottage. That's what her apartment was missing, Elspeth decided. It was all still too new, too sparse. She hadn't expanded to fill it yet, hadn't accumulated enough of a life there. But there was time. Especially now she'd decided to make it more of a permanent arrangement.

"So, have you found anything useful?" she said. She kicked off her boots, propping her feet on the coffee table.

"Move those, if you want," said Peter, indicating the heaped folders on the sofa. "I won't be much longer."

"It's all right," said Elspeth. "Tell me what you're looking for. I might be able to help."

"Nothing specific. I'm just going through the family records of the key suspects, seeing if anything obvious jumps out," he said. "The problem is knowing where to start. Some of these records go back to the fifteenth century. Lee Stroud was meticulous."

"Start with the people themselves," said Elspeth, "and work backwards from there. If there is anything worth knowing, it'll most likely be in the last few generations. I can't imagine people are going to hold on to grudges that go back much beyond their grandparents."

"All right, good point," said Peter. "I suppose I was just getting lost in all that stuff about Agnes, trying to unpick what had happened in the 1640s, who the victims had been."

"No joy?"

"No, it's all here, but it doesn't make anything clearer. There's no familial relationship to the current victims, so far as I can tell."

"Then maybe it's the killer, rather than the victims, who bears some relationship to Agnes? Is there a chart for the Levetts?" said Elspeth.

"Hang on, I'll take a look."

"Right. And I'll make a start with…" she picked up a folder at random and opened it "… the Abbotts. Now this should be interesting."

She opened the folder out on her knees and started leafing through. It was filed in chronological order, oldest to youngest. It seemed Stroud had traced the Abbott family line back as far as the 1450s. There were pages of the tree for each era, each contained in a plastic wallet along with supporting documentation. She unfastened the clip and paged ahead, jumping right to the end. Here she found another plastic sleeve, and she slipped it out of the folder, sliding out the thin sheaf of pages, much of which consisted of photocopies of birth and death certificates, and printed pages from the online census. She opened out the folded A3 page containing the most recent portion of the family tree.

It appeared to go back as far as the Victorian era, with Thomas Abbott's children listed in the bottom right-hand corner being the most recent additions.

Of immediate note was Nicholas Abbott, right in the centre of the page. Stroud had already updated the record to show his death date, and written beneath it in bright red ink were the words:

Cause of Death: Murder

Elspeth peered at it in wonder. Stroud had managed that pretty quickly. He must have written it in on the day that he, himself, had died.

She followed the line across, discovering that Nicholas had once been married, but that his wife, Sarah Abbott, née Winthrop, had divorced him twenty years ago. Good for her. They'd had no children.

The surprising thing, however, was that another

line was appended to Nicholas Abbott, connecting to another woman's name: Sally Jameson. According to the chart, she had borne a child to him in 1991, while he'd still been married to Sarah. The child's name was omitted, with the word ILLEGITIMATE written instead, in black capital letters.

Elspeth sat back for a minute, considering this. Sally Jameson had once, presumably, had an affair with Nicholas Abbott, and had carried his child. Was it Christian? She'd heard no mention of his absent father. If so, had Nicholas acknowledged him or left Sally to fend for herself? She presumed he had not accepted the boy as his own, judging by the fact that it wasn't until seven years later that his wife had finally left him. How had Sally stomached it all these years, with Abbott coming into her tearoom, making lewd remarks about the waiting staff, inappropriately touching Daisy in front of everyone? She'd obviously seen it happen, if it was as frequent an occurrence as Daisy had made out. Is this why she'd never thrown him out, or called the police? Because he had some sort of hold over her? On top of that – how had Lee Stroud found out about the affair? Had Sally told him?

"Peter?"

"Mmm-hmm?" he mumbled, still poring over the Levett file.

"Has anyone mentioned Christian Jameson's father in all of this?"

"No. Not that I'm aware of," he said.

"Is there a file for the Jamesons?"

He looked up, bleary-eyed. "Yeah, it's on the sofa somewhere."

She twisted around, opening a few of the files until she found the one she needed. This one also went back to the fifteenth century. She skipped to the end and found the chart she was looking for. There it was again: Sally Jameson was listed as having given birth to a child by Nicholas Abbott in 1991. This time, the chart read: CHRISTIAN JAMESON.

"Peter, you need to see this," she said. "I think I've found something."

"Hold on," he said, raising his hand. "Just a minute. I've found something too."

"Well, you go first."

"I've been following the Levett family tree. It seems Agnes had a sister, who'd married into another local family a few years before Agnes was tried and executed," he said. "What's interesting is that, if you follow the family tree, within three generations the family name became Heddle."

"The same as Daisy," said Elspeth. "So Daisy has a direct familial link to Agnes."

"There's more," said Peter. "Unlike most people in the village, the Heddles and Abbots have lived around Hallowdene for centuries. There's so much intermarriage that it seems almost inevitable, but according to this, the Jameson family are also directly linked to the Levetts, descended on the female side."

"It's the Jamesons I wanted to tell you about," said Elspeth. She handed him the Jameson chart. "Here."

He stared at it for a moment. "What am I looking at? I've been at this for hours."

"Sally Jameson, down the bottom there," she got up, walking around behind him and indicating with her finger. She traced the line across to the father of Sally's child. "Look at that."

"Nicholas Abbott," he said. "Now that is interesting. So Christian…"

"… is Abbott's son," she finished.

He placed the chart on the floor before him, and then glanced at his watch. It was close to midnight. "Looks like I'll be paying Sally Jameson a visit in the morning," he said.

"I think that's enough of charts and family trees and other people's business now, don't you?"

He sighed, and looked up at Elspeth. "I suppose so. Tea?"

She smiled, and cupped his face in her hands. "Peter?"

"Yeah?"

"Take me to bed."

Elspeth woke to the sound of a trilling phone.

At first she tried to ignore it, surfacing slowly from her comfortable dream, but the sound was a persistent irritation, and in the end, heaving a sigh, she rolled over and grabbed it from the bedside table. Beside her, Peter had propped himself up on one elbow, peering at her with bleary eyes.

It was Daisy. She thumbed to accept the call.

"Hello?"

The breathing on the other end sounded ragged, desperate. Daisy was crying. "Ellie?"

"Daisy? What's wrong?" Elspeth was awake now, the fear in Daisy's voice sending a shiver down the length of her spine.

"I... I didn't know who else to call. I'm sorry."

"What is it? What's happened? Are you okay?" She glanced at the clock. It was just after 2 am.

"I'm not sure. I blacked out. I've been out in the woods. I saw something..."

"Daisy, do you need an ambulance, or the police?" She sat up, swinging her legs out of bed. Behind her, Peter shifted, concerned.

"No, no. I just... I just need to talk to someone. I'm not sure what's going on, but I'm scared. Look, I'm sorry, I shouldn't have called."

"Where are you?" said Elspeth.

"I'm at home now. I'll be all right." She didn't sound convinced.

"Stay where you are. I'm coming over."

"No, really, it's okay."

"It doesn't sound okay. I'll be there in half an hour."

"All right. Thanks, Ellie. I'm sorry."

The line went dead.

"I've got to go," she said, turning to Peter.

"Then I'm coming with you." He pushed back the covers, starting to get out of bed.

"No. Whatever it is, she needs to talk about it. She told me as much earlier, and I put her off, telling her we could talk in the morning. If I turn up with you in tow, she'll think I've brought the police."

"I can't let you go over there alone at two in the morning!" he said.

"It's fine, Peter. I know what I'm doing." She tugged on her skirt and pulled her blouse over her head. "I'll call you. I promise."

"I don't like this, Ellie," he said, although it was clear he knew that he'd already lost the argument before it had started.

"If she's in trouble, I can't leave her," said Elspeth. She leaned over and kissed him on the cheek. "Go back to sleep."

"As if that's likely," he said, as she ran out the door.

CHAPTER THIRTY-THREE

Hallowdene was silent.

No one walked its ancient streets. Even the cats that usually prowled the rooftops and verges had sensed the disturbed atmosphere and slunk away to seek comfort in their owners' homes. It seemed to Elspeth as if she had somehow entered an eerie, otherworldly reflection of the place she had come to know during the last few days; as if this was an empty place, devoid of all life. There wasn't a single light on in any of the windows, and she had the bizarre notion that the entire village was drawing its breath in anticipation.

She turned the Mini onto the main street, past Richmond's and down the incline towards Daisy's cottage. Overhead, streamers had been hung from the lamp-posts in preparation for tomorrow's festivities – the fayre was still going ahead, as far as she knew – and they fluttered nonchalantly in the breeze. They seemed out of place here, now – colourful and celebratory, jarring against the silent stillness that seemed to have settled over the village at this hour.

Elspeth had a near-overwhelming urge to turn the car around, put her foot down and get as far away from the place as possible, but she stayed resolutely on course, all the time conscious of just how upset Daisy had sounded on the phone. The woman's heaving cries had been raw and primal, and Elspeth had known instantly that something was very, very wrong.

Now, as she drew near, with Daisy's cottage caught in the beam of her headlamps, she was filled with trepidation. What was she going to find?

She wished she could have brought Peter, too, but it would have seemed like a betrayal of trust. Daisy had been clear that this wasn't a police matter – that it ran deeper, was more personal than that. Perhaps she should have brought him anyway and told him to stay in the car. Well, it was too late now.

She pulled the car to a stop, cranking the handbrake. A light was on inside the house, the first she'd seen since entering the village.

Hesitant, she climbed out, locking the car doors behind her. The night air was cool against her skin. She glanced around, sensing a presence, but the street was deserted. She went to the door and rapped with the knocker, keen to get inside as quickly as possible.

She couldn't understand why she felt so spooked, but something about the atmosphere of the place just didn't seem right. It was probably the aftershock of what had happened to Steve Marley there just a few hours ago, she decided; the events turning what was once a pretty and idyllic village into something dark and suspect.

The door opened almost immediately, and Daisy fell into her arms, wrapping Elspeth in a tight embrace. She gave a racking sob, and Elspeth hugged her on the doorstep for a moment, before gently pushing her back inside.

"I'm here, Daisy. Whatever it is, it's going to be okay." She hoped this was true, that she could offer the woman more than empty platitudes.

Daisy stood in the hall in her striped pyjamas, but it was clear she hadn't been anywhere near her bed. Her feet were criss-crossed with a web of vicious cuts and scrapes; the hems of her trousers sodden with mud. Her lip was bloodied, and she was sporting a shining bruise on her left cheekbone that looked as though it was threatening to turn into a black eye. Elspeth's first thought was that she'd been attacked. "Who did this to you, Daisy?"

"*I* did. At least, I think I did," said Daisy.

"I'm not sure I quite understand," said Elspeth. "You'd better start from the beginning. First, though, let's get you cleaned up."

Daisy nodded, her bottom lip trembling. Elspeth led her through to the kitchen, sat her down on a chair and rummaged around cupboards until she found what she was after: TCP, a clean cloth, a bowl for hot water. She set about cleaning up Daisy's wounds. For her part, Daisy seemed to go along with it all in a kind of daze, barely responding to Elspeth's ministrations.

This wasn't the Daisy she'd come to know. She was meek and scared and uneasy. What had happened to her to reduce her to this? Elspeth decided not to press too hard, not until she'd finished tending to her wounds. Daisy barely spoke a word, except to mumble a brief 'thank you'.

When she'd finished, Elspeth put the kettle on and made them both a mug of tea, and then suggested they move through to the lounge. The first thing she noticed was the electric hum of the stereo amp, still switched on, despite the fact that the record had finished playing. The second was the small bloodstain on the floorboards in the centre of the room.

"What happened here?" she said, switching off the amp and sitting down beside Daisy on the sofa. "Did someone get in? Did they hurt you?"

"No. I mean, not in the way you think," said Daisy. She sounded hesitant, nervous. "The thing is, I don't really know how to explain it. I think I must be going mad." She sobbed again, and then caught herself, fighting back the tears. "It's Agnes," she said. "She's in my head."

Elspeth swallowed. That wasn't at all what she'd been expecting. "Go on," she prompted, gently. "Tell me."

Daisy studied her face. "You're going to think I'm crazy," she said. "I've been having these blackouts, you see, and hearing this whispering voice..."

"A whispering voice?" Elspeth thought of what Carl had said about the supposed victims of Agnes's curse in the 1640s. They'd heard the witch's whispered voice soon after she'd been interred.

"Let's just run through some basics," said Elspeth. She was no expert in these matters, but she had to rule out the idea that Daisy was simply having some kind of breakdown. "Tell me your name."

Daisy rolled her eyes. "I knew you'd say I was mad."

"I don't think you're mad," said Elspeth. "I'm just trying to make sure you're okay, and I shouldn't be calling an ambulance."

"All right," said Daisy. "I'm Daisy Heddle. And you're Elspeth Reeves."

"And who's the prime minister?" She'd heard people asking questions like this on TV. She hoped she was doing the right thing.

"A complete tosspot as usual," said Daisy. "Can we stop with the silly questions now?"

"Yes, we can stop," said Elspeth. "Now, you'd better start at the beginning."

Daisy told her about Lucy Abbott, about the dizziness and the visions, the blackouts and her consequent unexplained appearances in the woods. She detailed how she'd found herself in the ruins of Agnes's house, at the site of the witch's hanging, and in the copse where Agnes had carried out her ritual. She explained, too, about Cuthbert Abbott and what she'd seen of his role in all that had occurred. Finally, she told Elspeth of Agnes's terrible, knowing look, of the animosity in her eyes, the burning desire she still harboured for vengeance.

"I know it sounds incredible," she said. "And you probably think I'm making it all up like some silly little girl, or trying to cover my tracks with an unbelievable story. But I had to tell someone. I'm so scared, Ellie. I don't understand what's happening to me, and I don't know what to do. If it's real, then Agnes's spirit – it means to wreak havoc on us all. If it's not real... then I really am going mad."

Elspeth sat there for a long while, sipping her tea, taking it all in. What was there to say? She didn't know what to make of Daisy's story, but it did explain a lot – her secrecy and inability to give an account of her movements, the wound on her palm, her unusual tiredness. And who was *she* to judge? She'd seen things that others would never believe – a man controlling a woman through the manipulation of her reflection, people who had died by their own hands at that same man's behest. And she'd sensed something here, too, something sinister and untoward. She couldn't ignore that.

Could it really be that the stories were true; that Agnes's unquiet spirit was the force behind everything that had been happening in Hallowdene? Had Jenny Wren and her team disturbed something dark and primal when they'd moved that old stone up on the hill?

She thought, too, about what she and Peter had discovered that night about Daisy's ancestral relationship to the Levetts. Could Agnes be working through the vessel of her descendant? Did that mean Daisy had, perhaps unknowingly, been involved in some of the recent deaths? She decided not to give voice to that particular concern. Not yet.

"I believe you," she said, after a while. "I don't think you're mad."

"You don't?" Daisy's relief was evident, and the tears came again in racking sobs. Elspeth comforted her as best she could.

"I saw things during the Carrion King case that I can't readily explain, and it was enough to shake my entire view of the world. There are things out there that defy easy explanation. Perhaps this is one of them. I don't know what's happening to you, but I do know that you need to get help."

"What sort of help?" Daisy looked worried.

"I don't know, but perhaps you need to start with a doctor, just to be sure these blackouts aren't causing any lasting harm. And you need to tell the police the truth, too, about your recent whereabouts."

Daisy almost recoiled. "I thought you said you believed me. You know what will happen if I go to the doctor or the police. They'll assume I'm mad, and lock me up, and feed me with pills."

"We can talk to Peter," said Elspeth. "He was there, with me, and he saw what happened during the Carrion King case. He'll understand."

Daisy looked sceptical. "I don't know…"

"How about you sleep on it," said Elspeth, "and we can talk again in the morning, just like we'd planned?"

"All right," said Daisy.

"I can sleep on the sofa again if you like?"

"No, no. It's all right. It's probably best if I'm alone for a while. It'll give me a chance to think things over." She touched Elspeth's arm. "I can't tell you what it means to have someone to talk to about this."

Elspeth smiled. "It'll be okay. We'll work it out." She stood. "Now you're sure you don't want me to stay?"

"No. Thanks."

"All right. I'll call you in the morning."

She left the house, trudging out to the car, feeling utterly drained. It was nearly 4 am. She sat behind the wheel, and dialled Peter.

"Ellie?"

"Yeah, it's me."

"What happened? Is she okay?"

"No. Not really. I think we're going to have to talk later. And you're going to need to be open-minded."

"You can come over now, if you want. I'm up."

"No, I'm too tired. Heighton is closer. I'll run home, grab some sleep and a shower, and give you a call when I'm up. Okay?"

"If you're sure…" He sighed. "Look, I'm just pleased you're okay."

"See you."

CHAPTER THIRTY-FOUR

Her phone buzzed on the floor beside her bed, rattling as it vibrated across the floorboards. It had to be Elspeth, calling to arrange to meet. Surely it wasn't morning already?

Daisy rolled over, moistening her lips. They were still swollen, and her head felt as if it were full of cotton wool. She opened her eyes. Sunlight was filtering in through the gap between the curtains.

She reached out for her phone. She had the feeling it had been buzzing for some time. She glanced at the name on the screen. *Lucy.* She rejected the call, sinking back into the pillow. What the hell was Lucy doing, calling at five in the morning? She'd only been in bed for an hour. The sun would be up soon, and she'd have to emerge and face up to it all – Elspeth, the police… maybe a doctor too.

She felt better for sharing the burden with Elspeth, but the idea of talking to that detective about it… just the thought of it caused her chest to tighten and her stomach to clench. Still, she knew Elspeth was right.

Whether they believed her or not, she couldn't carry on as she was. She needed help, and where else was there to start looking for it?

The phone started buzzing again. Lucy wasn't going to give up. With some reluctance, Daisy accepted the call and put the phone to her ear. "Hello?"

"Oh, God, Daisy. Why weren't you picking up?"

"It's been a hell of a night, Lucy. I'm sorry, but it's 5 am and—"

"You've got to help me," said Lucy, cutting her off. "Please!"

Daisy sat up in bed.

"What's the matter? What's happened?"

"I don't know. It's just… I'm scared, Daisy. I think I might have been followed."

"Followed? What do you mean?"

"Look, I was going to tell you, I've been out with this girl from Heighton. I *wasn't* cheating, and I just got home, and there was this spooky voice and I don't—" She suddenly stopped dead.

Spooky voice. Daisy felt the hairs stiffen on the back of her neck.

"Lucy? Lucy?"

Nothing.

"*Lucy?*"

"*Without grace or remorse.*"

The voice whispered down the telephone line.

Daisy threw her phone across the room, screaming in fear. It thudded against the wall and dropped to the floor. She lurched out of bed, tearing her pyjamas off and throwing on a pair of leggings and a sweater, and then, shoving her feet into some trainers, set out for the manor at a run.

The sun was just beginning to poke inquisitively over the horizon when she made it to the top of the incline, casting long shadows across the grounds of Hallowdene Manor. The birds had risen with the light, and chirped merrily, and Daisy couldn't shake the impression they were laughing at her. Overhead, crows were wheeling.

Her lungs were burning, every muscle in her body screaming after the run up from the village. Nevertheless, she felt alert – more than she had in days.

She approached the door to the manor house. It was hanging open. What was she going to do? Knock? It was still early, and the house appeared to be asleep. She couldn't hear any sounds from within. She wished now that she'd held onto her phone – but after she'd heard Agnes's voice...

The thought of Agnes hardened her resolve. Lucy was in danger. She had to do something.

Tentatively, she pushed the door open. It swung wide, creaking on ancient hinges. She stepped over the threshold, her trainers making no sound on the old floorboards. It was gloomy inside, the only sounds coming from the ticking of an old grandfather clock, further down the hall. The air was still.

Daisy hadn't yet got her breath back, and her ragged gulps kept time with the ticking of the clock.

"Lucy?" she said, her voice sounding small and uncertain. "Are you there?"

She'd only been in the house a couple of times, when Hugh and Petra had gone away and Lucy had invited her over. Those were the times she'd seen Lucy at her best, unencumbered by the weight of the divisive relationship she was forced to endure with her stepmother.

"Lucy?"

She ventured a little further down the hall, feeling like a trespasser. What would she do if Lucy wasn't there? She supposed she could wake the household, see if Lucy had returned to her room?

Ahead, the hallway opened out, beyond the mouth of the small entrance passageway. She rounded it slowly, taking in the vast feature staircase, sunlight streaming in through the stained-glass window to pool, like mottled butterflies, on the silent corpse spread out on the floorboards at the foot of the stairs.

A kitchen knife jutted from Lucy's back, right between the shoulder blades. She was lying face down in a pool of glossy blood, her hair loose and matted with the stuff. Her head was turned to one side, and her eyes were frozen open in rigid panic. Her mobile phone lay a few feet from her outstretched hand, screen down on the floorboards.

Daisy screamed, unable to contain the abject horror. She ran to Lucy's side, lifting the girl's head in her hands, searching for any sign that it wasn't too late, that she hadn't somehow allowed this awful travesty to occur. She could hear the accusation in Lucy's words now, running through her mind: "why weren't you picking up?" If she'd answered her phone sooner, if she hadn't been so wrapped up in her own stupid mess, none of this might have happened.

She wailed, rocking back and forth on her knees, the lifeless head of her lover resting on her lap, the girl's blood all over her hands, her clothes.

Running footsteps sounded from the stairwell and she looked round to see Hugh Walsey, dressed in a T-shirt and shorts. He was standing on the bottom step, gaping at the appalling scene, his mouth hanging open in horror.

"What have you done?" he said, his voice barely above a whisper. "What have you done to my Lucy?"

CHAPTER THIRTY-FIVE

Peter's first thought was for Elspeth, and the near miss that she'd had. If she'd stayed at Daisy's any longer than she had, things might have worked out very differently indeed.

He knew she was going to be gutted – she'd really believed that Daisy was innocent, that whatever the young woman had been keeping from them all had to be unrelated to the murders. Christ, she'd spent one night getting drunk with her and slept on her sofa. He kicked himself for being so stupid. How could he have let her get so close to a killer? And what was he going to say to her now?

There was no doubt in his mind what had happened here. The scene had been like something from *Carrie* – Daisy standing in the hallway, drenched in Lucy's blood. It was all over her hands, her clothes – her face, even, where she'd tried to wipe away her tears.

She was claiming innocence, of course, saying that she'd received a call from a panicked Lucy after Elspeth had left, and had rushed up to the manor to find her like that. The call history on her phone certainly seemed to confirm there'd been a call, as well as corroborating her assertion that the two of them had been lovers.

Despite the apparent evidence, Hugh and Petra Walsey were strenuously denying the idea that their daughter might have been involved in such an affair. They maintained that their daughter was as heterosexual as they come and could never have been involved with this 'mixed-up young woman', who'd clearly dreamed up a whole fantasy about their daughter, and had murdered her when that fantasy had somehow been shattered. They knew Daisy only as a casual friend of Lucy's and the waitress from Richmond's – insisting that if Daisy had made advances towards Lucy, they would have been spurned.

Peter didn't know what to think – it wasn't beyond the realms of possibility that what had occurred here had been the result of a fight between lovers, and he only had Daisy's word on the content of the call that had taken place between them. It was still a possibility that Daisy had been involved in the other murders, too. He hadn't yet been able to rule her out.

He gave a weary sigh, trying to shake life back into his tired body. He'd only just got back to sleep when the call had come through to attend the scene. He'd been at the manor within twenty minutes, driving like a maniac through the near-empty streets. The first response unit had beaten him to it and secured the scene, but he'd only been minutes behind them, running in to find Daisy trembling in the corner, a pair of handcuffs clamped around her wrists.

Now, he was standing outside on the driveway, waiting for the ambulance crew to remove the body. The fourth this week. *Fourth!* He worked his jaw, trying to remain calm and professional, all the while suppressing the urge to scream in frustration. Could he really have missed it? Could a twenty-something girl have pulled the wool so convincingly over his eyes? He'd even visited her house, admired her art. The painting of his own girlfriend!

It was at times such as this that he wished he smoked. At least it would have given him something to do.

Inside he could still hear Petra wailing, every inch the distraught stepmother. Hugh Walsey was taking it all surprisingly calmly, but Peter recognised the signs of shock, and knew that the cool, collected exterior wouldn't last. In the meantime, Patel and Griffiths were with him in the drawing room, taking a full statement.

Daisy, meanwhile, had been bundled into the back of a squad car and ferried immediately back to the station, where a couple of SOCOs could document every inch of her clothes, take her fingerprints, and then clean her up and deliver her for questioning when he and Griffiths arrived.

He pulled his phone from his pocket, glanced at the screen. It was 6.30 am. He couldn't put it off any longer. He made the call.

"Peter?" Elspeth sounded sleepy on the other end of the line.

"Yeah, it's me."

"It's a bit early, isn't it? I've only been in bed for a couple of hours. Is everything all right?"

"No. I'm sorry, Ellie. There's been another murder."

"Peter, what's happened?" Her voice was suddenly full of trepidation.

"Lucy Walsey's been killed, up at the manor house. And Daisy was found crouched over the body, dripping in blood."

For a moment she didn't say anything. And then: "Shit!"

"Ellie, I really am sorry."

"I should have stayed with her. Peter, it's my fault. I could have stopped her. If I hadn't been so tired, so keen to get home…"

"Ellie, stop. This is not your fault. There was nothing you could have done. Christ, I'm just pleased you were well out of the way before it happened. If it had been you…" He trailed off. He didn't even want to think about it.

"Peter, we've got to talk. The things she said last night… I think there's more to it than you might imagine. Even if she did it, I don't think she was in her right mind."

Peter sighed. "I don't think anyone who's done what she's done *could* be in her right mind," he said.

"Look, can we meet?" she said. "How much longer are you going to be tied up there?"

"Not long," said Peter, "but I've got to question

Daisy with Griffiths. I'm going to be a while. And besides, you're going to have to come into the station too. You were with her last night, and they'll want to ask you some questions. It'll help us put a timeline of the evening together."

"Who's they?"

"Griffiths, probably. I'd do it myself, but since we're... well, you know."

"I know," she said. "But we do need to talk. You and me. Alone."

"What is it, Ellie? You sound spooked."

"It's about Agnes Levett," she said. "I've got a horrible feeling Lee Stroud was right, and Jenny Wren really did disturb something she shouldn't have when she lifted that stone." She sounded perfectly serious.

"Ellie, you're talking about a 350-year-old spirit rising from the dead," said Peter, keeping his voice low as a uniformed constable walked past.

"I know. I know. It sounds mad. But remember what I said about an open mind. If there's one thing the Carrion King case taught us..."

"Okay," said Peter. "Open mind. I promise."

CHAPTER THIRTY-SIX

Giving her statement proved to be a fairly perfunctory matter. She'd sat with DS Patel in a small interview room at the station, outlining everything that had occurred the previous evening: from her night in with Peter – skipping over the part where she'd helped him sort through potential evidence – to the phone call and her hurried drive over to Daisy's house.

She explained what she'd found when she arrived – Daisy in a dishevelled, emotional state – and how the woman had seemed when Elspeth had left her a short while later. She felt obliged, given the circumstances, to tell the police about the content of her conversation with Daisy, too, although she couldn't help but feel as if she were betraying the young woman's trust in doing so. She focused on what Daisy had told her about the dizziness and blackouts that had led to her wandering alone in the woods in recent nights. She'd allow the police to draw their own conclusions from that.

She also related Daisy's account that she'd been in a relationship with Lucy Walsey, and that it had

remained a secret to protect Lucy, who'd feared how
her stepmother might react to the news of her sexuality.
Elspeth realised now that Lucy was the young woman
she'd half-recognised from the painting in Daisy's
studio, reading her book and looking coyly at the viewer.
Patel had rather pointedly asked Elspeth to describe the
nature of her own relationship with Daisy, and she'd
been clear and brief: they were becoming friends, and
Daisy had given no indication that she was prone to
violent or disturbing behaviour.

She still found it hard to believe that Daisy could
be responsible for Lucy's death. It seemed so *wrong*,
so unlike the woman she had come to know. The only
possible explanations she could fathom were that Daisy
was seriously unwell and therefore not in sound mind,
or was innocent and had been wrongly accused, or else
had been acting under the supernatural influence of
Agnes's spirit. Given what she'd learned that evening,
Elspeth was tending towards the third explanation, no
matter how incredible it seemed.

This, of course, she kept to herself. She'd discuss
that with Peter as soon as the opportunity arose.

He'd been unable to get away after she'd finished her
interview, and so Elspeth had paid a visit to Meredith at
the offices of the *Heighton Observer*, where she'd logged
in and updated the ongoing story of what the media
were now calling the 'Hallowdene Murders'. She didn't
mention Daisy in her account of Lucy's death; the police
hadn't formally released that information, and she saw

no reason to give the other news outlets an early reason to begin their character assassination of her friend.

Following her brief stint in the office, she returned home and slept fitfully on the sofa until finally being woken by a call from Peter, just before 4.30 pm. He'd managed to finish up at the station – at least for a short while – and suggested they meet at Lenny's for coffee. She countered by suggesting the Old Dun Cow and so now she was standing at the bar, ordering a pint of bitter and a gin and tonic while Peter found them a quiet table at the back.

She paid the barman – a wiry little man with a bushy beard that seemed to have the effect of elongating his head – and carried the drinks over to where Peter was sitting in a little nook beside the fireplace. The fire itself was out, although the stink of sooty residue and ash still lingered beneath the smell of stale beer. In the background, a fruit machine chimed endlessly, and a few early starters had begun to gather, chatting away merrily over their first round of drinks.

"I'm sorry about earlier," said Peter. "Griffiths was on the warpath, and these sorts of things generate a ton of paperwork…"

"I understand. Don't worry about it." She took a sip of her drink, and puckered her lips. The barman had obviously been feeling generous – the glass contained considerably more gin than tonic. "How's Daisy?"

"Better than you might think," said Peter. He drained almost half of his beer in a single gulp. He really had

had a difficult day. "Although it does mean my main lead has evaporated," he added.

Elspeth frowned. "You mean you don't think she did it?"

"I *did*," said Peter. "I was convinced of it. Anyone would have been. You should have seen her at the scene, Ellie. It was harrowing. She was covered in all this blood…" He trailed off, taking another pull on his beer. "But the evidence doesn't stack up, no matter how we look at it. You've corroborated Daisy's movements until 4 am, and I know that's correct because of the call log on my phone. Judging by the estimated time of death, Lucy was killed before Daisy could have realistically made it to the manor house. The blood had already started to congeal."

"So Daisy found her like that?" said Elspeth. "The poor woman."

"It looks that way. There were none of Daisy's prints on the murder weapon, and the call logs show that she was telling the truth about Lucy's panicked phone calls – there were six missed calls on her phone. Lucy must have been terrified, and instead of calling us, she called Daisy, who was in no fit state to help her." He looked angry, not so much at Lucy, but at his inability to do anything about it. "Daisy thinks she was scared to call her parents because they'd want to know why she'd been sneaking out. They'd warned her about it just the other day, and they clearly didn't know – or hadn't accepted – that she was gay."

"And she and Daisy were a couple?"

Peter nodded. "A quick look at their phones confirmed they were in a relationship, despite what Hugh and Petra Walsey say. They were meeting regularly. The texts even show that the reason Daisy had been wandering about the village so late at night was because she'd been meeting Lucy. There's nothing about their relationship that suggests Daisy had a motive to kill her."

Elspeth felt a flood of relief. "What about the other murders? Is she still a suspect?"

"*Everyone's* a suspect until I can prove otherwise," said Peter, "but there's no forensic evidence to place her at the scene of either Nicholas Abbott's or Lee Stroud's murders, and the forensic report on Steve Marley suggests that he was killed only half an hour or so before I got to him. She couldn't have been responsible for that, either."

Elspeth took another swig of her drink, feeling somewhat vindicated. "I'm so relieved. Where is she now?"

"We've sent her home, with a warning not to leave the area."

"She must have been terrified. Imagine finding the person you love with a knife in their back. Imagine not being able to help them."

Their eyes met. Peter swallowed.

"I presume she told you about the blackouts?" said Elspeth.

He nodded. "Yeah. We had a doctor look her over,

but there's no obvious medical explanation. At least without further tests."

"But there is another explanation," said Elspeth.

"Ellie…"

"Hear me out. What if Lee Stroud was right? What if Agnes's spirit *was* responsible for those deaths in the 1640s, and what if she's doing the same again now? Think about it. There's no obvious link between the victims. Agnes is working to create chaos amongst the villagers, generating a climate of fear."

Peter looked pained. He was having a hard time going along with this, she could tell. "So you're saying a *ghost* strangled Nicholas Abbott, or bludgeoned Lee Stroud, or stabbed Lucy Walsey in the back? Come on, Ellie. I know that stuff with the Carrion King was hard to explain—"

"Impossible to explain," said Elspeth, cutting him off. "You know that. And I'm not saying that a ghost did it. I'm saying that a malign force might have influenced a living person to do it. A trace memory of what had lived before, now whispering into people's ears, pushing them to do something they'd never otherwise consider. Just think about it for a minute. It makes sense when you consider what's been happening to Daisy." She outlined everything that Daisy had told her the previous evening regarding Agnes, waking up in the ruins of her house, her 'memory' of the ritual and the role that Cuthbert Abbott had played in his wife's death.

"She might simply be disturbed, Ellie. If she'd told

us all of that, we might have been able to get her some help." Peter was frowning.

Elspeth could hardly blame Daisy for not revealing *everything* to the police. She knew it sounded unbelievable. But then most people hadn't seen the things Ellie and Peter had seen, or had to come to terms with real evidence of the supernatural. "Look, I *know* how it sounds, but think about what happened with the Carrion King. The things we saw... the *mirror*. You know that there are things in this world that defy rational explanation. You've seen it with your own eyes."

"All right. Say for a moment that it's true, and that Agnes, or whatever 'trace memory' is left of her, has been causing these blackouts, working through Daisy as a means of seeking vengeance for being wrongly accused. Why pick on Daisy? Why not someone else from the village?"

Elspeth mulled this over for a moment. "Perhaps it's the familial link you found yesterday: the connection between the Levetts and the Heddles. Could that be it? Agnes working through the remnants of her family to exact her revenge?"

"I suppose it makes sense," said Peter, "if you allow for the notion that the witch's spirit could even still exist. But there's one other thing you're forgetting. We've just more or less ruled out Daisy as a suspect. So even if this were true, and Daisy was being influenced in the way you describe, she couldn't be working alone."

"Yes, but there's another familial link, isn't there?"

said Elspeth. "One we haven't talked about yet."

"The Jamesons," said Peter.

"We know that Sally was in the village hall when Steve Marley was killed, too," said Elspeth.

"But Christian wasn't there," said Peter. "Plus, if Stroud's charts are correct and Christian knew the truth, he certainly had a reason to be at odds with Nicholas Abbott. It's just conjecture, but there could be something in it. I was planning to go over there this morning, but what with everything that happened..."

"Let's go now," said Elspeth.

"Now?"

She pushed her drink across the table. She'd hardly touched it. "Come on. I'll drive. The parade will be starting soon. If nothing else, it'll be a good spectacle."

Peter downed the last of his pint. "Okay," he said. "But if anyone asks, I'm off duty."

Elspeth grinned. "I'm not sure you're *ever* off duty," she said.

CHAPTER THIRTY-SEVEN

Hallowdene village was awash with people, many of them dressed in colourful costumes, in animal masks made from papier mâché and fake fur. Children danced around their parents' legs, dribbling ice cream or munching on candyfloss clouds.

A row of classic cars had been lined up on show along one verge; a fire-eater was working a crowd on another. The pub had thrown open its doors and people were wandering through the streets with plastic pint glasses filled with lager and local cider. At the far end of the village, over by the edge of Raisonby Wood, a large crowd had gathered, presumably to stake out a good spot for the start of the main parade. A number of enterprising villagers had set up bric-a-brac stalls outside their houses, arranged with piles of unwanted toys, DVDs and books. Others were handing out free plastic cups of water to passers-by or sitting out on the pavement on folding chairs, drinking beer from mismatched glasses. The atmosphere nevertheless seemed somewhat subdued, as if people were forging ahead regardless, wilfully attempting to affect an air of nonchalance, but unable to shake their unease at the horrors that had occurred amongst them in the course of the last week. The roads through the village had been closed, and Ellie had been forced to circle around for ten minutes until finally locating a man in a yellow coat, who'd ushered them into a farmer's field. She'd parked the Mini in the oozing mud, alongside a white Mazda that had been definitively spattered up both sides.

They hurried through the crowds towards Richmond's, fighting against the flow of people making their way down towards the village green. Elspeth didn't really expect to find either Sally or Christian at the tearooms, given Sally's prominent role in the festivities, so she was surprised to see that she was just in the process of locking up as they arrived. Peter moved quickly to intercept her.

"Ms Jameson," he said. "I'm pleased to catch you."

"I'm in a bit of a rush," she said, a little brusquely. "I'm needed down in the village for the end of the parade. I only came back to fetch some more change for the float." She waved a bag of coins as if to underline her point.

"I understand," said Peter. "I just need a few minutes of your time."

The woman sighed. She glanced at Elspeth. "Thank you for what you did for Daisy," she said. "The poor girl's in pieces–" she turned her glower on Peter for a moment, before looking back at Elspeth and softening again "–but we appreciate your kindness."

"I didn't really do anything," said Elspeth, feeling her cheeks reddening.

"You were there for her when she needed someone."

Elspeth nodded. "Where is she?"

"At home," said Sally. "Catching up on sleep."

"I need to ask you a couple of questions," said Peter.

"What, *now*?"

"It'll only take a moment. I have to ask you about Nicholas Abbott."

Sally looked flustered. "Look, I've already told you everything I know."

Peter looked sceptical. "Not everything, Ms Jameson. Is it true, for instance, that Abbott was Christian's father?"

All of the colour seemed to drain out of Sally's face. She stammered for a moment, and then took a deep breath. "I'm not sure what you've heard, but—"

"Is it true?" said Peter, firmly.

She nodded meekly. "But it's not how you think. It wasn't some big affair behind Sarah's back, or anything like that. It was a terrible mistake. A fumble down the back lane one night. It's all very sordid and embarrassing."

"Does Christian know?"

"Yes, he knows," she said. "It's why he's been so angry recently. He found out from Lee Stroud. Lee just blurted it out one afternoon after Christian manhandled him out of the tearooms. Christian had hurt him, and he lashed out in retaliation. He wanted to hurt Christian back, I think. He told him he was just like his father

– vicious and uncaring. That he had bad genes. You can imagine how it played out from there – Christian grabbed him by the collar and wouldn't let him go until he'd explained himself." She sighed. "Lee was devastated, afterwards. He knew he'd crossed a line. Plus, I think he genuinely cared for Christian. Back at the start, soon after he was born, Lee was there for me. He helped me get back on my feet. He had more to do with the boy than his own father, and deserved respect."

"So you and Lee Stroud had been close," said Peter.

A trumpet blared somewhere down in the village, and Sally looked away, glancing over her shoulder. She seemed anxious. "Once. Lee was a dear friend. He was the only one who knew about Nicholas. He helped me when I needed someone."

"But things had changed between you in recent years?"

Sally shrugged. "He had this theory that everything moves in cycles, repeating itself over and over again throughout history. That's why he was so interested in the legends of the witch and all the local families. But it just became too much. A true obsession. It was all he would talk about. After a while I stopped listening." She sighed. "He did care for me, though, in his own way. Poor sod."

"So Nicholas never acknowledged the boy?" said Peter.

Sally shook her head. "He didn't see why a quick fumble with a local girl had to impinge on his life up at the manor. He was a real bastard. The thing is, I didn't want him to. I didn't want my boy growing up with him as a father. So when Christian was old enough to ask, I told him his father had been a one-night stand with a man I couldn't remember, and whom I had no way of contacting."

"How did he react when he found out Nicholas Abbott was his real father?" said Elspeth.

"He was furious, as you might expect. He begged me to tell him it wasn't true. But I thought by now he deserved to know the truth. Even if it meant he'd never talk to me again," said Sally. She dabbed at her eyes with the cuff of her blouse.

"Did he confront Nicholas?" said Peter.

"Of course. And the result was just what you'd expect. Nicholas refused to acknowledge the truth. He said Christian was a 'grubby little commoner' trying to extort money, and to keep his dirty lies to himself."

"I presume Christian didn't take kindly to this?"

"He was mortified. It was the first time I'd seen him cry in years. All his life he'd pined for a father, and now, when it turned out he'd had one all along, the man wouldn't even look at him."

"Was he upset enough to lash out?" said Peter.

"Of course not," said Sally. "Christian didn't kill Nicholas. I've told you, he was at home that night watching TV in his room. It was blaring all night."

"Did you actually *see* him?" pressed Peter.

Sally hesitated. "Well, not *exactly*… but of course he was there. Look, Christian might be a bit hot-headed from time to time, but he'd never really hurt anyone."

"Can you tell us where Christian was last night, Ms Jameson?" said Peter.

"Yes, he was out with his friends in Heighton."

"All night?"

"I presume so. He must have stayed over. He didn't make it back until breakfast time this morning, and said he'd caught the early bus so he could help out in the kitchen. He's considerate like that," she said.

Peter and Elspeth exchanged a glance. So Christian had been out all night. He could have been up at the manor.

"Do you know how we could contact Christian's friends, their names?" said Peter.

Sally shrugged. "You'd have to ask Christian, I'm afraid. He doesn't really talk about them." She looked again down the hill towards the village. "Look, I really *must* be going."

"Just one more question," said Peter. "Can you tell us where Christian is now?" Elspeth could hear the tension in his voice.

"He's down at the fayre. Where I should be."

"Can you give him a quick call for us? Just to find out exactly where he is, so we can have a word?" Peter was doing a remarkable job of remaining calm. All Elspeth wanted to do was scream at her to hurry up.

Sally made a show of picking her phone out of her bag and thumbing through the functions. She held it up to her ear. It rang out, going to voicemail. "He's not picking up," she said, sliding the phone back into her handbag. "I'm sorry. It's loud down there."

Peter nodded. "Did he say anything that might help us find him?"

Sally shrugged. "Only that he was going ahead to find Daisy."

"Oh God," said Elspeth, grabbing Peter's arm. "Daisy."

"I don't understand," said Sally, "what about Daisy?"

But Peter and Elspeth were already running, hurtling down the incline towards the bustling village.

CHAPTER THIRTY-EIGHT

The parade was in full swing.

Onlookers lined both sides of the main street through the village, culminating in a massed gathering on the green, eager-eyed revellers awaiting their first glimpse of the witch. Children sat on their parents' shoulders, calling out excitedly to those below. It was nearly six, and the sun was still full in the sky.

The players were nearing the heart of the village now, a riotous procession of bizarre figures drawn from pagan legend – the Green Man, wearing a suit of rustling leaves; a woman bowed low by the weight of the antlers strapped to her head, pulled along by a man wearing druidic robes; a straw bear; a man dressed as a fox; another with a bird skull mask, a fan of peacock feathers erupting from his hat; four villagers in grey, featureless robes, their solemn expressions turned towards the earth as they bore the gnarled and twisted form of the witch upon their shoulders. The booming thud of two massive drums accompanied the slow march of the parade, and the ringing bells of Morris dancers followed in their wake like a sinister call to arms.

Elspeth was forced to pause as the procession marched past, unable to squeeze through the press of the crowd. The leering effigy of Agnes Levett seemed to peer down at her as it was carried by, lips twisted in a knowing grin. There was an electric atmosphere down here, a palpable sense of expectation and drama.

Perhaps Lee Stroud had been right all along, she thought. History does repeat itself. Right now, she might have been a spectator back in the 1640s, a villager come to watch the hanging of the hateful witch.

The procession passed, and she felt Peter's hand on her arm, tugging her on through the crowd.

"We'll never find her in this crowd," said Peter. "Have you got her number?"

"Yes! Hang on." She pulled her phone out of her bag, scrolling through her recent calls. "Here it is." She dialled. It rang for a minute, and then Daisy answered.

"Ellie?"

"Daisy! Where are you? I'm here in Hallowdene, looking for you."

"What? I can't hear you – the parade's really loud." Daisy's voice sounded as if it were muffled, underwater. Elspeth cupped a hand over her other ear.

"I said: where are you?" She raised her voice, shouting into the handset.

"Oh! I'm just by the village hall—" The line suddenly went dead.

Elspeth peered at the screen. It was blank and

unresponsive. The battery! "Oh no, no, no!" she yelled in frustration. She tried to turn it back on, but all she got was a blinking image of an empty battery and a power cable, urging her to plug it in.

"It's no use," she said, running back over to join Peter. "Battery's dead. She's by the village hall. She sounded okay. Maybe we can still get to her first."

"Right," said Peter, looking back in the direction of the village green, where the parade sounded as if it were reaching a climax.

"Everyone's gathering on the green," said Elspeth. "Come on. We've got to find a way through."

Peter gave a brisk nod, and they set off again at a run.

The crowds by the village green had grown denser, and she elbowed her way through, eliciting a stream of angry curses. Faces seem to loom down at her from all sides, hemming her in. The world lurched from under her, closing in, narrowing focus, until there was just her and those staring, laughing faces all around her – the fox and the bird, the jack-in-the-green, a pantomime dame, a goat-headed woman. She felt as if she were going to throw up.

"Ellie."

Peter was ahead of her now, grasping her by the hand, pulling her forward. She shook her head, trying to clear the after-image of the looming faces, the dizziness. "I'm okay. Keep going."

"Just stay with me, okay?"

She nodded, doing her best to keep up.

She turned at the clanging of a bell. The effigy of Agnes had now reached the village cross, where four men were holding her up to rapturous applause from the gathered throng. Things were coming to a head.

"That way!" she called, nudging Peter in the back and jabbing at a gap in the press of people ahead. "We can go around."

"All right," said Peter, nodding in agreement. "Let's go."

He clasped her by the hand again, and they set off through the baying crowd.

CHAPTER THIRTY-NINE

The village hall seemed to radiate a sense of deep unease that set Elspeth's teeth on edge. She paused in her approach, holding Peter back by his hand. The air, too, had grown noticeably colder, as if the hall had been cast in a long shadow, set apart and isolated from the rest of the village. A paper sign on the door of the hall suggested that the tearoom and exhibition had closed temporarily while the parade took place. No one milled about outside, and there was no sense of any sound or movement from within the building itself. She supposed people had been drawn down to the green, where the entire village was now cheering as the effigy of Agnes was paraded before them like some latter-day offering to the ancient gods.

Yet there was more to it than that. She could sense that disturbing presence again, unseen but pervasive: watching, influencing, repelling.

"She knows we're here," said Elspeth.

"What?" said Peter. He was frowning.

"Can't you feel it?"

He rubbed the back of his neck. "I... perhaps. Look, we have to find Daisy and Christian." He released his grip on her hand, pulled the door open with a creak. "The lock's been broken. Careful." He slipped through. With a deep breath, Elspeth followed.

Inside, the atmosphere was quiet and oppressive. The hall was empty, with disposable cups and paper plates abandoned haphazardly on Formica-topped tables, chairs left scattered, a few coats still draped over their grey plastic backs. The hall had clearly been given over to a makeshift tearoom, a pit stop for hungry villagers who didn't want to stray too far from the action of the fayre.

Up on the stage, the display case containing Agnes Levett's bones was caught in a stream of sunlight that was streaking down from an upper window, dust motes whirling in the otherwise still air. Beside it cowered a terrified-looking Daisy, slowly backing away from Christian Jameson, who was brandishing a kitchen knife in his right fist. His expression was half lost in shadow, but Elspeth could see that his lips were curled in a rigid smile. Daisy was bleeding from a long gash in her left forearm.

"Christian!" called Peter, extending his arm, warning Elspeth to stay back. "Put the knife down. Now."

Elspeth saw Daisy's eyes flicker in their direction.

"The police are here, Christian. It's over," said Elspeth, the tremor evident in her voice.

He said nothing, his lips still fixed in the same rigid smile, his eyes transfixed by the sight of the terrified woman before him.

"Christian!" bellowed Peter. He'd been slowly approaching the stage, arms held out to either side, getting close enough to try to intercept the man if he made any sudden movements towards Daisy.

Christian turned his head to look down at Peter, and the look of malice in his eyes was cold and distant.

"*Without grace or remorse.*"

The whispered words seemed to emanate from Christian, but he hadn't moved his lips.

Elspeth swallowed.

Agnes. She was here, in the room. She was making all of this happen.

Daisy had continued to back away while Christian was distracted, and Elspeth realised with horror that she was about to go backwards over the lip of the stage, tumbling down towards the hard floor below. Peter's eyes were locked with Christian's, attempting to anticipate the man's next move.

Daisy took another step backwards.

"Daisy, look out!" bellowed Elspeth, running forward, arms outstretched to catch the other woman if she fell.

What happened next seemed to pass in slow motion, as if, just for a moment, the world had stopped turning.

Daisy's foot caught on the lip of the stage, and she tottered backwards, waving her arms and screaming.

Elspeth's call seemed to stir Christian into action, and he leapt after Daisy, swinging his knife around in front of him, intent on plunging it into Daisy's chest.

Peter, seeing the danger, swept up a chair and launched it at Christian as he lurched towards the front of the stage.

Elspeth saw it all unravel, unspooling before her like the flickering scenes of a movie as she ran.

Daisy landed in her arms, and they both crumpled to the floor, sprawling awkwardly, knocking the wind from Elspeth's lungs.

The chair collided with Christian, full in the chest. He stumbled back, arms wheeling, and then lost his footing and fell backwards into the glass display case. It exploded in a shower of sparkling fragments, collapsing under the man's bulk. He seemed to sink into it, landing in a heap of jagged glass and old bones. Agnes's skull rolled across the stage, coming to rest at the top of the steps, vacant eyes staring down at Elspeth and Daisy.

Peter glanced at Elspeth, who was still sprawled on the floor beneath Daisy, and then jumped up onto the stage.

Christian was already stirring from amongst the pit of shattered glass. His back was streaming blood, jagged fragments of glass pitting his flesh where it had embedded itself during the fall. He looked demonic, frenzied, insane. He'd dropped his knife in the fall, and it lay a few feet from him on the stage, equidistant to Peter.

Elspeth saw their eyes meet, and then they both launched themselves toward it, Peter attempting to kick it away, Christian scrabbling at the boards, trying to get a grip. His fingers closed around the handle just as Peter's boot connected with his wrist. He rolled, crunching broken glass, and the knife skittered away again.

Peter took a step back, warily, as Christian rose out of the ruination like some bloodied phoenix. He was holding a jagged shard of broken glass. Blood dripped from his fingers. He opened his mouth in a silent scream.

"*Without grace or remorse.*"

He launched himself at Peter, roaring with feral animosity, swinging the broken shard in a wide arc like a dagger. Peter saw it coming and ducked at the last moment, sidestepping the attack and sweeping his trailing leg out to catch Christian off balance.

Christian went down heavily, crashing to the ground. Peter was standing ready, arms raised in defence, expecting Christian to rise and attack again at any moment. But the other man wasn't moving.

"Christian?" said Peter, warily.

The only reply was an awful, wet gurgling sound. Elspeth got to her feet. She could see a pool of glossy blood spreading beneath Christian on the stage. "Peter! He's hurt."

Peter motioned for her to stay back as he cautiously approached the prone form of the other man. "Christian?"

No reply.

Tentatively Peter dropped to his haunches and shook Christian by his shoulder. Christian shuddered in response, but still seemed unable to move. Peter cautiously rolled him over onto his back, and at once, they saw the horror of what had happened.

In the fall, Christian had accidentally plunged the broken fragment of glass into his own throat.

Blood gushed, spurting violently from the opened artery. Christian's mouth worked back and forth for a moment, his eyes flickering in shock, and then his whole body seemed to shake, and he lay still.

Beside Elspeth, Daisy screamed, and Elspeth grabbed her and bundled her into a fierce hug.

Peter was attempting to staunch the flow of blood, but it was like something from a nightmare, flowing up his arms as he tried to keep it at bay. It was spreading everywhere, pattering the boards, and Elspeth knew it was too late.

"Give me your phone," she said to Daisy, who looked at her with a dazed expression. "Quickly!"

Daisy continued to stare at her for a moment.

"Daisy, now!"

This seemed to shake the woman into action, and she slipped her hand into her pocket and pulled out her phone. Elspeth snatched for it and hurriedly called for an ambulance and police backup. When the call was done, she stumbled over to where Peter was still trying desperately to hold back the tide of blood. His face was ashen. Elspeth could see that Christian was dead.

"Come on," she said, turning and leading Daisy away towards the other side of the hall. "Come on. It's okay. It's over now." She settled Daisy into a chair and wrapped someone's abandoned coat around her shoulders. "You don't have to worry any more."

Daisy looked utterly dazed. She nodded, but didn't seem to know what to say.

Behind Elspeth, on the stage, Peter had taken the velvet drape from the display case and was in the process of covering Christian's body.

He looked up, saw her watching him, and gave a wan smile. "They'll be here in a minute," he said.

Elspeth sighed, and dropped into a chair beside Daisy. It was going to be another long night.

CHAPTER FORTY

They sat in the White Hart, fingers interlaced across the table top, sipping their drinks while David Bowie sang about suffragettes on the jukebox. It was quiet in there, as usual, and the other patrons were keeping their own council, sitting in small groups, chatting amongst themselves.

The events of the previous day seemed distant, now, like a horrific nightmare, although the image of Christian Jameson, the glass shard buried in his throat, seemed to rise unbidden in her thoughts every few minutes. She'd barely eaten, plagued by a constant feeling of nausea. She knew that image would haunt her for the rest of her life.

She'd spent the day with Dorothy in Wilsby-under-Wychwood, napping on the sofa, drinking cups of tea, sitting in the garden with Murphy the cat on her lap. It had all seemed so normal, so mundane, surrounded by the familiar shushing of the trees, the buzzing of insects, the chatter of her mum. Dorothy had talked about her work at the garden centre, about the fact that Nigel had been round for a curry and things seemed to be developing between them, and they'd idled away the afternoon, just being still. She could tell that Dorothy was concerned for her; that even she was beginning to wonder what sort of life Elspeth had come back to here, getting swept up in such terrible events for a second time.

Yet Elspeth, for all the horror of it, knew that she had made a difference; that she'd been there for Daisy and helped her even when the world seemed to have turned against the young woman. That she'd believed her, and had helped Peter to see the truth, too, and that had to count for something. That was her job – to help people to see the truth – and she wasn't about to stop now.

She'd file her article the following day – an expansive piece about everything that had happened in Hallowdene, from the dig to the fayre to the murders. And she'd started to make notes about the book she was considering writing, about folklore and unexplained phenomena, too, although that would come later. She'd texted Abigail that morning and received the usual bubbly reply. Things there were good. The storm had passed, and she knew that when she next went to London to visit, it would be fun again, because she'd already made up her mind that she could come home afterwards.

Across the table, Peter seemed to be peering into his half-full pint of beer, but she knew that he was really seeing something else. He was having trouble coming to terms with what he'd seen at the village hall. He'd said as much on the walk over from her mum's house – that he needed to find a way to explain what had happened. She'd help him with that, too. In time.

"How was Sally?" she asked, and the question seemed to startle him. He blinked, and looked up.

"Just as you'd expect, really," he said. "I think she knew the truth, deep down – that Christian was probably responsible. But she'd buried her head in the sand. If she didn't acknowledge her suspicions, they couldn't be real, if you see what I mean?"

Elspeth nodded. "She's a mum," she said. "It's only natural."

"She's still denying it, of course. But the facts are there. She just needs a bit of time."

"I doubt it's something she'll ever get over," said Elspeth. "What a thing to have to live with."

They were silent for a moment.

"We found the missing camera in Christian's room," said Peter, before taking a gulp of his beer. "It's a difficult thing to watch. It shows him bludgeoning Lee Stroud to death and dragging his body into the grave."

Elspeth shuddered.

"It also shows Daisy up at the site later that night, completely unaware of what's lying there in the trench."

"God, how awful. I presume that must have been during one of her blackouts," she said.

Peter nodded. "She certainly doesn't seem to be acting like herself. It's as if she's watching something off-camera. There's a glimpse of something, too – a flickering light. The tech guys think it's just a problem with the recording, but I can't help wondering if it's something more."

It had to be the night Daisy first saw the vision of Cuthbert Abbott, emerging from the manor house with his dying wife in his arms.

"Anyway," said Peter, "Griffiths is happy. Christian has a motive for every murder. He must have been harbouring such resentment against Nicholas Abbott after finding out the man was his father and being turned away like that. And Lee Stroud knew all about it, and was the one responsible for raking it all up. Christian must have realised that the camera had uploaded the footage from the dig site to the cloud, and that Steve Marley was likely to realise it, too. When he found Steve already watching it… well, that was his death sentence."

"What about Lucy," said Elspeth, "and Daisy, for that matter?"

Peter shrugged. "We think Christian must have had a crush on Daisy. His phone was full of photos of her that he'd taken without her knowing. Bit of a chip off the old block, it seems. We think he must have killed Lucy when he found out about her relationship with Daisy, and then turned on Daisy when it became clear she was never going to look at him that way."

Elspeth frowned. "All very neat and tidy for the police reports."

"You say that like it's a bad thing," said Peter.

"Come on, you know that's not really what happened. Or at least, there's much more to it than that."

Peter looked uncomfortable. "What *did* really happen, Ellie? I'm trying, but I just can't understand it."

Elspeth shrugged. "I'm hardly an expert. But I felt it, Peter. There was something wrong in that village, in that hall yesterday. You can't just ignore that. And then Christian – he wasn't right."

"Of course he wasn't right. He was threatening Daisy with a knife. He'd killed four people."

"You know what I mean," she said. "The way he looked at you. That whispered voice. He didn't move his lips…" She broke off, remembering again the sight of the man with the piece of glass in his throat.

"I know," said Peter, levelly. "I know."

"I think perhaps that Agnes, or whatever twisted remnant that was left of her, was using him: playing on his existing fear and hatred to drive him to such extremes. She wanted vengeance, to cause chaos and fear amongst the villagers. She used Christian to do it, homing in on his own dark thoughts, amplifying them. The familial link you found – it's probably why she chose him."

"Then why didn't Daisy turn murderous, too? You seem convinced that she had fallen under the influence of the witch as well," said Peter.

"Maybe she was just better at resisting it?" said Elspeth. "Maybe she wasn't harbouring such ill will towards others in the village? That's all I've got. I don't know what else to say."

"If you're right about all this, what's to stop it

happening again? I can't see anyone allowing the bones to be re-interred beneath the witch stone."

"Carl," said Elspeth. "Carl Hardwick. I spoke to him this morning. He and Iain are seeing to it that the bones are cleansed before they're handed back to Jenny."

"Cleansed?"

"Yes. Some old spell or ritual for exorcising the bones of ghosts and spirits. He's a bit of an expert in such things. He's promised to talk to Daisy, too, to help her understand what happened to her."

Peter nodded. He seemed unconvinced, but Elspeth could tell that he wasn't really satisfied with the story the police had settled on, either. At least, she supposed, it was over, and no one else was likely to be at risk. She just wished they'd been able to get to Christian sooner, to help him, or at least prevent him from carrying out any further attacks.

"So, this is going to make for another high-profile story," said Peter. "Might make ripples. You might expect a few new job offers on the back of it." He sounded wary – scared, even. More than he had even yesterday, when confronted with a murderous man with a kitchen knife.

"I suppose so," said Elspeth, "but if I do, I'll be turning them down. All that business with Abi, about London – I'm not interested. This is my home, now. I wouldn't give it up for the world. I think I've finally found my niche, right back here where it all started."

He grinned, squeezed her hand. "God, I was hoping you'd say that."

"What about you, though? Another high-profile case solved. You made a difference, just like you said you wanted to. That promotion must be a certainty now?"

"Maybe," he said. "But what do I want with all that?" he looked suddenly serious. "When you left the other night, to go to Daisy, I couldn't help thinking about what would happen if you didn't come back…"

"Peter…"

"I know. I know, it's stupid, and I trust you, and you can handle yourself. But all the same, it got me thinking – I don't want to be apart from you, Ellie. I'm not sure I could bear it."

He was eyeing her intensely. She looked away, released her grip on his hand. "I can't be the one to hold you back, though. You'd only resent it, maybe not now, but later, and—"

He reached over and took her hand again. "Ellie, I've made up my mind. I've told Griffiths. I'm here to stay."

She looked up and smiled. "I was hoping you were going to say that," she parroted.

"Besides," he went on, "Griffiths is getting itchy feet. She's said as much. Another six months to a year, and there'll be an opening at Heighton. Maybe I'll make DCI after all. And let's face it, for all that talk of shoplifters and teenage louts – we've had a pretty busy time of late. Certainly enough to keep me busy for a while."

"Then it's decided," she said. "Home."

"There is one thing," said Peter. "I was just thinking – maybe don't get too settled in that apartment, eh? I much prefer it here, in Wilsby, and it's close to your mum…"

"Hang on a minute, don't get ahead of yourself," she said, with a grin. "But yeah, I've only got another three months on the lease. Let's see how things go, yeah?"

"Yeah," he said, beaming. "Let's see how everything works out." He stood, smoothing the front of his shirt. "You coming?"

"Where?"

"I fancy a little walk in the woods," he said. "Besides, we've got some unfinished business."

"We have?"

"Yeah, we never finished that game of tag when we were seven. You fell and bloodied your knee while I was chasing you, and you went home to get a plaster."

"I remember," she said, laughing. She downed the end of her drink.

"Well, there's something else you should know," said Peter. He patted her gently on the shoulder. "You're 'it'."

He legged it for the door.

"You bugger," she said, rushing after him into the night.

ACKNOWLEDGEMENTS

First of all, I'd like to thank all the readers who picked up and supported *Wychwood*, the first novel in this series about Ellie and Peter. I can't tell you how much your support has meant.

Likewise all the bloggers and reviewers who supported the blog tour and helped to get people talking about the book. It made a real difference.

This time around, I owe a debt of gratitude to my editors Cat Camacho and Joanna Harwood for their encouragement and support, and to my agent, Jane Willis, for being a constant rock.

Cavan Scott remained a steadfast friend throughout, helping me to bounce around ideas and encouraging me to push on when it still looked like I had a mountain to climb.

Finally, my thanks go out to my family, who are never less than extraordinary in their support and love.

Until next time, folks!

ABOUT THE AUTHOR

George **Mann** was born in Darlington and has written numerous books, short stories, novellas and original audio scripts. *The Affinity Bridge*, the first novel in his Newbury & Hobbes Victorian fantasy series, was published in 2008. Other titles in the series include *The Osiris Ritual*, *The Executioner's Heart*, *The Immorality Engine* and *The Casebook of Newbury & Hobbes*.

His other novels include *Ghosts of Manhattan*, *Ghosts of War*, *Ghosts of Karnak* and *Ghosts of Empire*, mystery novels about a vigilante set against the backdrop of a post-steampunk 1920s New York, as well as an original *Doctor Who* novel, *Paradox Lost*, featuring the Eleventh Doctor alongside his companions, Amy and Rory.

He has edited a number of anthologies, including *Encounters of Sherlock Holmes*, *Further Encounters of Sherlock Holmes*, *Associates of Sherlock Holmes* and the forthcoming *Further Associates of Sherlock Holmes*, *The Solaris Book of New Science Fiction* and

GEORGE MANN

The Solaris Book of New Fantasy, and has written two Sherlock Holmes novels for Titan Books: *Sherlock Holmes: The Will of the Dead* and *Sherlock Holmes: The Spirit Box*.